Dancing in the Moonlight

Lynne Shelby

S

Copyright © 2025 Lynne Shelby

The right of Lynne Shelby to be identified as the Author of the Work has been asserted by her in accordance with the the Copyright Designs and Patent Act 1988.

All rights reserved. This work is protected by copyright. Apart from any use permitted under UK law, no part of the work may be reproduced, stored or transmitted in any form, or by any means, without prior permission in writing from the author.

All characters in this work are fictitious and any resemblance to real persons, living or dead, is purely coincidental.

Paperback ISBN: 978-1-0683584-0-1

Ebook ISBN: 978-1-0683584-1-8

Shaldo Books

Chapter One

When I open my eyes the next morning, I'm alone. He's left for the airport without waking me for one last kiss. Slowly, I sit up and swing my legs over the side of the bed, shivering as the cold air touches my bare skin. It's then that I see the tiny silver statuette of a ballerina, no more than an inch high, on my bedside table. I pick her up, marvelling at the detail of her face and hair, and her minute ballet shoes. There's a note, too, a piece of torn paper, folded in half, with my name written on it. I pull the duvet around me, unfold the paper, and read: *I hope she brings you good luck in auditions. F xx*

I smile at that. He has gone, as I always knew he would, but he's left me with something to remember him by . . .

Ten Years Later

Taking a deep breath, I pushed open the door of the London Dance Studios, and went inside, giving my name to a girl sitting at a table in the entrance hall, with a clipboard and a stack of numbered cards in front of her. She ticked me off her list of auditioning dancers, handed me a card with my number – thirteen, lucky for me, I hoped – and pointed me in the direction of the changing rooms, where I found a crowd of women swopping street clothes for dance gear in a cloying fog of hairspray. To my disquiet, I saw that most of them were younger than me by at least five years – and would probably need a lot less time than I did to warm up. Hurriedly, I stripped off the jeans and jumper that I'd put on over my leotard and tights, tied up my long dark hair in a pony tail, pinned on my number, slipped my feet into my dance heels, and headed off to a small mirror-walled studio that was being used as a waiting area – there were some thirty or so dancers in there already.

Dumping my bag on the ground, I began a series of warm-up exercises. A few of the other auditionees, none of whom I knew, were doing the same, but the majority of the young men and women in the room were sprawled on the floor in poses that only dancers or contortionists are flexible enough to achieve, and chatting with their friends. As yet more bright young things glided into the studio, superbly toned girls – one slender, elfin creature in a red leotard, with her dark blonde hair in a bun as though she was attending a ballet class, looked young enough to still be in school – and boys with the physiques of athletes, I gritted my teeth and made myself keep stretching.

I was sitting in the box splits, my upper body lying full length and at right angles to my legs, when I heard a male voice say, 'Hey, Nell.'

Tilting up my head, I saw my friend Justin Ofabemi, smiling down at me. I'd known he was auditioning at the same time as me, but I was still absurdly pleased to see a familiar face amongst all these youthful strangers – it occurred to me that at twenty-seven, he was closer to their age than mine. I sat upright, and he sat beside me, his gaze darting around the studio.

'Just checking out the competition,' he said, with a grin.

'I don't know any of them,' I said. 'Do you?'

'I've worked with a few. There are some fierce dancers in this room.' Again, Justin's gaze travelled over the other auditionees. 'I *so* want this job,' he said.

You're not the only one, I thought. Since I'd first put on a pair of tap shoes, I'd dreamt of dancing on a West End stage, but, unlike Justin, who had a string of West End credits, it had never happened for me. Picturing the good luck card made for me by my daughter Savannah, and now stowed carefully in my dance bag, I told myself that this time, auditioning for new musical *Speakeasy*, it would be different.

'Do you know how many dancers they're looking for?' I asked Justin.

He shrugged. 'All I've heard is that the show's going into the West End for a six-month run, and that it has a hot-shot choreographer.'

At that moment, the girl with the clipboard came into the room. Instantly, the chattering performers fell silent and every face turned in her direction.

'OK, guys,' she said. 'The audition panel is ready for you. If you'd like to follow me to Studio One. Please make sure you bring all your belongings with you.'

Although it was a much larger dance space than the waiting area – with skylights in its high ceiling, mirrored walls, and a pianist sitting at her piano – with fifty performers in it, Studio One was crowded. Hastily, Justin and I added our bags to the pile by the back wall, and managed to edge our way through the auditionees jostling for position, until we'd secured spaces close enough to the front of the throng that the audition panel would have a clear view of us when we danced. Justin was on my left, and directly to my right I saw the girl in red – close up, she was exquisitely beautiful, and definitely couldn't have been much more than eighteen. As though becoming aware of my scrutiny, she turned her head towards me. I gave her a friendly smile. For an instant, the hint of a smile flickered across her face in return, and then she looked down at the floor, her body rigid and her hands tightly clenched. I knew plenty of performers who got dreadfully nervous before an important audition – I was feeling a bit jittery myself – but I'd never seen anyone look quite so terrified. I couldn't help but feel sorry for her, even if she was a rival for my place in the ensemble.

Justin leant towards me. 'I don't recognise anyone on the audition panel,' he said, in an undertone. I looked towards the three people seated at the long table at the front of the studio: one woman, who looked to be in her late forties, the monochrome black of her clothes relieved by a brightly coloured scarf tied around her iron-grey hair, a bearded man of about the same age, and another man, younger than the other two. The woman and the bearded man, I didn't know. As for the other guy . . . My head reeled.

'Finn,' I said, my voice scarcely above a whisper. 'The younger guy's name is Finn Harris.'

'You know him?' Justin said.

'I used to –' My stomach twisted into a knot. 'W-what is he doing here?'

Justin raised his eyebrows. 'I'd imagine he's here to audition us,' he said, 'as he's on the panel.'

'But – but he can't be,' I said. This could *not* be happening to me. My heart thudded in my chest. 'I – He – When I knew him, he was a dancer like you and me.'

'Not much like you and me anymore, apparently,' Justin said.

Suppressing a sudden urge to run from the studio, I looked back towards Finn, who was leafing through some papers in front of him on the table. He looked older – unsurprisingly, as a decade had passed since I'd last seen him – his dark hair was slightly shorter and his formerly smooth-shaved chin was shadowed with stubble, but I'd have known him anywhere. Even as I wondered if he'd recognise me after all this time, he lifted his head and looked around the room, and the next instant he caught my gaze and held it, his mouth lifting in an achingly familiar smile. All at once, desire lanced through me, causing me to inhale sharply, and my heart to race, as though my body's muscle-memory was reacting to him in the same way it reacted to a piece of music I'd danced to long ago – and then, with another smile, he looked away. I let out a long breath, and told myself very firmly to get a grip.

'Are you all right, Nell?' Justin said. 'You look a bit distracted.'

'Just a touch of audition nerves,' I said. 'I'll be fine once we start dancing.'

Gradually, my heart slowed to a normal pace.

Now, all three members of the audition panel focused their attention on the fifty performers standing in front of them. The grey-haired woman got to her feet – now she was standing, I saw that she was tall for a woman.

'Good morning, everyone,' she said, her voice, reverberating around the studio. 'For those of you who don't know me, I'm Olivia Warren, Director of *Speakeasy*. We've not got a lot of time, so I'm going to hand you straight over to Finn Harris, our Choreographer.'

I watched as Finn got up from behind the table and came and stood at the front of the studio, his tight white T-shirt revealing that he'd kept the body of a dancer, even if he was no longer performing. *Focus, Nell*, I told myself.

'Morning all,' he said, his face creasing into a disarming smile that belied the power he wielded over the hopefuls assembled in front of him. 'Today, I'll be teaching you a short jazz routine. After we've seen you all dance, we'll be making a cut, so please dance full out. Show us what you can do.'

I'd worked with a lot of choreographers, but the routine that Finn proceeded to teach for the first round of the auditions, was both the most difficult and the most interesting jazz dance I'd done in a long while. He taught it extremely quickly, marking it through only once before asking the pianist to play the music, so that we could dance it twice with him demonstrating. Then he went and rejoined his colleagues behind the table.

'From the top, please,' he said.

As music once again filled the studio, thankful that my fifteen years as a jobbing dancer had accustomed me to learning dances in a very short time before I had to perform them to live audiences, I threw myself into the routine, focusing on dancing Finn's choreography exactly as he'd demonstrated it, while also keeping a confident smile on my face. I had to push myself, but I soon realised that not only could I do this, but I was enjoying the challenge. A girl in front of me did not fare so well, turning the wrong way, and stumbling as she tried to correct herself. The boy beside her forgot the routine entirely and with a shrug of his shoulders, stood still.

As soon as the music faded, Finn said, 'And again, please.'

Again, the music soared; again, fifty dancers jumped and turned, kicked and leapt. By the time the music stopped, I wasn't the only one who was breathing hard.

'Good job, everyone,' Finn said. 'Stay where you are, please. We'll let you know who we're keeping as soon as we can. By the way, you can sit down and relax.'

As one, the auditionees sank to the floor – although I very much doubted any of us could be described as relaxed – while the audition panel talked among themselves. They kept their voices low, but from the expressions on their faces, it looked to me as though they were having trouble reaching a consensus – several times, I saw Finn shaking his head at something the bearded guy said. A few of the dancers resumed their conversations with their friends; most stared fixedly at the audition panel.

'How do you think you did?' I asked Justin.

'Hard to tell,' he said. 'You?'

Deciding I'd known him too long to be anything but honest, I said, 'I've no idea if it was enough to get me through to the next round, but I do think I danced that routine as well as I could.' *And if I get cut now, I'll be gutted.* 'Finn's choreography was demanding – but I enjoyed dancing it.' *Finn's choreography.* Saying his name aloud so casually after all this time felt very strange.

'Excuse me,' a female voice said, quietly, 'but do you know what happens now?'

I swivelled around to find the girl in the red leotard looking at me tentatively. As she had been standing out of my line of vision when we danced, I'd no idea how she'd coped with Finn's choreography, but she certainly looked a lot less tense than she had before we'd started dancing.

'Once the audition panel have made their decision, they'll read out the numbers of whoever they want to keep,' I said. 'At least, that's what usually happens. I'm Nell by the way.'

The girl smiled shyly. 'I'm Florence.' She hesitated, and then said, 'So what about the dancers whose numbers they don't read out? Do they just leave?'

'Yep,' Justin said. 'They tell themselves they are *not* going to cry. Then they head for the nearest bar and get drunk.'

'I see,' Florence said. After a moment, she added, 'I hope you don't mind me asking all these questions, but I've never been to an audition before.'

'No, not at all,' I said. Her first audition, and it was for a West End musical! No wonder she was so nervous. 'Ask away all you want. And just so you know, the getting drunk if you get cut isn't compulsory.'

'But I recommend it,' Justin said.

Florence laughed, and then gasped. 'Oh – I think they've made their minds up.'

A hush fell over the studio, as director Olivia Warren, holding a piece of paper, walked out from behind the table.

'I'm going to read out the numbers of the people we want to see dance again,' she said. 'If you hear your number, please stay in the studio. If I don't read out your number, we don't need to see you again today.' She looked down at the paper in her hand. '2, 5, 8, 13 . . .'

Thirteen. I'd made the cut. Weak with relief, I glanced towards Justin who was number twenty-two.

'I didn't hear a thing after they read out my number . . .' I said.

'No need to drown my sorrows as yet,' Justin said.

Florence was beaming from ear to ear. 'I'm through,' she said, breathlessly.

Those performers not lucky enough to have got through the first cut – over half the people in the room – were already filing out of the studio, some putting a brave face on it, holding their heads high, others despondent, shoulders hunched. The girl who'd stumbled out of the turn was in tears. One of the boys picked up her bag as well as his own and led her out.

Olivia's voice rang out over the dance space: 'Listen up, guys. We're going to take five and then Finn will teach you a tap routine. Please wear tap shoes.'

There was a flurry of movement as the dancers swarmed to the back of the studio to retrieve tap shoes from their bags. I took a moment to swallow some bottled water, glancing towards Finn, who was still sitting at the table . . .

Slowly, I sit up and swing my legs over the side of the bed, shivering as the cold air touches my bare skin. It's then that I see the tiny statuette of a ballerina, no more than an inch high, on my bedside table. I pick her up, marvelling at the detail of her face and hair, and her minute ballet shoes. There's a note, too, a piece of torn paper, folded in half, with my name written on it. I pull the duvet around me, unfold the paper, and read: I hope she brings you good luck in auditions. F xx

I smile. Finn has gone, but he's left me with something to remember him by . . .

'OK, guys, the break's over.'

The sound of Finn's voice jerked me out of the past and back into the present. At the other end of the studio, he pushed back his chair and walked around the table to stand once again in front of the auditionees. The image of our last night together still vivid in my mind, I felt my body grow warm.

'We're going to crack on,' Finn said. 'Give yourselves plenty of space to dance in, please.'

The twenty or so dancers who'd made the cut ran into the centre of the dance floor.

Telling myself very firmly to focus on the task in hand, I slid my feet into my tap shoes and joined them, once again standing between Justin and Florence.

If Finn's jazz routine was hard, his tap routine was danced at a speed that made it even harder. We danced the entire routine twice with the music, and then – while I fought to get my breath back – Finn returned to his chair behind the table and began an intense conversation with Olivia. After what seemed an age, although it was probably only about a minute, the Director stood up.

'We've seen all we need for today,' she said. 'Thank you all very much.' She resumed her seat and her conversation with Finn, writing in a notebook as he spoke to her. With a clatter of tap shoes, the auditionees began heading across the dance floor, collecting their belongings from the back of the studio, and making for the door. Some wore confident smiles, others looked as exhausted as I felt.

'Does that mean that none of us got through to the singing round?' Florence said to me and Justin in a quavering voice, as we stood waiting for what had become a bottle-neck at the back of the studio to clear, so that we could find our bags.

'No, not at all,' I said. 'If you've got a recall, one of the production team will let you know through your agent.'

'But don't sit by the phone,' Justin said. 'My agent told me that they're auditioning every day this week. Most likely, no-one will hear anything until they've seen everyone they've called in.'

Florence's blue eyes grew round. 'They're seeing *more* people! I couldn't believe how many were here today. Are auditions always like this?'

'West End dance auditions are,' Justin said. 'No – make that all auditions. I don't know why I put myself through them. Actually, I don't know why I ever became a dancer. Do you, Nell?'

'Oh, I never wanted to do anything else,' I said. 'Also, when people told me that dancing was a demanding, overcrowded profession, with hundreds of people chasing every job, I didn't believe them.'

'Neither did I,' Justin said.

'There's also that incredible high you get when you're on stage,' I said.

'And the applause,' Justin said. 'Don't forget the applause.' We exchanged smiles.

From behind us, a male voice said, 'Nell, do you have a sec?'

Finn.

I swung around, and fund myself standing so close to him that our bodies were almost touching. My face grew hot, and I took a step back.

'Sorry – I didn't mean to startle you,' Finn said. 'Can I have a word?'

'Yes, of course,' I said. What did he want with me? Why was he singling me out like this? My heart started hammering in my chest.

'Come with me,' Finn said, ushering me into the centre of the dance floor, far enough away from Justin and the other dancers still in the studio that they couldn't hear whatever it was he wanted to say to me.

'You danced well today.' He looked directly into my eyes. 'But you need to relax your shoulders more in the tap routine.'

'Oh. OK,' I said. I'd forgotten how hard it was to think coherently with Finn Harris's grey eyes gazing at me. 'Was I hunching my shoulders? I didn't realise.'

'I doubt anyone else would have noticed,' he said, 'but I did, and once I saw it . . .'

'You couldn't unsee it?' I said.

He nodded. My heart sank. He was going to tell me that this was where my dream of finally dancing on a West End stage came to an abrupt end.

'You were a bit tense, I think?' Finn said. 'I get that. I haven't forgotten what it's like to audition.'

Just tell me the dream is over, I thought, *and let me get out of here.*

'I'm going to put you through to the singing round, regardless,' Finn went on. 'If you get through that – which isn't up to me – but *if* you get through to the final round, then I'll be seeing you dance again, so remember what I've told you today, yeah?'

I gaped at him. I hadn't danced my best, but he was going to put me through to the singing call anyway.

'Thanks for the advice,' I said. 'I really appreciate it.'

'You're a good dancer, Nell. You always were.'

'Well, as you're now a choreographer casting a West End show, I won't argue with you.'

He laughed at that. 'It's good to see you again.'

'You too, Finn,' I said, looking up at his face, almost reaching up to push back the unruly lock of hair that still fell over his forehead, just as it had ten years ago.

'We were good together,' he said.

'Ah –' *What* exactly *did he mean by that?*

'When we were students, you were always my first choice of dance partner.'

Dancing, I thought. *That's all he's talking about. Dancing.*

'Maybe,' Finn went on, 'we could have a catch up over a coffee sometime?'

'Great idea,' I said. *No, that is* not *a great idea.*

With a smile, Finn turned away, and went to re-join his colleagues, at the other end of the studio. Realising that I was the only auditionee still present, I walked quickly across the dance floor, the sound of my tap shoes echoing loudly in the empty space, picked up my bag, and without looking back, clattered out of the door. Suddenly, my legs were shaking so badly that it was all I could do to stagger to the changing room. Apart from a couple of girls, one blonde and one dark-haired, both in their early twenties, who were re-touching their make-up in the mirrors, everyone else had left.

I sank down on a bench. How could I possibly go on auditioning for *Speakeasy* now that I knew Finn Harris was the Choreographer? I should tell Amanda Crewe, my agent, to withdraw me from the auditions. That's what anyone with any sense would do . . .

The voice of one of the girls standing by the mirrors intruded into my thoughts and I realised that they were looking quizzically at me.

'Sorry, I was miles away,' I said. 'What did you say?'

'Me and my flatmate were watching you in the audition,' the dark-haired girl said. 'We thought you coped with that difficult choreography extremely well, didn't we, Nicole?'

'We did, Marisa,' the blonde girl said.

'Thanks,' I said, feeling just a tiny bit patronised. 'It's very sweet of you to say so.'

'I only hope that I'm still dancing when I get to your age,' Marisa said.

'So do I,' Nicole said. 'Everyone says that a dancer's career is short, but I want to go on dancing as long as I can.'

'Women of your age are so inspiring,' Marisa said.

I smiled weakly, not sure whether I was amused or irritated. Just how ancient did these young women think I was?

Fortunately, because I'd had quite enough of their conversation, Marisa and Nicole took one more look at themselves in the mirrors before making their exit, leaving me with their artless yet stinging remarks echoing around my head – and perturbed that their view of me as a dancer approaching her sell-by date wasn't far from the truth. I was only thirty-four, but for anyone in my profession, like a footballer or an athlete, that was *old*. So far, I'd escaped the sprains and pulled muscles that can plague a dancing career, but inevitably, now that I was in my thirties, my level of physical fitness wasn't at its peak. For the first time, I admitted to myself that no longer being able to effortlessly shoulder my leg or jump into the splits was something I was going to have to deal with in the not-too-distant future. How much longer did I have before the auditions and the dance work dried up and I had to decide what I was going to do with the rest of my life?

A cold shiver ran down my spine.

Speakeasy could be my last chance to dance in a West End musical.

The door to the changing room opened, and more girls came in – the next batch of auditionees, presumably.

'Anyone know if it's tap or jazz first?' one girl called out.

'It's jazz then tap,' I said. 'I've already auditioned.' Taking off my tap shoes, I started pulling on my jeans and jumper.

'What's the choreography like?' another girl asked me.

Despite my uneasy thoughts, I couldn't help smiling. 'It's amazing,' I said.

What I should do was pull out of the *Speakeasy* auditions and keep well away from the Finn Harris. What I was going to do was try my best to get into the show.

Chapter Two

Letting myself into the tiny terraced house that had been my and Savannah's home for the last five years, I called out, 'I'm back.' Savannah appeared in the living room doorway, a delighted smile on her small face. I swept her into my arms for a hug.

'Hey, you,' I said, as she wriggled out of my embrace. 'How was school?'

'Fine,' she said, with her customary dismissal of her academic education. 'Did you get a recall?'

'I did,' I said. 'That card you gave me brought me luck.'

Savannah beamed. 'Come and see the dance I've made up,' she said. Taking my hand, she led me into the living room, where my younger sister Marianne was sitting on the sofa, the electronic keyboard that had once been hers and was now Savannah's, in front of her.

'Will you play my music again so I can show Mum my dance?' Savannah asked, clasping her hands together in front of her in the gesture that in the language of ballet meant 'please.'

'As you asked so nicely,' Marianne said. 'How did the audition go, Nell?'

'I'm through to the singing round.'

'Oh, well done.'

Shrugging off my coat, I sat down on the sofa. Savannah walked to the centre of the carpet and stood ready in third position. As the first notes sounded from the keyboard, she began to dance around the room, making the steps look easy, although I knew they were anything but that for a child of her age. By the time the dance ended, with her sinking gracefully down to the floor and bending over her outstretched leg so that her forehead was resting on her knee, my throat was feeling just a little tight. I was sure there weren't many nine-year-olds who could dance with real expression like my daughter.

'That was lovely, Savannah,' I said, giving her a round of applause. Marianne joined in, clapping her hands with admirable enthusiasm for one who I suspected had watched that dance many times over the last couple of hours.

'Will you show me the dance you did in your audition?' Savannah said.

'I will,' I said. 'Right now, I need to start cooking our dinner, but I'll show you later.'

'OK,' Savannah said. 'Can I go and play in my room?'

'Of course,' I said.

Savannah trotted out of the living room. I heard her running lightly up the stairs.

'Thanks for picking her up from school,' I said to Marianne. 'There was no way I could've got back in time. You're a life-saver.'

'No worries,' Marianne said. 'You know I'll look after her any time, when I'm not at work.' She smiled. 'But not this Saturday – I have a hot date.'

'With James?'

'No, not with James,' Marianne said. 'I split up with him weeks ago. It's a guy named Anders I'm seeing on Saturday. Do keep up, Nell.'

'I try,' I said, 'but with a love life as complicated as yours, it isn't always easy.'

'What about your love life? Anything I should know?'

'Actually, I spent most of today in the company of a very good-looking guy, who has often held me in his strong arms. No, wait – that was my friend and sometimes dance-partner, Justin.'

Marianne sighed. 'When did you last see any action that wasn't on the dance floor?'

'A while ago. I – I don't remember.'

'That's what I thought,' Marianne said. 'You need to get out there. Tell you what, if it goes well with Anders, I'll ask him if he's got any single friends who'd like to meet my beautiful sister.'

'Please don't.' Could anything be more mortifying?

'But why not?' Marianne persisted. 'We could double date. Mum and Dad would have Savannah, you know they would.' She hesitated, and then added, 'You've been on your own for such a long time.'

'I'm not on my own,' I said. 'I have a daughter.'

'You know what I mean,' Marianne said.

'Listen, Marianne,' I said. 'If someday I happen to meet a nice guy who sweeps me off my feet – great. But if that day never comes, that's absolutely fine. I'm perfectly happy as I am.' I glanced at my watch. 'I really must get the dinner on. Would you like to stay and eat with us?'

'Thanks, but I should make a move,' Marianne said. 'I'm off to a conference on the legal aspects of bank asset securisation tomorrow and I still need to pack.'

'Ah – I hope you find it – er – entertaining,' I said. As usual, when Marianne mentioned anything to do with her work, I had no idea what she was talking about, but I tried to be supportive.

Marianne laughed. 'I doubt it'll be riveting, but those of us who work in City law firms have to know about these things.'

We went out into the hall. Marianne put on her coat and called out goodbye to Savannah. I opened the front door.

'That nice guy you mentioned,' Marianne said. 'I hope you meet him very soon.'

I rolled my eyes. 'Goodbye, Marianne.'

''Bye.' Marianne headed off down the front path, and with a cheerful wave, got into her car, and drove off.

I went into the kitchen, and had assembled the ingredients for a lasagne, when my gaze fell on my laptop, which I'd left on the kitchen table. On impulse, I sat down and googled Finn Harris. Apart from the basic details of the names of shows he'd appeared in or choreographed, there was very little to discover about him online – although he had a social media profile it was 'friends only.' It struck me that if social media had been as pervasive ten years ago as it was now, me and Finn would most likely have been 'on-line friends' and keeping my secret from him would have been a lot harder. As it was, all he knew about my life since he'd last seen me was what he'd have read on my CV – no more than I'd found out about him on the internet. Telling myself that whatever Finn had been up to in the past ten years was none of my concern, I switched off my laptop, and started chopping onions.

'Bedtime,' I said to Savannah, picking up the remote and turning off the TV. 'I'll come up in ten minutes to say goodnight.' Savannah pouted, but headed upstairs. I loaded the dishwasher – such was my glamorous showbiz life – and then I went up to Savannah's room, where I found her sitting up in bed, reading a book.

'It's time you went to sleep now, sweetheart,' I said.

'Can't I read some more?' Savannah said. '*Please*. I've just got to a good bit.'

I did sympathise – I was annoyed if I was interrupted in the middle of a good book – but unless there was a very good reason for Savannah to stay up late, I took a firm line on bedtimes on a school night.

'Not tonight,' I said. 'You have school tomorrow.' Without further protest, Savannah put the book on her bedside table, and settled down under her duvet. I was very lucky, I knew, to have such an amiable child.

'Did you really like my dance?' she said.

'I did,' I said. 'You're a *very* good dancer.'

'I love dancing so much,' Savannah said, adding, 'Can I have a mobile phone? *Please*, Mum. Everyone in my class has one.'

Inwardly, I groaned. Savannah hadn't asked for a mobile phone in weeks. I'd thought she'd forgotten all about it.

'Everyone?' I said, raising my eyebrows.

'Yes,' Savannah said. This seemed to me very unlikely. My gaze travelled around my daughter's pink and white bedroom, and I smiled at the sight of the ballet-shoe patterned curtains, the dolls' house, and the music box which opened to reveal a ballerina revolving in time to the music. Savannah was still so young. Surely, she didn't need a phone of her own?

'Maybe we could think about getting you a phone for your birthday,' I said, buying myself time.

'OK,' Savannah said, apparently satisfied with my evasive answer.

I bent over her and kissed her cheek. 'Goodnight, Savannah.'

'Night, Mum.' She shut her eyes, and was practically asleep before I'd switched off her bedroom light. For a long moment, I stood there watching her, my beautiful little dancer. Then, very quietly, I closed the bedroom door.

When Finn had left London bound for Berlin, I'd never imagined that the next time I saw him, I'd be auditioning for a West End musical that he was choreographing.

When I'd made the decision not to tell him that he had a daughter, I'd thought I'd never see him again.

Chapter Three

'Do you remember that time I took my sons to a dance class?' Zelda said to me, as we sat on the park bench, watching Savannah push Charlie, aged five, on the swings. Theo, a year older, having declared that he could push himself, was now looking enviously at his brother. One-and-a-half-year-old Esme, worn out by fresh air and the excitement of feeding the ducks, was asleep in her buggy, well insulated in a snowsuit and a blanket. Martin, Zelda's husband, was back at their house, watching the sport on TV.

'I remember you telling me Theo refused to go in the door,' I said.

'While Charlie ignored the poor teacher and just ran around the studio,' Zelda said. 'I was mortified.' She sighed. 'My best friend gets to sit in a nice warm community centre, watching her daughter skip across a stage; I stand shivering on a touchline, watching my sons get covered in mud. Knowing my luck, Esme will want to play football like her brothers.'

I laughed. 'At least no-one can ever accuse you of being a pushy Stage Mother.'

'No – I'll be a pushy Football Mother,' Zelda said. 'Now, tell me all about the *Speakeasy* auditions – quickly, before my sons decide to start mauling each other and I have to go and drag them apart.'

'Ah, yes, the auditions,' I said. 'The first round was dance. It was tough, but it went OK, and I got a recall for the singing. I had to prepare two songs.'

I'd always seen myself as a dancer, but, as I'd been told repeatedly by my first dance teacher, Miss Rachel – now Savannah's dance teacher – if I was to have any hope of dancing on a West End stage, I also needed to be proficient in singing and acting as well, and when I'd gone to performing arts college I'd taken classes in all three. Even so, it was years since I'd been required to sing professionally – in panto – and the day before the *Speakeasy* singing call, I'd looked out my old sheet music and asked Marianne to come round after work so that she could play my favourite audition pieces for me on Savannah's keyboard. I'd actually spent more time listening to her talk about the new man in her life than I had practising my singing, but it was enough to reassure me that I could still hold a tune.

A week later, I was standing in the corridor outside Studio One, awaiting my turn to go in and sing for the panel – everyone with a recall for the singing got their own individual time slot – telling myself that auditioning for Finn was no different to auditioning for anyone else. I would *not* let his presence unnerve me.

It had been something of an anti-climax when I'd been called into the studio to find that the audition panel for the singing round consisted of Olivia Warren and the bearded man, who'd introduced himself as Jonathan Gower, Musical Director – and that Finn was conspicuous only by his absence. I'd handed my music to the accompanist, sung the whole of one of my songs and half of the other, before Olivia stopped me, thanked me, and told me that was all they needed to hear.

Now, I said to Zelda, 'The singing went OK, too, I think. At least, the Director and the MD were smiling. I'll just have to wait and see if I get a final recall.'

'It all sounds very promising,' Zelda said. 'Who is the show's Director?'

'Her name's Olivia Warren,' I said. Having by now googled all the creative team, I was able to add, '*Speakeasy* will be her third West End show. The Musical Director is Jonathan Gower. He's worked in the West End many times.'

'And who's the Choreographer?'

I'd dreaded Zelda asking that question, but knowing I couldn't put my revelation off any longer, I took a deep breath and said, 'Finn Harris.'

'*Finn!*' Zelda gasped. 'He's back in England?'

'Evidently,' I said.

'But – if he's the Choreographer – if you get cast in the show – you'd see him every day.'

'I guess I'd see him most days, while the show is in rehearsal. Once it opens, his job as choreographer is finished.'

'But what if he finds out . . ?' Zelda let the rest of the sentence hang in the air.

'He won't,' I said. 'How could he? I'm not going to tell him. And the only other person who knows he's Savannah's father is you.' I looked towards Savannah who was now pushing the boys on the roundabout – although she was small and slight for her age, she had them whizzing round at what seemed to me an alarming speed. 'Not too fast, Savannah,' I called. Waiting until the roundabout slowed, I turned back to Zelda and said, 'I'll admit it was a massive shock to walk into that audition and see Finn again after all this time, but now that I've had a chance to get my head around it, I don't see any reason why working with him would be an issue.'

'Seriously?' Zelda shook her head as though to clear it. 'You won't feel at all *awkward* working with Finn Harris?' She pushed her unruly blonde curls back from her face.

'I *want* to work with him,' I said. 'If the dancing we did at the audition is anything to go by, his choreography is brilliant. Anyway, I've not yet been cast. I don't even know if I've got a final. I'm waiting to hear from my agent.'

Zelda gave me a long look. 'Do you *want* him to find out? Is that it?

'Absolutely not,' I said, shocked. Surely she knew me better than that? 'I made the decision not to tell him ten years ago, and I'm not going back on it now.'

We both fell silent. Savannah, having abandoned the roundabout and the boys, was now on a swing, her long dark hair flying out behind her as she swung herself higher and higher. I resisted the urge to shout at her to be careful.

Zelda checked the time on her phone. 'We should make a move,' she said. 'The roast will be ready.'

'Lovely,' I said. 'I'm starving.' We got to our feet, and, with Zelda pushing the still sleeping Esme in her buggy, started across the grass toward the children's playground. Then Zelda came to an abrupt halt.

'Nell –' she began.

'What is it?'

'There's something I want to say to you, but you have to promise you won't get mad.'

I arched my eyebrows. 'As if.'

'Do you know if Finn has moved back to England permanently? Or is he just here to choreograph this one show?'

'I have no idea,' I said. 'An audition was hardly the occasion to ask him about his future travel plans.'

Zelda hesitated, but then she said, 'If he's back in England for good, whether or not you get into *Speakeasy*, I think you should tell him about Savannah.'

'Never going to happen.' I wasn't mad at her, but if she pursued this line of conversation, I very likely would be. 'Leave it, Zelda. Please.'

Zelda opened her mouth as though to speak, but evidently thinking better of it, gave me a brief nod of her head. Then her eyes widened.

'Oh, for heaven's sake!' she said. 'Theo! Charlie! Stop that right now!'

I spun around to see Theo and Charlie hitting each other with branches fallen from a nearby tree.

'No TV later if have to tell you again,' Zelda called.

Both boys dropped their improvised swords.

Zelda sighed. 'Remember how we used to spend Sundays when we shared a flat? Never getting up before noon. Meeting friends for a pub lunch. Wine. All of us going back to someone's house. Music. Flirting. More wine.'

'If you could turn the clock back,' I said, 'would you want to?'

'Hmm, let me think about that,' Zelda said. 'These days I get trips to the park, a Sunday roast with my family, my best friend and her daughter, followed by a game of Snakes and Ladders. No, I wouldn't go back.'

I glanced towards Savannah who was now performing an arabesque, the climbing frame substituting for a ballet barre, and I smiled.

'Me neither,' I said. 'And even if I could, I wouldn't do anything different. And we still have wine.'

A week passed. I did the school run. I went for coffee with some of the other 'school mums.' I went over the dances from the first round of the *Speakeasy* auditions, both in my head and in my living room. I willed my agent, Amanda, to phone me with the news that I'd got a final recall, but my mobile remained obstinately silent.

On Saturday, I ferried Savannah to her tap, jazz and ballet classes at the Rachel Mullings School of Dance, and later we did some baking together. Sunday, I caught up with some household chores, took Savannah to a school-friend's birthday party, supervised her homework – hopefully without revealing that I had no idea how to do the arithmetic without a calculator – and once she'd gone to bed, collapsed in front of the TV with a glass of red.

Either I'll hear from Amanda tomorrow, I thought, *or I've not got a final recall.*

On Monday morning, I got a text from Justin – he had a final. I told myself there were any number of reasons why he might have heard when I hadn't, but, while I was genuinely pleased for him, my heart sank.

Reminding myself that sitting on the sofa staring at my phone wouldn't make it ring, and that while I might spend most of my working hours in a sequined leotard and high heels, with feathers in my hair, I also had a home to run, I went out into the hall and opened the cupboard.

'It's showtime!' I said, and got out the hoover.

It was late in the afternoon, just when I'd decided that I *almost* definitely hadn't got through to the final, that my phone rang – and the screen showed me that the caller was Amanda. Although I knew that she was unlikely to be ringing me if I'd *not* got a recall, it was with no small amount of trepidation that I hit the answer icon.

'Hey, Nell,' she said. 'Just a very quick call to let you know you're in the final for *Speakeasy.*'

'Oh, thank you, Amanda,' I gasped. 'That's great. Thank you so *so* much for phoning.'

'Of course.' Amanda sounded bemused. Understandably, I supposed, as calling a dancer to inform them they were in a final for a West End musical was all in a day's work for her. 'I'll email you the details,' she continued.

'Thank you.'

'Well, I'll say goodbye for now.'

"Bye, Amanda. And thanks again.' My hand shook as I put down my phone.

I had one more chance to show Finn – and the other members of the audition panel – what I could do. One more chance to achieve my dream of dancing on a West End stage.

No pressure there, I thought, as I started going over Finn's tap routine in my head.

Chapter Four

On the morning of the *Speakeasy* Final, I'd double-checked that everything I needed was in my dance bag – including another good luck card from Savannah, who, as always when I had such an early morning start, had stayed the night with her grandparents – and had got as far as unlocking the front door, when a sudden thought struck me. Ten years ago, Finn had given me a good luck charm; I could do with some of that luck now.

Running back upstairs and into my bedroom, I stood on a chair, and lifting my memory box from the top of my wardrobe, emptied its contents out onto my bed. I had a moment's panic when I didn't immediately find the tiny ballerina – it must have been years since I'd last taken her out of the box – but then I spotted a glint of silver, and found her under an old theatre ticket. Placing her on the flat of my hand, I went to the window so I could see her more clearly in the daylight, marvelling at the detail etched in the silver just as I had when I'd discovered her on my bedside table. What, I wondered, would Finn make of my keeping her all these years? Recalling that this was not the time for daydreaming, I stowed the little dancer in my dance bag, and headed off to what was increasingly feeling like a date with destiny.

As always at this time on a week day morning, the tube was jam-packed with commuters, and I had to stand for the entire journey into central London, hanging on to the overhead rail, apologizing when my over-sized bag bashed into a businessman's newspaper – quite why anyone would attempt to read a paper in a crowded underground carriage I couldn't imagine – and trying not to mind when a woman stepped on my foot, but I reached Covent Garden station, crowded as always with tourists and shoppers headed for the craft stalls in the piazza, in good time. Cutting through the side streets, passing the dance shop where I bought my first pair of pointe shoes, I arrived outside the London Dance Studios just as they opened. A cluster of dancers who'd arrived before me, immediately vanished inside. I was about to follow them when I spotted a girl standing a short distance away, half-hidden by a lamp-post, and recognised her as Florence. I waved, and waited for her to join me, but she remained where she was. I beckoned to her, but she shook her head. Assuming that she was waiting for someone else, I made to go inside the studios, when I saw her stagger, and put a hand on the lamp post as if to hold herself upright. I'm not proud of myself when I admit that I hesitated – I didn't know the girl, I was about to go into the most important audition of my dancing career, if not my life – but in the next instant I knew that I couldn't in all conscience just walk away without checking she wasn't about to collapse in the street, and hurried over to her.

'Hey, Florence,' I said, as I reached her. She was, I noticed, very pale. 'Is everything OK with you?'

Florence nodded. 'Y-yes. Th-thank you. I-I just felt a bit dizzy, that's all' She smiled feebly. 'I'm so nervous about the final. I never expected to get this far.'

'Loads of performers get jittery before an audition,' I said. 'It'll pass. Have you got any water?'

'Oh – yes – I do.' She bent down, retrieved a bottle of water from the bag at her feet, and drank. 'I'm all right now.'

'Good to hear,' I said. 'Right. Let's go in and get warmed-up.'

'You go ahead,' Florence said. 'I-I'll see you inside.'

I shot her a look, strongly suspecting that if I went inside without her, she'd never make it through the door. I told myself that it made no matter to me – if she didn't come in, there would be one less dancer competing for a place in the line – but I knew that if I left her there I'd feel guilty all day. A ten-years-old memory surfaced . . .

I'm standing outside a dance studio, in an anxiety of indecision, watching the other dancers streaming in to the final audition for a new West End musical. I wanted it so much, but now I'm here, I can't bring myself to go in the door.

'Nell! You got through to the final round, too!' A girl from my year at college plants herself in front of me on the pavement. 'Let's do this!' she says.

And even although I know that if what I suspect is true – as a dancer, I am very conscious of changes in my body – then

I'm wasting everyone's time, including my own, I go into the audition...

'You need to come in now if you're going to have time to warm up properly,' I said, to Florence. When she didn't respond, but stared towards the studios biting her bottom lip, I added, 'You've got a chance to get cast in a West End show today – don't throw it away.' I turned on my heel, and started walking towards the studios. To my relief, Florence fell into step beside me.

Inside the studios, we were met by the same girl holding a clipboard who'd been at the first round of auditions.

'May I have your names?' she said to me and Florence.

'Nell Avery,' I said.

'Florence Newton.' Florence's voice was scarcely above a whisper. The girl consulted her list and ticked off our names. Today, she didn't give us numbers. I supposed the audition panel must all know who we were by now.

'Please be ready to dance in Studio One by nine o'clock sharp,' the girl said. 'Please wear heels.' Before I could thank her, she turned her attention to the dancer behind us in the queue. 'Name, please?'

Taking the hint, Florence still at my side, I walked briskly to the changing rooms, where half a dozen or so girls were readying themselves for the final. Hurriedly stripping off my shirt and jeans, I adjusted the straps on my leotard, and put on my dance heels. Squeezing past a girl re-doing her lipstick, I found a space in front of the mirrors and inspected my reflection. For a thirty-four-year-old woman who'd got up at the crack of dawn, I looked pretty good, I thought – even if my waist was an inch thicker than when I was twenty. I pulled my leotard higher up towards my hips so that my legs looked longer.

'Ready?' I asked Florence, who was wearing knee-length leggings and a crop top, revealing a stomach that was positively concave.

'As ready as I'll ever be,' she said.

With Florence trotting at my heels, I made my way to Studio One, where twenty or so dancers, rather than chatting with their mates, were doing some sort of warm-up – it was getting serious now. Looking around the room, I saw that this time, there were a few people I knew – a girl I'd worked with occasionally on corporate gigs, a boy who'd partnered me in an advert – and others I remembered from the dance round. There was also a girl I recognised from having watched her perform several times in the West End, which reminded me that however well I'd done to get to the final, I was up against some stiff competition. Then I spotted Justin lying on his side with one leg raised behind his ear, while chatting to another guy who was sitting in box splits.

'Let's join Justin,' I said to Florence.

'Oh – I don't want to intrude on you and your friends,' she said.

'You won't be intruding,' I said. Picking a path across the studio between the lithe dancer bodies all over the floor to the front where Justin was lying, I sat next to him and started my own warm-up. Florence sat a short distance away, and did the same.

'You'll remember Florence from the dance round,' I said to Justin. Florence smiled shyly.

'Of course,' Justin said. 'Hey, Florence.' Sitting up, he gestured towards the other guy. 'This is Matt Brooking. Matt – Nell.'

'Hi, Nell and Florence,' Matt said. He looked to be in his early twenties – a few years younger than Justin – with a shock of light brown hair, and the toned physique typical of a male dancer. He was good-looking, I thought – in a boy-next-door sort of way – and vaguely familiar.

'Have we met before?' I asked him.

'I don't think so,' he said, 'but I'm guessing you've met my older brother. People say I look like him.'

'He's Kieron's brother,' Justin said. 'You must remember Kieron – my ex.'

'Oh – yes,' I said. 'I can see the resemblance now. How is Kieron? What's he up to these days?' I had a vague idea that after he and Justin had split up – amicably – Kieron had gone travelling.

'He's working for an events company,' Matt said. 'Which is great for me as he puts a lot of gigs my way.'

From nowhere it came into my head that Events Management was a job that I could consider when I could no longer dance for a living. I'd danced at enough events to know how to run them.

Justin said, 'Nell, there's a couple of girls who've just come in who're trying to get your attention.'

Giving myself a mental shake – now was *not* the time to be thinking about the demise of my dance career – I looked over my shoulder to see two girls standing by the door, the blonde girl waving and smiling at me across the room, the other, dark-haired, raising a desultory hand. For a moment I couldn't think who they were, and then I recognized them as Nicole and Marisa, who'd been so impressed that I could still dance, despite my great age and decrepitude. I fixed a smile on my face, and waved back. I was relieved when they didn't come and join me, Florence and the boys, but found themselves a space on the other side of the studio.

'Friends of yours?' Justin said.

'Not so you'd notice,' I said.

'Ah – the audition panel have arrived!' Matt said.

While I'd been distracted, Finn, Olivia and Jonathan had entered the studio, and arranged themselves behind their table, followed by the pianist who settled herself at the piano.

'I wish I knew how many dancers they're looking for,' Florence said.

'My agent said they want ten guys and ten girls,' Matt said.

I counted the number of auditionees who'd made it through to the final: twenty female dancers and twenty male dancers.

Half the dancers in the studio would not get cast in the show.

The audition panel conferred briefly among themselves, and then Finn pushed back his chair, stood up, and walked slowly around the table to stand before the auditionees. Every dancer in the room fell silent and sat up a little straighter.

'Morning all,' Finn said. 'If you'd like to stand in rows of eight across the studio, please.'

I sprang to my feet and ran forward, staking my claim to a place in the front row, almost directly in front of Finn. His hair was tousled this morning, I noticed, just as it was ten years ago, when I'd woken up next to him . . . My pulse began to race. *Focus, Nell*, I told myself firmly. *You've only got one shot at this*. Gradually, my pulse calmed to a normal rate – or at least to what was normal for a dancer in the final for a West End show with adrenaline coursing through her like wildfire.

In the wall mirror, I saw Justin, standing on my left, his face fixed in a smile that was just a little tight.

I turned my head towards him and mouthed, 'Break a leg.'

He mouthed back, 'And you.' Matt, I saw, was standing on his other side. I couldn't see Florence at first, but then I saw a flash of red amongst the reflections of the dancers massed behind me, which could have been her.

This is it, I thought. *The next few hours will decide if I finally get to dance on a West End stage.*

'OK, guys,' Finn said. 'The first two rows stay where you are – everyone else move to the side of the studio. First group, we'll start with the jazz routine I taught you last week, with the music.'

In the mirrors I saw a couple of dancers glance uneasily at one another – evidently they'd expected to have time to go over the routine before dancing it. The pianist played the introduction.

Finn said, 'And five, six, seven, eight –'

Thankful that I'd practised the routine at home, I started to dance, letting the music lead me through the steps, the echo of Finn's voice in my head reminding me to relax my shoulders . . .

The music and the routine came to an end.

'First group to the side,' Finn said. 'The next two rows to the centre. Five, six, seven, eight –'

The dancers in the second group – who I now saw included Marisa and Nicole – sprang into action. I watched the two of them as they danced, and, annoyingly, was forced to admit that they were both good dancers, who knew the routine and performed it as Finn had taught it. Unlike one of the boys, who appeared to have given up any attempt at remembering the choreography and was improvising a routine all of his own.

'And the last row, please –'

The last group of dancers ran forward to dance, Florence among them. From where I was standing at the side of the studio next to Justin and Matt, I could see that she was biting her bottom lip, and darting nervous glances around the studio. *Break a leg, Florence*, I thought.

The pianist began to play.

'Five, six, seven, eight –'

The dancers went into the routine – and suddenly Florence's demeanour changed, a smile lighting up her whole face, her eyes shining, her slender body seemingly weightless as she leapt and twirled, performing Finn's choreography so beautifully that it was impossible to look away. It came to me then that this was one of those extraordinary moments in an audition, when you look at a young, unknown performer and see something in them – a raw talent, undefinable, unable to be taught – that sets them apart from everyone else. I glanced towards Finn, and from the way his eyes followed Florence as she floated across the floor, I was sure that he'd seen it too. Unless I was very much mistaken, the girl who'd been afraid to walk into the audition had it in her to become a star.

The music ended. Like the other dancers, Florence stood motionless. I was pleased to see that she was smiling broadly – as anyone should, having danced like that.

'Florence is very good, isn't she?' I said to Justin. He nodded in agreement.

'She's outstanding,' Matt said, gazing at Florence in awe.

Finn called out, 'Everyone take ten.' He rejoined Olivia Warren and Jonathan Gower behind the table, and the three of them plunged into an intense discussion, heads close together. The dancers milled around the studio, gulping down bottled water, and checking their appearance in the wall-mirrors. The boy who'd forgotten the routine sat on the floor by himself, his head in his hands. Florence trotted over to me and the guys, her eyes bright, and with no trace of her earlier nerves.

'Well done,' Matt said to her. 'You danced that routine brilliantly.'

'Oh – thank you,' Florence said, her face turning pink. 'What happens now, Nell?'

I glanced towards the audition panel. They were still deep in discussion.

'I suspect the panel are about to make a cut,' I said, having been to more than enough auditions to know that they all followed a similar pattern. I swallowed uneasily.

'Already?' Florence gasped.

'You'll be fine, Florence,' Matt said. 'Honestly, you don't need to worry.'

Even as Matt spoke, Finn stood up, holding a sheet of paper, and walked around the table. The studio fell silent and the face of every dancer turned towards him.

'Listen up,' he said. 'I'm going to read out the names of people we need to see dance again. When you hear your name, please come forward.'

The thought came to me that he was literally holding my fate in his hands.

'Lucas Halliday,' Finn said, 'Matt Brooking . . .'

The dancers whose names he read out, walked to the centre of the studio, as if walking from the wings at the side of a stage into the spotlight. My hands clenched painfully tight.

'. . . Hettie Parkes . . .' That was the girl I'd recognised as a West End performer.

'. . . Nell Avery . . .'

I exhaled sharply. I'd made the cut! Resisting the urge to perform a celebratory dance around the studio, I joined Matt and the others.

Finn was still reeling off names: '. . . Florence Newton . . .'

A beaming Florence ran lightly across the floor to me and Matt.

'Told you that you'd be OK,' Matt said to her.

'. . . Marisa Cutler . . .'

Smoothing her dark hair, the girl who'd so annoyed me walked into the centre of the room.

There were now only twelve dancers left standing at the back of the studio, including Justin, whose smile was beginning to resemble a rictus grin.

'. . . Nicole Whitby . . .'

Marisa's fair-haired friend had also got through.

'. . . and Justin Ofabemi,' Finn said.

Oh, thank goodness, I thought, as Justin strolled nonchalantly up to me, outwardly calm, as if he hadn't had a moment's doubt that he'd hear his name – although the patches of sweat under his arms told otherwise.

'Everyone else, we don't need to see you dance again today,' Finn said. 'Thank you all very much.'

While the dancers who'd made the cut murmured congratulations to their friends and acquaintances, the five girls and five boys who had *not* heard their names read out by Finn collected up their bags and coats, and trailed out of the studio. I'd been cut often enough to feel for them, especially the boy who'd forgotten the choreography, who was out the door ahead of all the rest. It was bad enough to fail an audition when you knew you'd danced your best – you could tell yourself that you simply weren't right for the gig or that the casting director was an idiot – but to get as far as a final and then mess up had to be a lot worse.

Finn said, 'Time to crack on, people. Everyone grab a partner.'

Without hesitation, I slid my arm through Justin's. If this round of the audition was partner work, I wanted to be dancing with a guy who I knew could lift a girl above his head without dropping her. All around us, the remaining auditionees were hastily pairing up. In the wall mirrors, I saw Marisa seize the hand of Lucas Halliday, whose name Finn had read out first, and who I'd noticed was a fierce dancer. However much she irritated me, I couldn't fault the girl's audition technique. Behind the other dancers, Matt held out his hand to Florence. With a shy smile, she took it. As if leading her into a ballroom, he drew her nearer to the front of the studio.

'If I could have your attention, please,' Finn said. 'I'm going to teach you another short routine. Nell, could you and your partner move forward, please. I know you pick up steps quickly, so I'll use you to demonstrate. If that's all right?'

At first all I did was gape at him, but then I smiled. I was in the final for a West End show, and the Choreographer had just asked me to demonstrate his choreography. I reminded myself that this particular choreographer had called on me because he knew me, not because he'd already decided to give me the job, but still . . . With the eyes of every other auditionee searing our backs, Justin and I stepped out of the line to the stand directly in front of Finn. It was as well smiling was mandatory at an audition, because I couldn't stop.

'Everyone got enough space to dance in?' Finn said. 'OK, folks, let's get started.'

The routine that he proceeded to teach – with me and Justin performing each move first and the other dancers copying us – wasn't complicated, but it included two demanding lifts that made me glad I was literally in safe hands. After we'd marked the routine through several times, Finn swopped a number of dance partners around – splitting up Lucas and Marisa, who did not look happy – and we danced it with him calling out the counts, and then twice with the music.

'And again, please,' Finn said.

Again, the men held out their arms, and the girls rushed into their embrace. I felt Justin's hands on my waist as he lifted me onto his shoulder, before setting me back on my feet, his arm supporting me as I bent backwards, so far back that my head almost touched the floor, before he raised me up and we spun away from each other . . .

The music crashed to a stop in one loud echoing chord.

The dancers ceased to move.

For a long moment, Finn regarded us silently from the front of the studio.

Then he said, 'Well done, guys. I'm not going to ask you to dance that routine again today. As I'm sure you'll be pleased to hear.' There was a faint ripple of laughter, that sounded just a little forced. Finn smiled. 'Stay where you are, please. We won't keep you much longer.' Turning away, he bent over the table to talk to Olivia and Jonathan.

I stood next to Justin, relieved to have a chance to get my breath back. The mirrors showed me that tendrils of wet hair had escaped from my pony tail and were now plastered to my face, and I could feel sweat trickling down my back. Not that I was the only dancer in the studio who no longer looked audition-ready. Guys had dark patches of sweat on their T-shirts, girls had mascara smudged around their eyes, and a number of dancers, exhausted either by Finn's choreography or the tension of auditioning, had sunk down onto the floor – not wanting him to think I lacked stamina, I resisted the temptation to do the same. I looked for Florence and Matt, but caught only a brief glimpse of them before another dancer moved in front of them blocking my view – they were both still standing at any rate. Beside me, Justin used his wristband to wipe his forehead.

'Remind me again why I put myself through the ordeal of auditions,' he said to me, quietly.

'I do it for the glamour,' I said, indicating my reflection in the mirror. He laughed softly.

At that moment, a hush fell over the studio as Olivia Warren and Jonathan Gower rose to their feet, and joined Finn in front of the wilting auditionees.

'First of all, I want to thank you all for auditioning for us – and for *Speakeasy*,' Olivia said. 'There was a time when I was standing where you are now, and I know how hard it is, believe me.' She paused, as if collecting her thoughts. 'There are a lot of very talented performers here today. Jonathan, Finn and I have some difficult decisions to make, but we *will* be casting the ensemble from the dancers in this studio. I can't tell you exactly when we'll be sending out offers, but I assure you we won't keep you waiting any longer than we have to. Now, all that remains is for me to wish you a safe journey home. Thank you very much.'

With that, the Director, Choreographer and MD resumed their seats, and their conversation. Through a haze of exhaustion, I looked at Finn, and wondered what he was feeling at that moment, knowing that for everyone he cast in the show, he was trampling on someone else's dreams . . .

Realising that I was the only dancer still standing in the middle of the dance space, I hurried to the back of the studio, hoping that Finn hadn't noticed me gawping at him. Edging my way through the swarm of auditionees retrieving their belongings, swopping mobile numbers, and promising to let each other know as soon as they heard *anything*, I located my bag and Justin, who was talking with Florence and Matt, and went up to them to say goodbye – and to express the hope that the next time we saw each other would be at the first day of rehearsals.

'Anyone fancy getting a late lunch?' Justin asked, as I reached them. 'There's a bar – the Troubadour – just around the corner from here that has a good lunchtime menu.'

'I'll come,' Matt said. 'I'm starving. Also, I could murder a pint.' To Florence, he added, 'Come with us, Florence? It's a long-standing theatrical traditional that after a final, a dancer heads for the nearest tavern.'

'Oh – That would be lovely,' Florence said, adding, 'The audition was *amazing*, but it all went so fast – I'm not ready to go home yet.' She was, I saw, still on a high from dancing.

'What about you, Nell?' Justin said. 'The first round is on me.'

I hesitated. Tempting as it was to go with them – to wind down from the audition over a glass of wine, speculating which of our fellow auditionees were likely to be cast – if I went straight home, I'd be in time to meet Savannah from school. On the other hand, she was expecting to be collected by her grandmother, and was perfectly happy about it. Having lunch with an old friend and making new ones, wouldn't make me a neglectful parent.

'Now that,' I said to Justin, 'is what I call a plan.'

Chapter Five

The four of us piled through the door of the Troubadour – a venue extremely popular with both performers and theatre-goers on account of its proximity to a number of West End theatres, and famous for the signed black and white photographs of well-known actors that adorned its walls – and discovered that we were not the only dancers to feel the need for post-audition rehydration. Looking round the crowded bar for an empty table, I spotted Hettie Parkes and another girl sitting in a corner, sharing a bottle of wine, a group of male dancers packed loudly into a booth and, perched on bar-stools, Marisa and Nicole. Fortunately, they were too absorbed in their own conversation to notice me, so there was no necessity for me to further our scant acquaintance.

'Someone's just leaving,' Justin said, pointing to two middle-aged women who were making for the door. 'Quick, grab their place.'

Plunging heedlessly through a group of men in business suits, and the closely packed tables, we shoved our dance bags under the empty table, and commandeered four chairs. The next few minutes were taken up with studying the menu, and trotting up to the bar to place our orders. Justin bought a round of drinks, returning from the bar with wine for me, lager for him and Matt, and cola for Florence. A waiter arrived soon after with our pizzas, burgers, and chips.

We talked over the audition, offering suggestions as to what might have led the panel to keep one dancer after the first harsh cut and not another, but agreeing that no-one could ever hope to understand the arcane decision-making process of a casting team. No-one ventured an opinion as to their own chances of getting into the show. Matt hoped that whatever decision Olivia, Jonathan and Finn made, they'd make it fast.

'It's the not knowing that's the worst,' he said, through a mouthful of burger, 'especially when you hear that other people have had offers.'

'Do they give feedback to the dancers who don't get cast?' Florence asked. 'Or is it just a *thanks but no thanks*?'

Justin gave her a long look. 'If they're not interested in casting you in the show, you probably won't hear anything at all.'

'They don't phone your agent to let them know?' Florence's eyes widened.

'Only very rarely,' I said.

'Mostly you're just left hanging,' Justin said. 'The trouble is, it's hard to know when to give up hope. Even when the full cast of a show is announced, if I know I did a good audition, I still sometimes have this insane notion that someone will drop out and I'll get the Call.'

Matt laughed. 'You and me both, mate,' he said. 'Not that I can imagine why anyone would drop out of a West End musical,' Despite the warmth in the bar, I shivered.

'Neither can I,' Florence said.

'The only viable reason I can think of for pulling out of any show is injury,' Justin said. 'Don't you agree, Nell?'

Deciding that it was high time I changed the subject, I shrugged and said, 'I'll get the next round. Same again?' My tactics worked, and further debate as to why a dancer might turn down a chance to perform on a West End stage, was cut short by the more pressing question of who wanted what to drink.

By now, the Troubadour was considerably less crowded, the lunchtime clientele, including the other dancers – except for Marisa and Nicole who were still ensconced at the other end of the bar – having departed and the pre-theatre diners not yet arrived, and I didn't have to wait long before I was served. Standing at the bar, waiting for my change, I looked back towards our table, and seeing Florence giggling at whatever Matt was saying to her, I wondered if she could be younger than I'd first thought. She was drinking cola. Was she even old enough to be in a premises that served alcohol? I drank a mouthful of my wine. Thank goodness I had a few years yet before I'd have to worry about Savannah going to bars and hanging out with good-looking boys like Matt. Who, even as I watched, got his phone out of his shirt pocket and passed it to Florence so she could key something into it – presumably her number. She then retrieved own phone from her bag and gave it to him, and he proceeded to do the same. Of course, he could have just asked for her contact details so that they could let each other know if they'd got an offer for *Speakeasy*, with no ulterior motive, but somehow, I doubted it.

'Hey, Nell.' Finn's voice intruded on my thoughts, making me jump. I spun around and found myself looking directly up into his handsome face. For a moment, I couldn't think what he was doing in the pub, but then it occurred to me that after the long day he'd had, he was probably in as much need of a restorative glass of wine as I was. 'May I buy you a drink?' he said, leaning nonchalantly against the bar . . .

I came to the nightclub with Zelda and some other friends, but I've lost them amongst the flashing lights, throbbing music, and the wildly gyrating bodies on the dance floor. I am standing at the bar when, suddenly, I spot Finn, a friend from performing arts college, making his way towards me through the crowd. I've seen him at auditions a couple of times since we graduated, but it's been a while.

'Hey, Nell,' he says, when he reaches me, raising his voice so that I can hear him above the music. We exchange air-kisses. 'Have a drink with me?' He smiles. 'I'm celebrating. I heard today that I've landed a role in a musical in Berlin . . .'

A chance meeting in a club off the Strand, Finn buying me a drink, and then another . . .

We leave the nightclub together, neither of us ready for this night to end, walking arm in arm along a narrow street that Finn thinks leads down to the river, laughing when we stumble on the uneven pavement, denying loudly that we've maybe drunk just a little too much. When we reach the Embankment, we fall silent, standing by the wall that runs alongside the Thames, looking out over moon-silvered waters, the street lamps like a string of fairy lights. A warm breeze caresses my bare arms.

'Nell –' Finn says. I turn my body towards him. He looks down at me with hooded eyes. 'You're so beautiful tonight,' he says, putting his hands on my waist, and drawing me close to him, pressing his hips against mine. I tilt up my chin, and he leans in for a kiss, tasting of wine and moonlight. I feel the heat of his desire through my thin summer dress, and my body catches fire...

Our first kiss down by the river, by the light of a full moon. That's how had started between us all those years ago. But those days were over and done.

'Thanks,' I said to Finn, 'but I've just bought a round.' I indicated my tray of brimming glasses. 'I'm with some other dancers –' I glanced towards Justin, Florence and Matt, who I now saw were openly staring at me and Finn, although, when they saw me looking in their direction, they quickly looked away.

'It's thirsty work, auditioning,' Finn said, with a smile. He paused and then added, 'Thank you for demonstrating the partner work for me today. It made my job a lot easier.'

'You're welcome,' I said.

The bartender came back from the till with my change, and Finn asked him for a glass of Chenin. His favourite wine, I remembered.

'I'm thinking you and Justin have danced together before?' he said.

'Oh, yes, I've worked with him on a lot of gigs. He's lovely to partner. He's a very talented dancer.'

'I noticed,' Finn said, dryly.

'Ah – of course,' I said, flustered. What was I thinking, wittering on like that? Obviously, Finn knew Justin was a talented dancer; he'd put him through to the final.

'The pair of you did a good job today,' Finn remarked.

Without thinking, I blurted, 'Good enough to get us into the show?'

Finn's gaze caught mine and held it. 'Nothing will be decided before the end of next week,' he said. 'Even when Olivia, Jonathan and I know who we want in the ensemble, the show's producers have to give their approval. All I will say, is that you certainly didn't do yourself any harm the way you danced today –' He broke off, as Marisa Cutler, pushing past the other people at the bar, planted herself in front of him.

'Hello, Finn,' she said, flicking her hair over her shoulder. 'I may call you Finn? I'm Marisa. Marisa Cutler.' She smiled, revealing very white teeth. I noticed that she had unusually long, pointed incisors that reminded me of a cat.

Finn raised one eye-brow. 'Yes, I know your name,' he said.

'I hope you don't mind my accosting you like this,' Marisa said, 'but I simply had to tell you how much I enjoyed auditioning for you today.' She put her hand over her heart, which inevitably drew attention to the ample breasts straining to break free of her low-cut top. 'Your choreography is awesome.'

For goodness' sake, I thought, *does the idiotic girl think flaunting her body at a choreographer is the way to get cast in a show? That's just plain* wrong – *on so many levels.*

'Er – thanks,' Finn said.

'Well, I won't take up any more of your time,' Marisa said. 'I just wanted to let you know how much I admire your work. I do *so* hope I get the chance to dance for you again.' With another pointy-toothed smile, and a vague nod in my direction, she sashayed back along the length of the bar and rejoined Nicole. I looked at Finn, and, with no small amount of satisfaction, saw that rather than watching Marisa's swaying hips, his grey eyes were looking at me.

'About you and Justin,' he said, picking up our conversation from before, as if it hadn't been interrupted, 'you did dance well together today, but it's unprofessional of me to discuss the audition with you, or with anyone other than the casting team, so please don't repeat what I said.'

'I won't,' I said. Ten years ago, we could and did talk to each other about all sorts of things, but we were different people now, in very different places in our lives – and there was a gulf between us that I couldn't cross even if I wanted to. Which I didn't. 'I should go –' I began, before realising that Finn was no longer looking at me, but over my head, towards the door. His face breaking into a smile, he raised a hand and waved. Twisting around, I followed the direction of his gaze and saw a woman edging her way between the tables towards us. She was tall and very striking, her hair a mass of dark curls around her heart-shaped face, her very short skirt revealing enviably long legs. And she was no more than twenty-five at the most.

'There she is,' Finn murmured, under his breath. Turning back to me, he said, 'Nell, I'd like to talk more with you, but –'

'You have a date,' I said, feeling that it was safe assumption to make. 'And I should get back to my friends.'

He nodded. 'Listen, I honestly don't know which way the casting is going to go – there are so many things we have to consider – and even if I did know, I couldn't tell you, but whether or not we end up working together on *Speakeasy*, I meant what I said the other day about us having a catch-up over coffee sometime.'

'That would be lovely,' I said. *But it's never going to happen.* I smiled and started back towards Justin and the others – and almost collided with Finn's stunning date. Fortunately, the wine that sloshed out of my glass, only went on me, not her, but the look she gave me could not be described as friendly.

'Sorry,' I said, standing aside to let her sweep imperiously past me, before continuing on my way.

From behind me, I heard her say: 'Finn, who was that woman you were talking to?'

And Finn reply: 'Just a dancer I used to know.'

Which was about right.

Chapter Six

Savouring the taste of my mother's home-made sponge cake, I settled back in the rocking chair that my father had made when I was about Savannah's age. While my parents' house had seen a number of changes over the years – the long through-room where we were now gathered had once been two small rooms, and there were many more photos on the walls – some things never changed, especially the array of melt-in-the-mouth cakes that my mother provided when her daughters and granddaughter visited on a Sunday afternoon.

'So, Nell,' my mother said, from her seat on the sofa, setting her cup down on the wooden coffee table, also made by my father, 'have you heard any more about that musical you auditioned for?'

Returning to our table in the Troubadour, I'd evaded my friends' questions about what Finn had said to me with the vague explanation that we'd trained together. After one more round, we'd left the bar and gone our separate ways, exchanging phone numbers and promises to let each other know if we got the Call that we all wanted so badly. I'd tried to put the show out of my mind, but during the two weeks that had passed since the final, I'd jumped out of my skin every time my phone rang.

'No, I've not heard anything,' I said. 'But if they wanted to cast me, I'm sure I'd have had the Call by now.'

'But it sounded as though the audition went really well,' my mother protested.

I shrugged. 'I may not be what the casting team are looking for.'

Savannah, seated at my parents' dining table, looked up from the picture she was painting.

'Why not?' she said, indignantly. 'You're a great dancer.' I smiled, delighted by my daughter's unshakable conviction that I was the best dancer *ever*.

'It's not only my dancing they'll be looking at,' I said. 'They have to think about matching me up with the other dancers. They may decide that the ensemble all have to be the same height, or that they have to be able to cover the leads.' *Or that they have to be under thirty*. Not wanting to spoil a lovely relaxed afternoon with the debate that would inevitably follow such an announcement, I refrained from informing my parents and Marianne that my age might count against me. It certainly wasn't a conversation to have in front of Savannah.

My father closed the Sunday paper he was reading and leant forward in his armchair. 'When you say *cover the leads*, do you mean understudies?' he said.

'Oh, no, Grandad,' Savannah said. 'Understudies just sit in the dressing room. Covers are like understudies, but they get to be in the ensemble as well.'

'Goodness, Savannah,' my mother said. 'You do know a lot about musical theatre, don't you?'

Savannah nodded happily. 'Mum told me.'

Marianne got up from the window seat – where she'd spent most of the afternoon glancing surreptitiously at her phone, as though attending a family gathering in the parental abode had caused her to revert to adolescence – and picked up her bag.

'Time I headed home,' she said.

I glanced towards the French windows, and saw that it was already dark.

'We should be getting off too,' I said. 'Come on, Savannah, you've still got homework to do. You can finish your painting next time we're here.' My daughter pulled a face at the mention of homework, but laid down her paintbrush.

After a brief hiatus while we exchanged cheerful assurances that we'd all get together again very soon, I retrieved my and Savannah's coats from the hooks in the hall and we followed Marianne out of the front door and down the path, my mother and father watching from the doorway.

'Phone us if you have any news about that musical,' my father called after us.

'I will,' I said.

'Fingers, toes and eyes crossed,' my mother said, which made Savannah laugh – I remembered her saying the same thing to me when I was a child – and my parents went inside and closed the door.

With Savannah dancing along the pavement ahead of us, Marianne and I walked to her parked car.

'You seemed a bit distracted this afternoon,' I remarked, as she unlocked the door. 'Expecting a phone call, were you?'

Marianne nodded. 'From Anders. He stayed over last night. For the first time.' She smiled dreamily.

I glanced hastily towards Savannah, but she was out of earshot, standing in first position in the pool of light from a street lamp, as though in a spotlight, raising one arm and then the other above her head.

'What is she doing?' Marianne said.

'*Port de bras* – arm exercises,' I said. 'So, Anders stayed over, and . . ?'

'When he left, he said he'd call me.' Marianne shook her head as though to clear it. 'I can't believe that I've spent the whole day clutching my phone waiting for a guy to call. This so isn't me. If he wants to see me again, he'll call. Whatever.' She opened the car door and slid into the driver's seat. 'I guess it's worse for you, waiting for your agent to call with a job offer.'

'It's tough being in showbusiness,' I said. 'But you do get to wear feathers and sequins.'

Marianne laughed. 'So that's why you became a dancer. I did wonder.'

'Yep,' I said. 'I did it for the glitz. Not that there was any other job I could have done. I'm not super-clever like you, with all your qualifications.'

'I'm no more intelligent than you are,' Marianne said. 'I just worked harder at school and passed more exams.'

'While I was practising my jazz hands, you were studying,' I said.

'I was a right swot,' Marianne agreed, with a grin. 'Mum and Dad had it so easy when we were teenagers, what with you dedicated to dance and me always with my nose in a book or playing the piano.' She paused, and then added, 'When I was fifteen, I had this wild idea that I could be a singer-songwriter.'

'I didn't know that,' I said, taken aback. As far as I was aware, Marianne's piano playing had never been anything more than a hobby.

'I never told anyone,' Marianne said, fastening her seatbelt. 'Anyway, it was just a passing phase, not a vocation – and here I am today, working in the City. I've no regrets, I'm good at what I do and very well-paid, but sometimes I can't help wondering what would have happened if I'd gone on with my music, the way you went on with your dancing.'

Without thinking, I said, 'There's no point in regrets. For whatever reason, you make a choice, and you'll never know what might have happened if you'd chosen differently.'

Marianne gave me a quizzical look. 'That's for sure,' she said. Fastening her seat belt, she added, 'When you get that Call you're waiting for, let me know immediately.'

Before I could remind her yet again that it was *if* not *when* I got the Call, she closed the car door, and started the engine. I watched her pull away from the kerb and drive along the street, until she turned the corner and was lost to my sight, heading back to her luxurious flat and the baby grand piano, which she'd told me she rarely had time to play. How different her life might have been if she'd made a different choice all those years ago.

How different might Savannah and my lives be if I'd done the same?

Savannah had gone up to bed, and I was in the kitchen, pouring myself a glass of wine, when my phone, which I'd left on the worktop, started ringing, the caller ID showing me an unknown number. Wearily, expecting it to be a scam call, I hit the answer icon.

'Evening, Nell,' the caller said. 'Finn Harris here.'

'Hey, Finn,' I said. Why was Finn Harris phoning me at nine o'clock on a Sunday night? Why was he phoning me at all?

'I hope you don't mind my calling you this late,' he said, 'but I've something to say that you're going to want to hear.'

Suddenly, my heart was thumping in my chest.

'Today,' Finn said, 'Olivia, Jonathan and I finalized the cast list for *Speakeasy*. You, Nell Avery, have a place in the ensemble. If you want it, that is.'

I almost dropped my phone. 'Oh – I – Oh, Finn –' Suddenly my legs were shaking so much that I had to clutch at the kitchen table to keep myself upright.

'I take it you do want the job, then?' Finn said.

'Where do I sign?' I said. I heard him laugh.

'I'm breaking all the rules, letting you know we've cast you before we send out contracts,' he said, 'and I'd appreciate it if you don't broadcast it on social media until you get a formal offer through your agent, but you and I go back a long way, and I wanted the pleasure of telling you myself.'

'Thank you, Finn,' I said. 'Thank you *so* much. Getting into *Speakeasy* – it means so much to me. Thank you for casting me – and for calling me tonight to let me know.' I was gushing, but at that moment, I really didn't care.

'You're welcome,' he said. 'I'm looking forward to working with you. See you in rehearsal.'

Scarcely able to believe I was saying it, I repeated his words back to him: 'See you in rehearsal.' My whole body tingled. I felt as though I was floating several feet above the ground.

'Goodnight, Nell.' He ended the call.

I am in the cast of Speakeasy.

I said it aloud, 'I am in the cast of *Speakeasy*.'

Taking my wine with me, I went out of the kitchen, and up the stairs, and opened my daughter's bedroom door. The light from the landing showed me that she was fast asleep. I looked at her, my beautiful child, and my heart brimmed.

'I did it, Savannah,' I whispered. 'I got into *Speakeasy*. I'm finally going to dance on a West End stage.' Careful not to wake her, I closed the door, and crept along the landing to my bedroom.

Placing my wine glass on my dressing table, I located my dance bag under my bed, took out my tiny silver dancer, and placed her on the palm of my hand.

She'd brought me luck at the auditions; hopefully she'd do the same during rehearsals and for the run of the show.

Chapter Seven

I stepped through the sliding doors that led into the Foundry – formerly a Victorian ironworks, now one of the few rehearsal spaces in central London with studios large enough for the entire cast of a full-scale musical – and found myself in a brightly-lit foyer. A lift and a wide staircase leading to other floors took up one wall, while another was covered with posters of the theatre companies who'd rehearsed there. A bespectacled young woman, who I assumed was the receptionist, was seated behind a desk, reading a book, and didn't look up until I was standing right over her.

'Hi,' I said. 'I'm Nell Avery, and I'm here for the *Speakeasy* rehearsals.' Oh, how I loved saying that. Excitement bubbled up inside me.

The day after Finn had phoned me, both Justin and Matt had texted to say they'd got into the ensemble, while Florence, sounding a little shell-shocked, had rung with the news that she'd got second cover for Kitty, the female lead – adding that she hadn't known what being a second cover involved, until her agent had explained to her that she'd be dancing in the ensemble, but would go on for

Kitty in the unlikely circumstance that the actress who was cast in the role, her understudy and the first cover were unable to perform. After we'd exchanged congratulations, Florence had told me that she'd hesitated to accept the cover role in case it was beyond her, but her agent had assured her she could do it. I was left with the distinct impression that she had no idea just how good a dancer she really was.

The rest of the week saw the arrival of the *Speakeasy* script – a story of gangsters, bootleggers and showgirls in 1920s New York, that I'd read with mounting delight as I counted the number of dance routines – and a costume fitting with a well-known costumier. I'd also received an email asking me to bring an object that might have belonged to my character to the first day of rehearsal – something I'd not been asked to do since prop-based acting exercises at college – and another email informing me that one performance during *Speakeasy's* six-month run would be a Gala Performance in aid of the Hillier Foundation, which supported a number of charitable projects. A third email had an exceptionally demanding rehearsal schedule attached. Fortunately, my parents, having congratulated me extensively on getting my dream job at last, were, as ever, happy to step in and look after their granddaughter while I was at work, and I knew Marianne would help out when she could. When I'd told Savannah that I'd got into *Speakeasy* she'd danced exuberantly all around our kitchen. I'd been unable to resist joining in.

Now, the Foundry's receptionist peered at me over her glasses, and said: 'You're in Studio Four, on the third floor.

There's a lift, but it's quicker to walk, if you ask me.' She gestured towards the stairs. 'Have a good day.'

'Oh, I'm sure I will,' I said, but she'd already returned her attention to her book. Evidently, the first day of rehearsals for a West End musical, did not hold the same momentous sense of occasion for her as it did for me.

I ran up the stairs to the first floor, before making myself walk slowly up the next two flights – it wouldn't look good if I rocked up to the first day of rehearsals out of breath. The door to Studio Four was wide open, revealing a large, airy room, with floor to ceiling windows along one wall, mirrored walls at either end, an electric keyboard in one corner, and in the centre of the room, a number of wooden chairs set out in a circle. Although I'd made sure to arrive at the Foundry ten minutes early, at least fifteen of my fellow cast members, dancers I recognized from the final, and a few people who I'd not seen before – presumably they were playing named roles rather than ensemble – had got there before me and were scattered around the studio, some chatting, others looking out over the London skyscape visible from the window. One guy was helping himself to coffee from the industrial-sized urn on a trolley by the door, while a stunning, red-haired girl, in her early twenties who'd not been at the audition, was studying the wall opposite the window, which was almost entirely covered in photographs and pages of newsprint. With a completely unprofessional thrill, I recognised the good-looking young guy with a floppy blonde fringe who approached her and, after they'd exchanged air-kisses, drew her into an animated conversation, as Leon Walsh, only twenty-three, but already a star of the West End stage and a Hollywood movie, and whose face was rarely out of the media. Just the other day, I'd read somewhere that he'd recently broken up with his long-term girlfriend, actress Kelsey Dickson. I'd never watched *Regency,* the popular TV series that had made her a household name, but I'd seen photos of her and Leon together.

From behind me, a woman's voice said, 'Are you going inside?'

I turned around to see Marisa Cutler staring at me, with her flatmate, Nicole Whitby, hovering beside her.

'Oh – it's you,' Marisa said, arching her eyebrows. 'I did wonder if you'd be here today.'

I thought, *does she have to sound quite so surprised to see me?* Almost immediately, I chided myself for reading too much into a perfectly innocuous remark. I'd taken against Marisa at our first meeting – and I was far from delighted to discover that she and Nicole had also got into *Speakeasy* – but now we were going to be working together, I knew I needed to make an effort to get along with them, even if we never became best friends.

'Hey, Marisa,' I said. 'Nicole.' I gestured towards the studio. 'I was just standing here for a moment, drinking it all in.'

'Ah, yes, the first day of rehearsal can be so overwhelming can't it?' Marisa said. 'Although, I'd have thought a dancer with your experience would take it in her stride.' With a smile that didn't quite reach her eyes, she glided into the studio and walked over to the window, Nicole trailing silently in her wake.

I told myself that no-one could possibly have intended to sound so condescending, but I had no hesitation in heading in the opposite direction to take a closer look at the pictures tacked to the wall. These turned out to be faded black and white photographs of street scenes labelled *New York, 1922,* and copies of newspaper articles describing the exploits of bootleggers and gangsters in lurid detail. There were also a number of drawings of stage sets, and others of men wearing double breasted suits and fedoras and women dressed in beaded dresses and bejewelled headbands. My pulse rate quickened as I realised these must be the set and costume designs for the show.

A female voice said, 'Don't you just adore 1920s fashions?' I turned my head to see that I was standing beside Hettie Parkes.

'They are rather fabulous,' I said. 'I'm Nell, by the way.'

'I'm Hettie,' she said. I refrained from telling her that I knew who she was, and that I'd seen her on stage, for fear of sounding like a deranged fan. 'All these picture references are great, aren't they?' she went on, pointing at a photo of a row of smiling chorines. 'I find a display like this really helps me to get into character – I must write some notes.' She produced a notebook and pen from her bag.

'Mmm,' I said. Dancing at corporate gigs and on podiums, there hadn't been time or the need for me to think about *getting into character* – and no inspirational photographs. *I'm going to have to up my game*, I thought. *I'm in the West End now.*

While we'd been talking, more members of the cast had come into the rehearsal studio, including Justin and Matt, who'd joined a small queue that had formed by the refreshment trolley. Leaving Hettie scribbling away, I went over to them, just as the queue shuffled forward and they reached the front.

'Well, this is all right, isn't it?' Justin said, passing me and Matt a coffee and filling another cup for himself.

'It really is,' I said. 'I'm very excited.'

Justin gave me a quizzical look. 'I guess free coffee and biscuits is quite exciting.'

'Oh – I thought you meant – I was talking about the show.'

He laughed. 'I know, Nell. Just teasing. I'm excited to be here myself, and I don't mind admitting it.' I punched him lightly on the arm.

Matt said, 'There's Florence.'

I glanced round the studio and saw Florence standing just inside the door, gazing around, wide-eyed.

'Hey, Florence, over here,' Matt said, hurrying towards her. When she saw him, her mouth lifted in a smile.

Justin put his head on one side. 'Am I right in thinking that young Matt has a bit of thing for Florence?' he said. 'Or am I right?'

'And they say that women gossip more than men,' I said. 'You *could* be right – they wouldn't be the first couple to fall for each other while dancing on the same stage – but who knows?'

'You heard it here first,' Justin said, with a grin. 'Oh my days, but it's good to be back in a musical with a large cast – the intrigues, the flirtations, the ill-advised liaisons – the possibilities are endless.

I rolled my eyes, but at that moment, a sudden hush falling over the studio announced the arrival of the creative team, and any further speculation about Matt and Florence's relationship status was necessarily put on hold.

It was Olivia, I saw first. Dressed all in black as she had been at the auditions, today with a purple scarf draped around her neck, a large tote bag on one arm, she strode into the centre of the rehearsal space, commanding the attention of the whole room before she'd said a word. The bearded Jonathan Gower, holding a bundle of music, a younger man with a beard considerably scantier than Jonathan's, holding a very large notebook, a young woman with an equally large notebook, and a grey-haired, middle-aged man, arranged themselves around her. Then, I saw Finn, today dressed in a sleeveless T-shirt and cut off trackies, coming into the studio a few paces behind the others. I watched him as he walked past me to go and stand next to Olivia, and it struck me how good he looked in his dance gear – just as he had ten years ago. The thought came to me that he'd still look pretty good out of it as well, but I pushed it to the back of my mind.

'Good morning and welcome, everyone,' Olivia said. 'Before we do anything else, I'm going to ask our Company Manager, to say a few words.'

The grey-haired middle-aged man stepped forward. 'Morning people,' he said. 'I'm William Fitzgerald, Company Manager, and the guy you come to if you have any problems. Problems to do with the production, that is. If you're heartbroken because you've split up with your boyfriend, I don't care – as long as you get to the theatre in time for the half.' His eyes twinkling, he added, 'Oh, and my phone number is for you let me know if you're too ill to perform – I don't want you calling me when you're drunk in a club at 2.00 a.m. to tell me how much you love being in the show, OK?' He smiled at the polite ripple of laughter that greeted his welcome speech.

'Thanks, William,' Olivia said. 'Now, I see some of you have already found the refreshments –' She paused as her words invoked more polite laughter. 'If anyone else feels in need of caffeine, please do help yourselves. And then, if you'd like to take a seat, we'll get started.'

As one, the cast of *Speakeasy* stampeded towards the circle of chairs – no-one it seemed was prepared to be known as the dancer who held up rehearsals while they got themselves a hot beverage – and hastily sat down in the nearest empty place. Justin and I managed to find chairs next to each other, while Matt – unlike everyone else, who'd walked round the outside as though taking part in a game of musical chairs – marched boldly across the circle to sit on my other side, saving the chair next to him for Florence.

'Aw – look at him, saving her a seat,' Justin whispered to me. 'Told you he has a thing for her.'

'All it proves is that he's been well-brought up,' I whispered back, placing my dance bag at my feet. Glancing around the circle, I saw that I was sitting almost directly opposite Finn, who was leaning back in his chair, his hands linked behind his head, one ankle resting on a knee. Even as I was thinking how relaxed he appeared for someone about to set the dances for a West End musical, his gaze caught mine and held it. I smiled, and he smiled lazily back at me. He was, I thought, extraordinarily attractive when he smiled. Becoming aware of a pleasurable fluttering in my stomach, I told myself to get a grip. I had eleven weeks of rehearsal ahead of me. I couldn't allow myself to go weak at the knees every time I felt Finn's grey eyes on me while I danced.

Olivia said, 'OK, guys, time to get this show on the road. We'll begin by going round the circle and introducing ourselves – and please say a few words about the object you've brought in that belongs to your character. I'm going to assume that everyone here knows who I, Finn and Jonathan are – at least I hope you do –' There was more laughter at this point. 'So, Samantha, I'll ask you to start us off.'

The red-haired girl who I'd seen earlier studying the photo-wall and talking to Leon Walsh, sat forward in her chair. She really was very striking, I thought, with the high cheekbones that always looked good under stage lights.

'Hi, I'm Samantha Ellis,' she said. 'And I'm playing Kitty.'

So this was *Speakeasy's* leading lady. Her name was vaguely familiar. I made a mental note to google her at some point.

'Kitty is a dancer living in New York,' Samantha went on, 'but she grew up on a farm in Oklahoma. When she moved to the city, she brought this with her to remind her of home.'

She held up a small bunch of corn stalks, tied with a blue ribbon. A murmur of appreciation went around the circle.

'Thank you, Samantha,' Olivia said. 'That's a great backstory.' She smiled at Leon Walsh, who was seated next to Samantha. 'Over to you.'

'Morning all,' he said. 'I'm Leon Walsh. I play, Nathan.'

I might have guessed which character Leon was playing. With his clean-cut good-looks, and his floppy blonde hair, he was perfect casting for Nathan, Kitty's musician boyfriend, and the show's male lead.

'Nathan plays piano in a speakeasy,' Leon went on, 'but like so many young men of his generation, he fought in the Great War. He was shot – and he still has the bullet.' There was a collective gasp as he held up a small metal object between his thumb and forefinger. He grinned and tossed the bullet – if it was indeed that – into the air, catching it with one hand before putting it into his shirt pocket.

'Thank you, Leon,' Olivia said, beaming at him.

'Someone's been doing their homework,' Justin whispered. I smiled weakly, and wished I'd done mine – or asked my clever sister to do it for me. I was a dancer in the ensemble, playing a nameless chorine. Asked to come up with an object that my 'character' might have about their person, all I could think of was to raid Savannah's dressing up box for a string of the beads that were a costume staple at every gig where I'd danced a Charleston. As to my character's back story, I didn't have a clue, other than she wore beads to parties.

'And next,' Olivia said, smiling at Leon's neighbour – who, I now saw, was Marisa.

'Good morning everyone,' Marisa said. 'I'm Marisa Cutler and I'm in the ensemble. Like Nathan –' she paused to smile at Leon '– my character did her bit in the First World War, as a nurse on the Western Front, caring for the wounded soldiers. Now she's putting the horror of the war behind her and throwing herself into all that New York in the Jazz Age has to offer – the parties, the music, the dances, the fashions –' She held up a string of beads. Inwardly, I groaned. Not only had Maria invented a backstory for her 'character' much more imaginative than anything I'd ever have come up with, she'd picked the same object as me. How could I possibly follow that? '

'Thank you so much, Marisa,' Olivia said.

'You're welcome, Olivia,' Marisa said. 'I do find researching a character so helpful.'

Olivia arched her eyebrows. 'Absolutely,' she said. 'That's why we do it. So, moving on –' She nodded encouragingly at the boy sitting next to Marisa.

'Hi, I'm Lucas Halliday,' he said. 'I'm the Dance Captain. I've brought in a newspaper . . .'

'Hi, I'm Hettie Parkes. I'm in the ensemble. I found this feather boa . . .'

'Sadie Price, understudy for Kitty . . .'

'Ensemble . . .'

'Annelise Kent, first cover for Kitty . . .'

'Swing . . .'

'First cover for Nathan . . .'

The introductions continued around the circle, coming inexorably closer to me, names and objects – a diamond necklace and a fur stole, both presumably fake, a bow tie, a cigarette holder, a wad of dollar bills, also fake, presumably – coming in quick succession. One girl had decided that her character was religious and always carried a prayer book, a male dancer declared that his character worked for the Mob, and brandished a plastic water pistol in lieu of a machine gun. I racked my brains for something original I could say about my beads without success.

The guy sitting on Florence's right, a man of about thirty, his slight paunch making me think he was an actor rather than a dancer, said, 'I'm Donte Travis. I play the villainous, Spencer Henderson IV, Wall Street financier, and determined to have his wicked way with sweet innocent Kitty.' With a wolfish grin, he held up a champagne coupe. Turning to Florence, in an American accent, he said, 'Have a glass of champagne, my dear.'

Florence giggled, and her face went pink, but then, to my surprise, she looked Donte straight in the eye and in an American accent as impeccable as his, she said, 'Oh my, Mr Henderson, I don't think I should. I've never had champagne before.'

'But I insist,' Donte said. 'Trust me, my dear girl, you'll love it.'

Olivia said, 'Keep going, Florence. Tell us who you are.'

'I'm Florence Newton,' Florence said, in her normal voice. 'I'm in the ensemble and 2nd Cover for Kitty. I – my character in the ensemble – is a gangster's moll.' She raised a hand so that everyone in the circle could see that she was holding a clutch bag and, reverting to an American accent, said. 'In this bag, Mr Henderson, is a pistol. I surely do hope that you are not going to force me to fire it.'

Donte raised one eyebrow, and twirled an imaginary moustache. 'There's no need for that, Miss Newton, you have slain me already.' He raised his glass as if in a toast.

Olivia, along with the entire cast of *Speakeasy*, broke into a spontaneous round of applause. Clapping my hands along with the rest, my gaze fell on Marisa. She, too, was clapping her hands, but without enthusiasm, her mouth a thin tight line. She did not, it seemed, enjoy seeing another dancer in the spotlight.

'And there was me thinking our Florence was such a quiet little thing,' Justin whispered to me.

'Thank you, Florence,' Olivia said, when the clapping had died down. 'And thank you, Donte – that was inspirational. And now, I think it's time we moved on.' She smiled at Matt.

'I'm Matt Brooking,' he said. 'I'm in the ensemble.' Holding up a whiskey bottle, and swopping to a broad New York accent, he added, 'You guys want some of this? I can git it for yer. But it'll cost yer.' Then his eyes widened. Placing the bottle on the floor, he raised his hands above his head. 'No! Don't shoot –' His body jerked several times, and he slumped back in his chair, remaining motionless long enough for a smiling Olivia to lead another round of clapping, before he sat up. 'My character is – was – a bootlegger,' he said. 'He made a lot of dollars supplying alcohol to the rich during Prohibition. Until the cops caught up with him.'

'Thank you, Matt,' Olivia said. 'That was a useful reminder for all of us that the glamorous Jazz Age had a dark underside.' Her gaze fell on me. 'And what have you got for us?'

Nothing that's going to get me a round of applause, I thought. I reached into the inside pocket of my bag to retrieve my beads and saw a glint of silver – my tiny dancer. On impulse, without conscious thought, I took her out of the bag and rested her carefully on the flat of my hand.

'Hi, I'm Nell Avery,' I said. 'I'm in the ensemble. My character is a dancer. Until now she's danced in . . . speakeasies and . . . as the entertainment at rich people's parties, but her dream has always been to get into the chorus line in a Broadway musical. She keeps this silver charm in her dance bag to bring her luck at auditions.'

Olivia face grew thoughtful. 'That's very interesting, Nell,' she said. 'Your character shows us that the dancers who lived in the 1920s might appear to lead lives very different to those of dancers today, but they still shared the same hopes and dreams.'

I nodded my head in agreement – I might have been wildly improvising when I came up with my character, but I didn't feel the need to admit this to *Speakeasy's* director.

'We theatrical folk have always been superstitious,' Olivia went on, leaning forward so that her elbow was on her knee and resting her chin on her hand. 'Tell us a little more about this lucky charm, Nell. Did someone give it to your character? Was it a lover, perhaps?'

I looked down at the tiny ballerina. 'Yes,' I said. I looked back up at Olivia, and saw to my dismay that she was still smiling at me encouragingly. I cast about for something else I might say, and found myself blurting out, 'He gave it to her just before he went overseas.'

'Ah – another young man sent to fight in Flanders fields,' Olivia sighed, and put her hand over her heart. Then, recovering herself, she smiled at Justin. 'And next,' she said.

'Hi, I'm Justin Ofabemi, and I'm in the ensemble. My character is the owner of a speakeasy . . .'

Relieved to be out of the spotlight, I bent down and carefully returned the tiny ballerina to my bag. When I sat up, I saw that Finn was staring at me, one eyebrow quizzically raised. It was only then it occurred to me that the silver charm might well have stirred memories for him that were better left forgotten. Inwardly, I cursed my stupidity – the last thing I wanted to do was remind him of the nights he'd slept at my side. Resolving to think more carefully before I spoke in future, I looked away from him, making myself focus on the imaginative biography that Justin had invented for his character, and, as the introductions moved around the circle, memorizing names – including that of the young bearded guy, Cameron Lewis, the Resident Choreographer, and the notebook-carrying young woman, Gwen Marsh, the Resident Director. Both of them would remain with the Company after the show had opened, unlike Olivia and Finn.

Once everyone had introduced themselves, Olivia again took centre stage, telling us a little more about her ambitions for the show, and informing us that while we'd all be working extremely hard over the next few weeks, she hoped we'd also find the experience of bringing *Speakeasy* to the stage an enjoyable one. I found myself smiling at her words and nodding my head. How could I *not* enjoy dancing in *Speakeasy*? All I had to do was to be mindful of what I said in front of Finn.

'And now,' Olivia said, reaching into her voluminous bag and taking out a bulging ring binder, 'I'd like us to go straight into our read-through.'

Hastily, I scrabbled in my bag for my own copy of the script, and along with everyone else in the room, turned to the first page.

'The curtains open to reveal a New York street scene,' Olivia said. 'Kitty is alone on stage. Take it away, Samantha.'

In a mid-West American accent, Samantha said, 'I am in New York City.'

I was in rehearsal for a West End show!

'It's been my dream for so long,' Samantha said. 'I can hardly believe I'm here,'

I could hardly believe I was there, either. Performing in a West End musical had been my dream for as long as I could remember. And now, that dream was coming true.

An hour and a half later, during which Kitty and Nathan had, despite the evil machinations of Spencer Henderson IV, fallen in love, Leon said, 'I'm going, Kitty. I'm leaving New York and going to Hollywood.' He paused, and then he said, 'What I want to know is, is will you come with me?'

'Oh, Nathan,' Samantha said. 'Of course, I'll come with you.'

'I love you, Kitty. I will always love you.'

'Oh, Nathan –'

'They kiss,' Olivia said. 'The curtains close.' She smiled, shut her folder, and leant back in her chair. 'Good job everyone. I think we can all give ourselves a round of applause, don't you?' Along with the rest of the cast, I clapped my hands.

'I think I'm going to like working for her,' Justin whispered to me.

'We're going to take an hour lunch break,' Olivia said, 'then we'll be going straight on with the rehearsal.'

William, the Company Manager, added, 'For those of you who don't know, there's a canteen in the basement. For those who haven't read their rehearsal schedule – you know who you are – after lunch, the ensemble are back here in Studio Four with Finn. Everyone else in Studio Five with Olivia and Jonathan.' William and the creative team exited the rehearsal space, along with Leon, Samantha and Donte.

'I didn't realise the principals and the ensemble rehearse separately,' Florence said. 'How does that work?'

'It's only for the first few weeks while we learn the big dance numbers, and they learn their solos,' Matt said. 'We'll all be in the same studio once we start putting the whole show together.'

'Ah – of course,' Florence said. 'Sorry to keep asking questions.'

'Not at all,' Matt said. 'You can ask me anything you like. I honestly don't mind.' Justin caught my eye and winked.

By now, the four of us were the only people left in the rehearsal studio. Suddenly aware that we were hungry, we headed down to the canteen, discovering that most of the Company had got there before us, including the creative team and the principals, who were all seated together at one long table away from everyone else. Queueing up at the counter for my sandwiches and coffee, I saw Marisa and Nicole plonk themselves down at the creatives' table. Marisa, it seemed, never missed a chance to put herself forward. Although, whether forcing her presence on a director and her entourage while they were relaxing over lunch would attract their attention in a good way was, it seemed to me, debatable.

Having paid for my lunch, I carried my tray over to the nearest empty table, followed by Justin, Florence and Matt, and shortly afterwards we were joined by Hettie Parkes and Annelise Kent, first cover for Kitty. Dancers might not say much on stage, but off-stage they are as talkative as any other performer, and we were soon chatting easily. I discovered that Hettie and Matt had both trained at the same performing arts college as me – although, naturally, I'd graduated some years before they did – and that Matt's first job out of college had been a prestigious National Tour, although this was his first time in the West End.

'Where did you train, Florence?' Matt asked.

Florence, who until then hadn't contributed to the conversation, went pink. 'I – I never went to college,' she said. 'I learned to dance at weekends at a small part-time performing arts school.'

Hettie's eyebrows shot up. 'It must have been an exceptionally good school,' she said.

'It had some brilliant teachers,' Florence said, 'but it was only for students aged up to sixteen. Since then, whenever I can, I've been taking classes at Limelight – do you know it?'

I nodded. I'd taken classes at Limelight myself, but while the occasional class at a dance studio was great for brushing up a dancer's technique between jobs, it was hardly the same as spending three years at a top college. Florence really was exceptionally talented, I thought, to have come so far without professional training.

Matt cleared his throat. 'Er, how old are you, Florence?' he said. 'If you don't mind my asking.'

'I'm nineteen,' Florence said.

It may have been my imagination, but I thought I saw an expression of relief flicker across Matt's face, which made me think that Justin was right, and the younger man's interest in Florence was not confined to her ability to execute a perfect fouetté. *Well*, I thought, as I regarded their fresh young faces, *if anything comes of it, they'll certainly make a cute couple.*

'When did you leave school?' Hettie asked.

'Last July,' Florence said. 'As soon my A Levels were out of the way, I started applying to theatrical agencies, but didn't hear anything for *ages*. Then Evelyn Swann at the Swann Barret agency accepted me onto her books, and got me the *Speakeasy* audition. And here I am.'

'Oh my days,' Hettie said. 'One moment you're a schoolgirl, the next you've signed with a top agent and you're making your West End debut.'

'It's the stuff of theatrical legend,' Annelise said.

Florence laughed, not taking Hettie or Annelise seriously – presumably she had no notion that her path to the West End stage had been both smoother and speedier than that of most performers.

Justin said, 'People are starting to make a move. We should go too.' Seeing other members of the cast already drifting out of the canteen, I nodded my head in agreement. Justin got to his feet and started to make his way between the tables to the door.

'Oh – I don't want to be late,' Florence said. Jumping up from her chair, she hurried after Justin, with Matt in hot pursuit, and Hettie and Annelise not far behind. Hastily, I drained what was left of my coffee, and was about to go after them, when Finn Harris sat down in the chair next to mine.

'Oh – Finn,' I said. 'I was just going to your rehearsal.'

'We don't have to go just yet,' he said. 'It's not as though it can start without me.'

'I guess not,' I said.

Finn leant towards me. 'That silver charm you talked about this morning,' he said, 'was it by any chance the one I gave you?'

'Y-yes,' I said. Did he remember the exact circumstances in which he'd given me the charm? Did he think I was purposefully trying to remind him? My face grew hot.

'I was too far away to see her properly this morning. May I see her now?'

My stomach clenched, but I reached into my bag and took out the tiny ballerina.

'Here,' I said, dropping her onto the palm of his outstretched hand while studying his face, trying to gauge his reaction. To my relief, his mouth lifted into a smile.

'I remember leaving her by your bedside,' he said, quietly. 'You were still asleep.'

Nooo, I thought. I was not going to sit here gazing at Finn Harris's handsome face and talk about *that*.

'Finn,' I said, 'what I told everyone about the charm this morning – it was my character talking, not me. I was acting.'

'Method acting?' he said.

'What?' I said.

'Method actors draw on their own experience to discover their character's motivation.'

'I am aware of what method acting is, Finn,' I said. 'No – I wasn't thinking about you and me. I simply said the first thing that came into my head.'

'But I did go overseas.' His eyes glinted with amusement. I bit my lip. He wasn't taking this conversation seriously, but I had to. I needed to keep a distance between us.

'Please don't think I'm trying to make something of it,' I said. 'I'm fully aware that you're *Speakeasy's* Choreographer and I'm one of your dancers. I'm not expecting more than a professional relationship with you just because ten years ago –' The words I hadn't spoken hung in the air between us.

'We were *friends* back then,' Finn said, in a tone that brooked no argument. 'Are you saying that because I'm now choreographing the steps that you dance, we can't be friends again?'

'N-no – I-I don't know what I'm saying,' I stuttered.

'So, as long as I swear to treat you no differently to any other dancer while we're working,' Finn said, 'outside the rehearsal room, we *can* be friends?'

My heart began to beat faster. It came to me that I was standing on the edge of a precipice and that one wrong move, a step out of place, a thoughtless word, and I'd tumble into the depths below. And yet, how could I tell the man sitting next to me – the man whose beautiful grey eyes were now gazing into mine – that I didn't want his friendship?

'Yes, Finn,' I said. His smile was contagious; I couldn't help smiling back at him.

'Ok, friend, shall we go out and grab a bite to eat together after rehearsal? My treat.'

'Oh – I –' Sharing a meal for two with Finn Harris – because that what the invitation amounted to – was *not* a good idea.

'Unless you have to rush off, of course.'

Every instinct for self-preservation screamed at me to take the easy way out and tell him that after rehearsal I had to shoot off home, but another part of me was already remembering the evenings we'd spent together in the past, and how much I'd liked him. Besides, I was no longer that care-free young woman who, in a haze of lust and alcohol, had fallen into bed with him. I was older, wiser, fully aware of my responsibilities and the boundaries that I'd be a fool to cross. And it wasn't as though I'd told Savannah or my parents any definite time to expect me back.

'We can always do it another night,' Finn said. That decided me. I could put him off for now, but not forever.

'No, tonight's good for me,' I said.

'Great,' Finn said. 'I'll look forward to hearing what you've been getting up to over the last ten years. Right now, though, I need to have a quick word with Olivia. Here's your good luck charm –' Taking hold of my hand, he placed the tiny dancer on my palm and closed my fingers around her. 'I'll see you up in the studio.' He got to his feet, and weaving his way across the now rapidly emptying canteen, caught up with Olivia just as she was heading out of the door, her purple scarf floating in her wake.

I took a moment to stow the silver ballerina carefully in my dance bag, and then ran upstairs to the rehearsal studio, fairly certain that Finn wouldn't be so keen to renew our friendship if I wasn't warmed up enough to dance his steps.

Chapter Eight

I stood beside Finn on the South Bank, one hand on the railings, the other clutching my wine, and gazed out over the dark waters of the Thames, several metres below. To my left, I could see the Wheel, glowing red and purple against the night sky, and the Houses of Parliament. To my right, fairy lights in the trees led my eye along the river to the arches of Waterloo Bridge, the National Theatre and, in the distance, the flood-lit dome of St Paul's and the glittering skyscrapers of the City. Out in midstream, a party boat cruised slowly past, trailing phosphorescence in its wake, its illuminated decks heaving with revelers. Behind us, a street musician began playing a saxophone, the music rising above the snatches of conversation coming from groups of tourists and commuters holding shouted conversations on their phones as they marched towards Waterloo Station.

'Did I wear you out today?' Finn asked.

'I do feel tired,' I said, 'but in a good way.' I couldn't remember when I'd felt so tired after one afternoon of dancing, but I wasn't about to admit that to him.

'I never promised that my choreography would be easy,' Finn said.

'Your choreographing is *fiendishly* difficult,' I said, 'but it's wonderful to dance.'

The ensemble had spent the afternoon learning *Good Morning New York City,* the show's opening number, a long, complicated routine, obviously intended to wow *Speakeasy's* audience from the moment the curtains opened. By the end of the rehearsal I was exhausted – I was sure I wasn't the only one – but I also knew that I'd pushed myself to the limits of my ability in a way I'd not done in years, and that it felt *good*. Finn had seemed pleased with this first day of rehearsals, sending his dancers off home with his thanks for their hard work, grinning as he reminded us that we'd get to do it all again tomorrow. After everyone else had gone, I'd waited while he'd made some notes, and then the two of us had left the studios together. At his suggestion, we'd made our way down to the river, and the food stalls that clustered along the South Bank from Waterloo to Westminster, standing in a pool of light from an old wrought-iron street lamp while eating fajitas from a Styrofoam tray, drinking rough red wine from plastic cups and talking over the rehearsal.

Now, Finn said, 'I hope you feel the same about my choreography when you're dancing it six nights a week.'

'How could I not,' I said, 'when I'll be dancing on a West End stage? It's a dream come true.'

'It's my West End debut too, you know,' Finn said.

'So it is!' I laughed.

'To *Speakeasy*,' Finn said, holding up his wine. I did the same and we touched the plastic cups together. Looking up at his handsome face, it struck me that I hadn't spent time alone in the company of such an undeniably attractive man in a very long while.

'*Speakeasy* isn't the first time you've choreographed a musical though, is it?' I said. 'I'm pretty sure I'm right in guessing that *choreographie* is German for choreography?'

'Have you been googling my credits?' Finn said, raising his eyebrows.

'I certainly have,' I said. 'It's only fair as you've read my CV.'

He laughed at that. 'I went to Berlin to dance in a musical, but when another dancer in my cast asked me for help choreographing his showreel, I discovered that creating dances was something I enjoyed doing, and – I'm not going to lie – that I was good at it. Fast forward, and I've choreographed three full-scale musicals, in Berlin, Hamburg and Stuttgart.'

'Well, you certainly made the right choice when you went abroad all those years ago.'

Finn nodded. 'In many ways it was a huge wrench to leave Germany and come back to England, but I knew that if I stayed much longer, it'd be too late for me to establish a choreographic career in London. I think most of the Brits working in German musical theatre – and there are a lot of them – get to the point when they realise they either need to go home or accept that they're always going to live overseas.' He shrugged and drained his wine, tossing the empty cup into a nearby bin. 'In the end, the decision was made for me. Four months' ago, *Speakeasy's* producers contacted my agent and asked if I'd be interested in choreographing a musical that was going into the West End. A couple of weeks' later, I was in London, workshopping *Good Morning New York City*.'

He'd been back for months and I never knew. Not that there was any reason why I should have known. He had no motive to contact me – that he knew of.

'How do you like living London now you're back?' I said.

'It's all good so far,' he said. 'For now, I'm renting a flat in Camden – an area I really like – but I'm looking to buy my own place. I want to make a life for myself here. See my parents, my brother and his family, and my sister more often – and not just on a phone screen. Catch up with old friends.' We exchanged smiles. 'And that's quite enough about me,' he said. 'What have you been getting up to for the last ten years? Do you still share a flat with – what was her name? Zelda?'

'The flat with the dodgy wiring and the mould growing in the bathroom?' I laughed. 'No, I moved out of there years ago, thank goodness. These days, I live in a house in north London with –' I broke off. I'd almost told him that I lived with Savannah. What was I *thinking*? I didn't want him to know I'd had a child. And yet, for the last ten years, she'd been the most important person in my life – how could I *not* mention her? I gulped down what was left of my wine, threw away the cup, and said, 'I have a daughter.'

Finn's eyes widened. 'A daughter? I never would have expected –' He ran a hand through his hair. 'I don't know why I'm so surprised. I guess I came back to England thinking everything would be the same as when I left. But, of course, while I've been away, everyone's gone on with their lives.' He fell silent for a moment, and then he said, 'What's your daughter's name?'

'Savannah,' I said.

'Does she dance?'

'She does,' I said. 'Actually, she's a very talented dancer.' I saw him glance at my left hand.

'Are you and Savannah's father together?' he said.

Somehow, I looked at him directly in his eyes. 'No, he's never been a part of our lives. I'm a single parent.' And that was all he was ever going to know. To change the subject, I said, 'What about you? Are you in a relationship?'

'No, not me,' Finn said.

'What about that girl I saw you with in the Troubadour?'

He shook his head. 'I took her out a few times, but she was never my girlfriend, and I've no plans to see her again. I'm single like you.' He paused, and then he said, 'Would you like another drink? We could find a bar, if you're getting cold.' His mouth curved into a warm, inviting smile, and in that moment, standing there with him in the lamplight by the river, something shifted between us, a spark of long-extinguished emotion re-igniting. I had a longing to reach up and tangle my fingers in his hair, to feel his mouth, tasting of spices and wine, on mine – and the way Finn was looking at me, I suspected very strongly that he had more on his mind than musical theatre.

Yes, I thought, *I would like to go to a bar and have another drink with this good-looking, straight man who has just told me he is single.* I didn't want the evening to end. Which was why it was best that I ended it here and now – before I did something stupid like forgetting that I couldn't let Finn Harris get close to me, and why.

'I wish I could, Finn,' I said, 'but it's getting late, and I have to be up very early in the morning to take Savannah to school before I come to your rehearsal.'

'Ah – of course you do,' Finn said. 'I wasn't thinking. How are you getting home?'

'Tube from Waterloo.'

'So am I.'

Together, we walked to the station, Finn talking non-stop about his plans for the following day – finishing *Good Morning New York City*, starting to set the Act I finale, *She Only Drinks Champagne* – me attempting to focus on what he was saying, all the while trying not to think about the moment by the river when I'd wanted very badly for him to kiss me. At Waterloo, as we were travelling on different tube lines, we said goodbye at the bottom of the escalators, assured each other that we'd had a good evening and that we must do it again sometime, and then went our separate ways. I spent most of my journey home on the train with my head all over the place, but by the time I was walking the short distance between the station and my little terraced house, I'd decided that I'd had a narrow escape – and nothing had really changed. The evening *might* have ended very differently, but it hadn't. Finn had *not* kissed me, even if he'd been tempted to. Lulled by the wine and the lamplight, I'd had a brief moment of madness – and I wouldn't let anything like it happen again. And in future, if Finn invited me out, I'd find an excuse not to go.

Chapter Nine

The music stopped. With relief, I stood still, pushing a strand of wet hair out of my eyes, while I got my breath back. Finn, standing at the front of the performance space, shifted his gaze away from his dancers and turned to speak to Cameron, who scribbled something in his notebook. Although I'd known that a large-scale musical like *Speakeasy* would have a Resident Choreographer – who, once the show opened and Finn's job came to an end, would ensure the dancers continued to perform his choreography to his exacting standards, exactly as he had set it – I hadn't realised that Cameron's job would include his acting as Finn's assistant during rehearsal. In all my years as a dancer, I'd never had any inclination to move from performing someone else's choreography to creating my own – apart from competition dances for Savannah – but now, my mind drifting as I waited for Finn's next instruction, I found myself wondering if Choreographer's Assistant, was another job I should consider for the future. It would at least keep me working in the theatre . . .

'That was much better,' Finn said, jerking me back to the rehearsal studio. 'That was good. We'll just go through it one more time.

Justin, standing next to me, whispered, 'That's what he said the last time.'

'And the time before that,' I whispered back.

Along with the rest of the ensemble, we walked quickly to the side of the rehearsal studio and waited for the music that would be our cue to run into the performance space – just as if we were in a theatre, standing in the wings, waiting to go on stage.

Finn sat astride a chair, resting his arms along the back. After dancing *On A Night Like This,* the big Act II finale number that lasted for a full ten minutes, twice through full out, I could have done with a sit down myself. Instead, as soon as the rehearsal pianist had played the intro, I sprang into the dance – as did Samantha, Leon, and the entire ensemble, twenty-two pairs of tap shoes making enough noise to almost drown out the music – the choreography sending me downstage, until I was dancing directly in front of Finn. Every time my shoe hit the floor, my muscles protested, but I forced myself to keep tapping, acutely aware of Finn's grey-eyed gaze travelling over me, telling myself that the only reason he was looking at my legs was to check I was dancing his steps correctly. And that as he hadn't asked me to have another drink with him in the past two weeks, he was unlikely to do so at all. Which was most definitely for the best.

The final chord sounded and faded away. Too tired to hold my finishing position, I let my arms fall to my sides, Studio Four's mirrored walls showing me that almost every dancer in the room was red-faced and breathing hard. Even Matt, who I'd never seen give a dance less than his all, even at the end of the day when most of us were beginning to flag, had a dark patch of sweat on his back. Only Florence seemed unaffected by the demands of Finn's choreography, standing in third position, her hair still in a tidy bun, waiting for Finn's next pronouncement. Oh, what it was to be nineteen.

'OK, people, we'll leave it there for today,' Finn said, getting to his feet. 'Next week, you're all rehearsing the songs with Jonathan, while I'm working with the principals, so I won't be with you again until the week after that, when we start putting the whole show together. Thank you all very much.' He picked up his bag, and he and Cameron began making their way towards the door. Marisa ran across the sprung floor and planted herself in Finn's path.

'I just wanted to thank *you* again, Finn,' she said, her voice loud enough to echo around the studio. 'These past two weeks dancing your choreography have been *awesome*. And I assure you I never have any trouble recalling dances, so if, when we start putting the show together, you need anyone to demonstrate for those who've forgotten, please do call upon me. I honestly wouldn't mind.'

I gaped at her. Everyone in the room was a professional dancer. Retaining choreography after two weeks of rehearsal was a given.

'I'll remember that, Marisa,' Finn said. His face deadpan, he continued walking with Cameron towards the door. Marisa fairly skipped to the back of the studio, where she was joined by Nicole, and the two of them made their exit.

In a low voice, Justin, said: 'Do you think she's after *him* or does she think that blatantly sucking up to a choreographer will further her career?'

I rolled my eyes. 'I've no idea. But it isn't working. I've noticed that every time she sidles over to him, he can't get away from her quick enough.'

Justin laughed. 'Are you going to the cast curry?' he asked.

I shook my head. 'All I want to do right now is soak in a hot bath.'

I couldn't remember when I'd last felt as exhilarated as I had during the past two weeks of Finn's rehearsals – but nor could I remember ever feeling so *exhausted*. While I was managing to keep up with the younger members of the cast, I knew I was pushing my body to its limits, and then some. Travelling back home in the evening, there'd been a couple of times when I'd nodded off on the train; fortunately, I'd woken up before I'd gone past my stop. On this Saturday night, as Savannah was at a sleepover party, I was planning to go to bed early and, as I didn't have to collect her from her friend Amy's house until the afternoon, sleep late on Sunday, my day off from rehearsals.

'But you have to come to the cast curry,' Justin said. 'It's one of the great theatrical traditions. Besides, if one of the ensemble doesn't come to the cast curry, it's very unlucky for the show.'

'I've never heard that particular theatrical superstition before,' I said.

'Neither have I, to be honest,' Justin said, with a grin. 'But that's what Matt told Florence. She wasn't coming to the curry either, but she is now. And you should definitely come too – you don't want to miss out on the chance to bond with your fellow dancers over a biriani.'

I laughed, but it struck me that Justin was right. I should go out and be sociable tonight. Skipping an all-cast get together because I was tired was not only feeble, but also not very friendly.

'OK, I'll see you there,' I said to Justin. 'But you have to promise to wake me up if I fall asleep face down in a bowl of pilau rice.'

Collecting our bags from the pile by the back wall, Justin and I went downstairs, and he vanished inside the men's changing rooms. I went into the women's, where the female half of the ensemble were getting ready for a night out. Finding nowhere to put down my belongings, I made my way through the dance bags and the chatter to the far end of the L-shaped room, and around the corner. With relief, I sank down onto an empty bench, slumping back against the wall, and closing my eyes. I'd just sit quietly for a minute . . .

'Are you sure you left it in here?' A shrill female voice tore me out of sleep. For a moment, I didn't know where I was, but then it came flooding back to me. I was in the changing room at the Foundry. I'd sat down and shut my eyes – and I must have drifted off.

'I'm not sure, Marisa, but I don't know where else it could be.' That was Nicole's voice. Apart from her and the first speaker, who I now realised was Marisa, the changing room was silent, and I guessed that everyone else had left. Yawning, I was about to call out and announce my presence, when I heard Marisa talking again.

'Well, hurry up and find it,' she said. 'We need to get to the restaurant. I don't want to get stuck at a table with someone like that little twit Florence. She never opens her mouth unless it's to say something stupid.'

That was my friend they were talking about. My body went rigid, and I clutched the bench with both hands.

'She's a good dancer, though, don't you think?' Nicole said.

'She's nothing special,' Marisa said. 'But she's far from the weakest dancer in the company. That would be Nell Avery. I can't imagine how *she's* going to cope with the demands of a West End show. She made so many mistakes when we were dancing *On A Night Like This*. I'm amazed that Finn didn't give her any notes.'

Anger lanced through me. I'd danced for nearly eight hours today without making one mistake. At least, none that I knew about.

'Poor Nell,' Marisa continued. 'It's a mystery to me why Finn put her in the ensemble when she's so obviously past it.'

Poor Nell? The blood began pounding in my head.

'And I'm not only talking about her dancing,' Marisa said. 'She looked *haggard* in today's rehearsal.'

Nicole giggled. 'I really need to find my phone,' she said. 'I'll just look through my bag one more time.' There was a short silence, and then she said, 'Oh – I've found it. It was there all the time. Sorry. What am I like?'

Marisa made no reply. I heard the girls' footsteps on the tiles, and the thud of a closing door.

I sat very still, my confidence in my ability to perform Finn's choreography leaching away from me. For the first time, it occurred to me to wonder if rather than my dancing, it was some lingering trace of affection for those few sweet weeks before he went to Germany that had made him cast me . . . No, I couldn't believe that of him. As for messing up his choreography, he wouldn't spare my feelings by not giving me corrections if I needed them. It was his job to get the best out of his dancers. His own professional reputation depended on it.

I let go of the bench, noticing that I'd been clinging to it so tightly that my knuckles had turned white. Checking the time, I was appalled to see that over half an hour had passed since I'd parted from Justin. He'd think I'd changed my mind about the meal and taken myself off home. Hastily I peeled off my leotard, put on my street clothes, and repaired the ravages that a day of dance had done to my make-up, my reflection in the mirror reassuring me that while I might not have Florence's natural youthful bloom, there was no way I was *past it*. Chiding myself for letting Marisa's words get to me even for a moment, I put on my coat, shouldered my bag and left the changing room. I arrived in the foyer just as Finn stepped out of the lift.

'Still here, Nell?' he said.

'Er, yes,' I said. 'I'm just on my way to the cast curry,' There was, I decided, no need to mention that I'd fallen asleep in the changing room. 'Are you going?'

'It wouldn't be the done thing for me to go,' Finn said. 'I'm not actually a member of the cast.'

'Ah,' I said. 'I forgot that you aren't – I mean, I forgot that the creative team don't go – I haven't forgotten that you're the Choreographer. Obviously.'

'Good to hear.'

'You know what I mean.'

Finn's eyes glinted with amusement. 'So, I'm not going to the cast curry,' he said, 'but I'll walk with you as far as the restaurant, if I may.'

'Sure,' I said. We headed out of the Foundry into the cold night air, and walked in a companionable silence along the pavement to the Tiger Moon restaurant.

'I've just come out of a meeting with Olivia and Jonathan,' Finn said, as we stood in the light spilling out of the restaurant's plate glass windows. 'They're very pleased with the way the rehearsals are going. As am I.' He smiled. 'I couldn't take my eyes off you today.'

I told myself that he was only talking about my dancing, but a shiver than had nothing to do with the cold tingled down my spine.

'I love dancing your choreography,' I said, tilting up my face towards his.

'You look good dancing it,' Finn said. His eyes met mine, and held my gaze. 'It suits you.'

My stomach tightened. It was a while since I'd had occasion to flirt with anyone, but I was fairly sure that was what Finn and I were doing. And it had to stop.

'I should go in,' I said, nodding vaguely towards the restaurant.

'Yeah,' Finn said, still looking directly into my eyes.

'See you, Finn.' I turned toward the restaurant and reached for the door.

'Nell –' Finn said. I turned back to face him. 'I meant what I said. Today, in the rehearsal studio, I liked what I saw.' Before I could answer him, he spun on his heel and strode off. My heart started racing, and for one wild, delirious moment I imagined myself running after him and demanding to know *exactly* what he meant by such remarks – before all the reasons why I had to keep him at a distance came flooding back into my mind. Telling myself firmly that in future I needed to avoid being alone with him, I pushed open the door of the restaurant and went inside.

Chapter Ten

'What kept you?' Justin said through a mouthful of beef jalfrezi, as I slid into the empty chair between him and Hettie.

'Oh, nothing much,' I said, smiling and nodding at Samantha and Leon, who were sitting across from me on the opposite side of the table. 'Finn caught me just as I was leaving the Foundry, and I couldn't get away.'

'Yeah, yeah,' Justin said.

'No, really,' I said, reaching for a menu. 'We were talking.'

'What about?' Justin said.

'About – about Finn's choreography.' I felt my face grow warm. 'Thanks for saving me a seat, by the way.'

'You're welcome,' Justin said. 'Although I did think you might have to fight Marisa for it. I told her it was taken, but I had to grab hold of the chair to stop her sitting down regardless. She was not best pleased.'

When I'd walked into Tiger Moon, it was to see the rest of the cast seated at three long tables in the rear of the restaurant, beneath a painted mural of a tiger stalking through a jungle. For a moment, I'd thought there was nowhere left for me to sit, but then Justin had leapt to his feet and, wildly waving his arm, had beckoned me over. Now, I saw that Marisa and Nicole were seated at the next table. Neither of them appeared to be enjoying each other's company.

'Not sitting next to you seems to have ruined her evening,' I said to Justin.

'Who wouldn't want me as their dining companion?' Justin said. 'Unless –'

'What?' I said.

'Could it possibly be that rather than my sparkling conversation, it was the chance of making new friends who can further her dancing career that attracted Marisa to the empty place next to mine.'

I raised my eyebrows. Apart from Samantha, her leading man, and Hettie, the others at our table were Lucas Halliday, the Dance Captain, understudy Sadie Price, Donte Travis – seeing him now, with a benign smile on his face, I'd never have imagined him playing a villain if I hadn't witnessed his transformation into Spencer Henderson IV at the read-through – and two of the ensemble, Toby and Edward.

'I don't see anyone here who has the power to further her career,' I said.

'Perhaps not directly,' Justin said, 'but it never hurt an ensemble dancer to be on good terms with stars like Leon, Samantha, or Donte. Not to mention that Sadie is married to a casting director.'

'And you know that how?' I said.

Justin merely grinned. 'In other news,' he said, 'you'll notice that Matt and Florence have the best seats in the house: next to each other.'

I glanced towards the third table and spied Florence and Matt sitting at the far end. He was talking, while she smiled and laughed.

'I can *so* see those two starring together in a long-running show,' Justin said.

'You are, of course, talking about their careers in musical theatre,' I said, my face deadpan.

'What else could I possibly be talking about?' Justin said. I laughed, raised my hand to attract the attention of a passing waiter, and asked him to bring me a chicken korma and a lager to go with it.

When the waiter had gone, Samantha leant across the table. 'Nell,' she began, 'we haven't had a chance to talk yet. I was wondering if you remembered me? We performed together once in panto.'

'We did?' I said, taken aback, for I had no recollection of meeting her other than on the first day of rehearsal.

'It was *Sleeping Beauty*,' Samantha said. 'You were one of the dancers. I was in the juvenile chorus, and completely starstruck . . .'

A theatre at Christmas time. Me and my dance partner standing in the wings, waiting to run on stage. A small group of children and teenagers – the pantomime babes and the juveniles – gazing at us wide-eyed. One girl, taller than the others, with long red hair, a talented dancer and singer . . .

'I think I do remember you,' I said to Samantha. 'Weren't you one of the older kids?

'That's right,' she said. 'I was fifteen. Dancing had only been a hobby for me until then, but performing in *Sleeping Beauty* made me want a career on the stage.'

Sleeping Beauty. It had been one of my all-time favourite jobs – not least because I was dating the actor who played the Prince, even if our relationship hadn't lasted beyond the end of the run. I was offered panto at the same theatre the following Christmas, but by then I was pregnant.

'Me and the other kids were all in awe of you dancers,' Samantha went on. 'On the last night, I plucked up my courage and asked you for your autograph.'

'I remember,' I said, as more memories surfaced. 'I was flattered. I also remember you saying that you didn't want to go back to school now the panto had ended because what was the point when all you wanted to do was dance and sing? And I couldn't think of a good answer. I wasn't much of a role model for a starstruck teenager, was I?'

Samantha laughed. 'You told me that I had to get through just one more year at school and then I should train in musical theatre at a performing arts college – which is exactly what I did. And now I'm starring in *Speakeasy*. I'm *so* glad I took your advice.'

Ten years ago, Samantha had looked up to me. Now, her stage career had far eclipsed mine. I'd have forgiven myself if I'd felt a pang of envy, but instead, hearing that I'd played a part – even if it was *miniscule* – in her success, made me glow inside.

Further pantomime reminiscences were interrupted by the return of the waiter with my meal, and by the time he'd gone, Samantha was talking to Sadie. I ate my curry, drank my lager, and listened while Donte told a very funny story about how he'd once been flown out to Hollywood to audition for a movie only to be told that there'd been a mistake and he was not, in fact, the guy they wanted to see. Leon bought everyone at the table another drink.

A couple of hours and several more rounds of drinks later, including shots bought by Leon for the entire cast, the evening drew to a close, and – after the typical chaotic interlude that ensues when any large group of people try to work out who owes what on a communal restaurant bill, while hugging and air-kissing and assuring each other they've had the best time – stars and ensemble made their exit from the restaurant

'Glad you came?' Justin asked, once we'd extricated ourselves from a reprise of fond farewells outside on the pavement.

'Yes, I am,' I said, as we started strolling towards the station. It had been a good night out. And with Savannah at her sleepover, I didn't need to feel guilty about it.

We'd only gone a few yards when, from behind me, I heard Matt say: 'Nell, wait up.'

I turned around to face him.

'Can I ask you a favour?' he said. Without waiting for my reply, he continued, 'I'm worried about Florence. She's been in the rest-room for ages. Would you mind going to check she's all right? I think she may have had too much to drink.'

'Have you been plying that girl with alcohol?' Justin said. 'Shame on you.'

'No, I have *not*,' Matt said, visibly bristling. 'I would *never* do anything like that.'

'Only teasing,' Justin said.

'Ignore him, Matt,' I said, shooting Justin a look. 'I'll go and make sure Florence is OK.' Leaving the two men standing on the pavement, hoping that Justin would have the sense to realise that Matt was not in the mood for jokes, I walked the short distance back to the restaurant.

A small group of my fellow performers were still clustered outside in the light spilling from the plate glass frontage, including Samantha, Leon and Hettie – and Marisa and Nicole – who regarded me curiously as I skirted past them and reached for the door handle.

'You're going the wrong way, Nell,' Marisa said. 'I hope you have a better sense of direction when you're on stage!' She laughed uproariously, as if she'd said something particularly amusing, but only Nicole joined in.

Looking back over my shoulder, I said, 'I'm going back for my phone, which I appear to have left in the restaurant. At least, I can't think where else it could be.'

Nicole said, 'That's a coincidence. I lost my phone earlier. But it was in my bag all the time.'

'What are you like?' I said, smiling brightly. To my immense satisfaction, Marisa started, and her eyes bulged in surprise. I went into the restaurant, and, unremarked by the waiters, who by this time of night were run off their feet, made straight for the women's restroom, and slipped inside.

At the far end of the room, Florence was sitting on the floor, slumped against the wall, under a row of hand-dryers. Her eyes were shut, and her cheeks were flushed. Next to her, the contents of her bag were scattered on the tiles.

'Florence!' I ran over to her and, crouching down beside her, put my hand on her shoulder.

She opened her eyes. 'Hello, Nell,' she said. 'I don' feel ver' well.'

Oh, my goodness, I thought, she's wasted. 'How much did you have to drink?' I asked.

She stared at me blankly.

'Never mind,' I said. 'Come on, let's get you out of here. You need to stand up –' Somewhat to my surprise, for she seemed pretty much out of it, Florence did as I told her, rising unsteadily to her feet. Hastily, I shoved her phone and other belongings back into her bag and slung it over my shoulder, along with mine. Taking hold of Florence by the elbow, I steered her out of the restroom and into the seating area of the restaurant. Two heavy dance bags and one drunk girl did not make for easy navigation through the tightly-packed tables – a disastrous collision with a tray of steaming tandoori chicken was only narrowly avoided – but we made it to the door and out into the street unscathed.

Unfortunately, as soon as we were outside, Florence came to an abrupt halt, and before I could stop her, sat down on the pavement.

'I'm havin' a rest,' Florence said. 'Just need a lil' rest.'

'Not here you don't,' I said, taking hold of her hands and attempting unsuccessfully to haul her to her feet.

Justin and Matt, who'd been waiting a short distance along the street, ran over to us.

'Florence?' Matt said. 'Florence, talk to me. Are you OK?'

'She will be once she's slept it off,' I said. To Justin, I added, 'I'm in need of your partnering skills. Specifically, your unrivalled ability to perform a difficult lift.'

Justin rolled his eyes, but with him on one side, and Matt on the other, the guys got Florence upright again. She swayed alarmingly, slumped against Mat, and shut her eyes. He put a steadying arm around her waist.

A male voice said, 'Do you need a hand?' I spun around, and almost knocked into Leon, who was standing behind me, unnoticed until he spoke. Samantha and Hettie had apparently gone home, but Marisa and Nicole were hovering at his shoulder.

'No, we don't need anything,' Matt snapped.

'Are you sure?' Leon said. 'Florence doesn't look at all well.'

'Florence,' Marisa said, 'is totally pissed.' She trilled with laughter, setting my teeth on edge, and removing any doubts I might still have had that she was *not* a nice girl. Matt glared at her.

'We've got this, Leon,' I said, 'but thank you.'

He inclined his head. 'I'll say goodnight then. To all of you. Ah – there's my ride at last.' With a brief but charming smile, he walked briskly over to a large saloon – with the logo of an upmarket car-hire firm on the passenger door – that had drawn up at the side of the road, and jumped into the back seat. The car drove off.

'We may as well go straight home too, Nicole,' Marisa said.

'But you told Leon you wanted one more drink,' Nicole said.

'I've changed my mind,' Marisa snapped, pivoting around and marching off at a furious pace in the direction of the station.

'Er – goodnight everyone,' Nicole said. Without waiting for our reply, she hurried after Marisa.

'Well, someone's evening didn't end the way she hoped,' Justin remarked.

I was inclined to agree with him, and opened my mouth to tell him so, before recalling that the four of us were still standing in the middle of the street, one of us was very drunk, and that this was hardly the time or place to indulge in scurrilous gossip.

'Focus, Justin,' I said. 'All we need to think about right now is getting Florence home.' Even as I spoke, I realised that I had no idea where her home was. 'Florence, look at me,' I said. Her eyes remained shut. 'Florence, listen, I need you to tell me your address.' To my frustration, her only response was to bury her face in Matt's chest. 'Do either of you know where she lives by any chance?' I said.

'I have her address,' Matt said. 'She lives in Finchley. Near the tube station. One stop along from me.'

Inwardly, I sighed. As a jobbing dancer who'd performed in venues scattered all over London, I'd ordinarily have no qualms about travelling home late at night on public transport, but with Florence in her present state of inebriation, I baulked at conveying her from our current location in Waterloo to Finchley on the other side of the city on the tube. If Matt hadn't been so quick to turn down Leon's offer of help, I thought, irritably, he might have given us all a lift home.

Aloud, I said, 'If you two wouldn't mind waiting while I call a cab, I'll take her home.'

'It's all right, Nell,' Matt said. 'It's late and you'll be wanting to get home yourself. I'll see she gets back safely.'

'It's fine,' I said. 'I don't mind taking her.' I'd no doubt that his intentions were purely chivalrous, but there was no way I was going to abandon a very drunk female friend in central London late at night – it just didn't feel right.

'I'd like to know she's home,' Matt said.

'OK,' I said. 'We'll both take her.'

'We'll *all* take her,' Justin said, firmly. 'Why should I miss out on all the fun?'

Half an hour or so later, the cab – into which Matt and Justin had bundled Florence before the driver could object to a drunk passenger – drove past Finchley Road station, turned off the main road into a residential side street, and drew up outside a large Victorian terrace house, with bay windows and a short flight of stone steps leading up to the front door.

'Time to wake up, Florence,' Matt said. Florence, who'd spent the journey lolling against him with her head on his shoulder, sat up, staring owlishly around her. Justin got out of the cab. Matt, holding Florence's waist, passed her to Justin, and joined them on the pavement. I followed, carrying everyone's dance bags, and paid the cab-driver, who sped off.

Dumping the bags at the foot of the steps, I said, 'Florence, you're home. Where are your keys?'

Florence smiled at me sleepily. Before Matt and Justin, who were standing on either side of her could stop her, she sat down on the bottom step, and in a pure soprano, started to sing:

'*Home, I must go, for the dawn it is breaking . . .*' Her voice trailed off.

'*My lover is gone,*' Justin sang, '*my heart it is aching.*'

'I don't know that tune,' Matt said. 'Which show is it from?'

'It's not a show tune,' Justin said. 'It's an old folk song. *He's gone for a soldier over the sea/When will he ever come back to me?*'

I took a deep breath. 'Guys,' I said, 'now is really not the time for street theatre.'

'Sorry,' Justin said.

'Florence,' I said. 'I'm going to look through your bag. For your keys.'

'Er, Nell,' Matt said, 'there's a light on in the house. We could just ring the bell.'

I glanced up at the house and saw that while the windows on the lower floors were dark, a window on the upper floor showed the flickering light of a TV screen. At least one of Florence's house-mates, whoever they might be, was awake.

'Now that's a plan,' I said. Picking up Florence's bag, I walked up the steps, waited for Matt and Justin to hoist Florence to her feet, and rang the bell. After a short while, a light came on in the hall, shining through the panels of stained glass in the front door, and then I heard the sound of a key turning in a lock. The door opened, and I found myself face to face with a grey-haired, bespectacled, middle-aged man, wearing a plaid dressing gown over striped pyjamas. He did not look happy.

'Er, good evening,' I began. 'My name is Nell. I'm a friend of Florence. We – me and some other friends – were out with her tonight, and I'm afraid she's had a little too much wine.'

The man's gaze travelled past me to Florence, Justin and Matt, who were still standing at the bottom of the steps. His eyes narrowed.

'Are you telling me you've brought my daughter home drunk?' he demanded.

'You're her father?' I said, stupidly. It simply hadn't occurred to me that Florence would still live at home with her parents, but that was where most girls of her age lived, unless they were off at uni – or performing arts college. 'I mean – of course, you are. She's only nineteen. Naturally, she lives with her family.' Until now, the only time I'd informed a parent that their child was intoxicated had been when Zelda had overdone the punch at a mutual school-friend's Sweet Sixteen party – the revelation hadn't gone down well. 'Yes, she's drunk,' I said.

'I'm very disappointed to hear that,' Florence's father said. 'I'd have hoped Florence's friends would behave more responsibly.'

I gaped at him. It wasn't *my* fault that his daughter was off her face. I resisted the impulse to inform Mr Newton that I was *not* the miscreant teenager he seemed to think I was, but had a daughter of my own.

Florence chose that moment to start singing again.

'Florence,' her father said, 'stop that caterwauling and come inside right now.'

At the sound of her father's voice, Florence fell silent, and, with Matt and Justin ready to catch her if she fell, tottered precariously up the steps and past her father into the hall. She made it almost as far as the stairs, before sinking down onto the carpet.

'I feel sick,' she said, suddenly.

'Angela!' her father shouted. 'Angela, I need some assistance here.' After a moment, a middle-aged woman, in an ivory silk dressing gown, appeared on the landing – she looked so like an older version of Florence that she had to be her mother. When she saw Florence sitting forlornly on the floor, the woman gasped, and ran down the stairs.

'What's happened?' she said, her hands fluttering about her face. 'What's wrong?'

'The silly girl has had too much to drink,' Florence's father said. 'These people –' he glared at me and the guys – 'have brought her home.'

'She's *drunk*?' Florence's mother said. 'But Florence wouldn't – she doesn't drink.'

'Evidently, she did tonight,' Florence's father said.

'I'm going to throw up,' Florence wailed, clutching her stomach. I saw that her face had turned a peculiar shade of green. Angela sprang into maternal action, seizing an empty fruit bowl from a console table that stood against the wall, and thrusting it towards her daughter.

And that, I thought, *is my cue to exit*. Florence's father presumably thought the same, for he'd put his hand on the door ready to close it. Matt and Justin were already retreating down the steps – wisely, it seemed to me.

'Well, I won't take up any more of your time,' I said to Florence's father. He spluttered something unintelligible. Raising my voice, I called out, ''Bye, Florence. See you at rehearsal.' She didn't reply, but then I hadn't really expected her to.

Angela, now sitting beside her daughter, stroking her hair, while she bent over the fruit bowl, called out: 'Goodnight. Thank you for seeing Florence home. It was very kind of you.'

'No worries,' I said, glad to discover that Florence had one reasonable parent. Without thinking, I added, 'After all, we've all had too much to drink at one time or another, haven't we?' I glanced towards Florence's father. The expression on his face suggested that he was about to implode. 'Not that I drink very often,' I said, hastily. 'Just the occasional glass of wine with dinner.' I spun around, and under Mr Newton's baleful glare, walked quickly down the steps. The front door slammed shut.

'Did you know Florence lives with her parents?' I asked Matt. He nodded. 'You might have warned me,' I said.

'Why?' Matt said, genuinely puzzled. 'I live with my parents.'

Oh, my days, I thought, *not only I am older than every other dancer in* Speakeasy, *I'm a different generation.*

Matt was staring up at the house, where every window was now in complete darkness. 'I was sort of hoping to ask Florence if she'd like to do something tomorrow,' he said, 'but once she'd started on the tequila, I didn't get the chance.' He sighed.

'You were planning to ask Florence out on a *date*?' Justin said. 'Just so I'm clear.'

Matt shrugged. 'I guess. I thought we could – you know – hang out together. Maybe check out Borough Market. What do you think, Nell? Would Florence like that, do you think?'

'Well, I did when I was her age,' I said, cringing at how ancient this made me sound, 'but you should really ask *her*.'

'I will,' Matt said. 'But maybe not tomorrow.'

'No, tomorrow wouldn't be a good time,' I said.

'Aw – *Speakeasy* has its first backstage romance,' Justin said.

'Not yet,' Matt said, with a grin. 'But here's hoping.'

'What about you, Nell?' Justin said. 'Anyone in the cast who caught your eye across a steaming plate of chicken madras tonight?'

'What?' I said. 'No, of course, not. *No*, Justin.'

'Someone *not* in the cast . . ?'

Finn, naked, lying next to me on my bed in the moonlight, reaching for me, his mouth lifting in a smile, his hands softly caressing my body . . .

'Don't be ridiculous,' I said.

Justin laughed. 'You are so easy to wind up,' he said.

'Guys, I don't want to worry you,' Matt said, nodding towards the house, 'but a light's just come on again, and Florence's dad is watching us through the window. I'm out of here.' He set off at a run in the direction of the station.

Realising that we'd been talking extremely loudly, and having no wish for another scolding from Florence's irate father, I seized Justin's hand, and the two of us ran after Matt, only slowing to a walk when we were around the corner and out of sight.

Oh, the glamour of showbusiness.

Chapter Eleven

'Do you like the bracelet I made?' Savannah said, as we walked up the front path. She held up her arm to show me the neon pink and yellow beads around her wrist. Too garish for my taste, but I could see its appeal to a nine-year-old.

I smiled. 'I do, sweetheart. It's so lovely and bright.' I unlocked the front door and we went inside the house. Savannah headed straight for the sitting room, and the TV. I went into the kitchen, and heated up a casserole. The way my daughter had been yawning ever since I'd picked her up from the sleepover, I suspected that if I didn't put some food in front of her very soon, she'd be asleep before she could eat it.

Carrying our plates into the other room, I placed them on our small round dining table. Savannah switched off the TV without being asked, and the two of us sat down to eat.

'So, tell me about the sleepover,' I said. 'Did you have fun?'

'Oh, yes,' Savannah said. 'Amy has the best jewellery-making kit. She has glitter pens as well.'

'Fabulous,' I said. 'I'm partial to a bit of glitter myself.' I peered at Savannah more closely. 'Is that pink glitter in your hair?'

Savannah nodded. 'It's Amy's big sister's glitter hair spray. She said we could have some. Amy's mum said to tell you that it washes out.'

'Good to know,' I said, with a pang for the days when Savannah returned from friends' houses with tales of dolls' tea-sets and playing 'shops.'

'Did you have fun at your party?' Savannah asked.

'I did,' I said. 'But it wasn't a party. It was a meal with some friends in a restaurant.' Savannah pulled a face, unimpressed with what I considered fun.

'We stayed up really late,' she said. 'We wanted to stay awake all night, but Amy's mum came into Amy's room and said it was almost morning and we had to stop talking and go to sleep.'

And that, I thought, was why Donna, Amy's mother, whose usual appearance at the school-gates was one of effortless elegance, had looked a little harassed this afternoon. And why her sociable husband, Patrick, had, for once, not asked the parents who'd come to collect their offspring from his house to stay for a drink. Not that I was feeling up to being sociable today myself, after my night out, despite having slept in until noon.

'Please can I have a sleepover?' Savannah said. A wave of parental guilt flooded through me.

'Not while I'm in rehearsal,' I said, laying down my knife and fork. 'I'm sorry, Savannah. Once *Speakeasy* opens, I'll be able to take days off. I promise you can invite some friends for a sleepover then.'

Savannah thought for a moment, and then she said, 'Can I have a sleepover for my birthday party?'

'Yes,' I said, mentally crossing my fingers. Her birthday wasn't until June, but as only two of the cast could take holiday at the same time, I'd have to put in a request to the Company Manager as soon as possible.

'Please can I have a phone for my birthday? You said I could have a phone.'

'I said I'd think about it.' Guilt could only make me go so far when it came to indulging my daughter. To forestall further requests for a phone, I said, 'What else did you do at the sleepover?' Savannah immediately began chattering away about Amy's light-up dance mat and Amy's sister's karaoke machine. Congratulating myself on my distraction techniques, I resumed eating my casserole.

'Time to say goodnight now, Savannah,' I said, going into her room and sitting down on her bed. Savannah, her hair now washed – the bath was covered in glitter – nestled down under her duvet.

'Amy's dad does magic tricks,' she said. 'He can make money disappear.'

'I hope he can make it re-appear,' I said.

'Oh, yes,' Savannah said. 'Amy's mum pretended to be cross when he made her 50p disappear, but he found it again behind her ear, and she laughed.' In a conspiratorial tone, she added, 'I know magic isn't real.'

'But it's fun to make-believe it is,' I said.

Savannah nodded. 'If I had a dad, I'd like him to do magic tricks and tell jokes like Amy's dad,' she said.

I sat very still. My heart began to pound. Savannah had never asked me any questions about her father and I'd never thought seriously about what I might say to her if she did ask. I wasn't ready for her to start asking now.

Savannah yawned. 'Please can I have a glitter pen set.'

I let out the breath that I hadn't realised I'd been holding. 'Absolutely,' I said. 'I'll go and order one on-line straight away.'

'Thank you,' Savannah said. I leant over her, kissed her cheek and hugged her. She gave me a kiss on my cheek in return.

'Goodnight, Savannah,' I said. 'Love you.'

'Love you, Mum,' she said.

Slowly, I stood up, and on shaking legs went to the door. 'Sleep tight. See you in the morning.'

I turned out the light, went downstairs to the sitting room, where I'd left my phone, and placed an on-line order for the glitter pens – and a sparkly pink pencil case to go with them. Then I sank down on the sofa.

Surely Savannah was still too young to start wondering about the absence of a father in her life? She was certainly too young to understand any explanation I could come up with, unless I told her an outright lie . . .

I stand by my bedroom window, and look out at the street. When Finn left for Germany, the leaves on the trees were just turning from green to gold; now their leafless branches claw at a darkening sky. Cars line the kerb bumper to bumper.

A gust of wind scatters pages of a dropped newspaper. For everyone else, it's a winter day like any other, but not for me. I place my hands on my stomach.

'I am pregnant.' There's no-one to hear me, but saying it aloud makes it real. When Finn went to Germany, he left me with more than a good luck charm. I am carrying his child. I've suspected it for weeks, but now I know for sure. My chest tightens. What am I going to do?

I turn from the window and pace about the room. I've always vaguely imagined that I would have children someday, but not now, and certainly not with Finn as the father. We're friends who fell into bed one night after too much wine – and went on having incredible sex for the rest of the summer – but we both knew from the start it was strictly no strings. Even if I wanted a steady relationship with him – and it's just as well I don't, given that he never stays with a girl for longer than a few weeks – he's hundreds of miles away. If I have this baby, I will be raising him or her or my own . . .

I picture a little boy with Finn's grey eyes, a little girl with my long dark hair . . .

I hear Zelda let herself into our flat.

'Nell?' she calls out. 'Are you home?'

'In here,' I call back, switching off the TV. Zelda comes into the living room, dressed in the uniform she wears as a museum guide.

'What a day I've had,' she says, flopping down in the armchair opposite mine. 'My last tour group had so many

questions, I thought I'd never get away. What did you do today?' I have to tell her sometime. It might as well be now.

'This afternoon,' I say, 'I called Amanda and told her to withdraw me from the musical I auditioned for last week.'

'You did *what?*' Zelda sits bolt upright. 'Why would you do that?'

'Because if I get an offer of a contract, I'll have to turn it down. I'd rather not know.'

'I don't understand,' Zelda says.

I take a deep breath. 'I'm pregnant.'

'Oh, Nell.' Zelda's hands fly to either side of her face. 'Are you sure?'

I nod my head. 'If I wasn't sure – and if I wasn't keeping it – there's no way I'd be walking away from a West End musical.'

For a long moment, Zelda regards me in silence, but then she asks, 'Is it Finn's?'

'Yes, Finn is the father,' I say. 'But I haven't told him, and – I've thought long and hard about this – I'm not going to.'

'But – but you have to tell him.' Zelda's eyebrows draw together in concern.

'I don't see why,' I say. 'Finn and I had a good time together, but it was just a casual fling. He wouldn't welcome the news that he's about to become a parent.'

'But surely he has a right to know?' Zelda says.

'No, he does *not*,' I say. 'It's my decision to go ahead with this pregnancy. I don't want anything from Finn. I'm not going to ask him to support me financially or in any other way. I'm raising *my* child on my own.' I catch Zelda's gaze and hold it. 'I've told you that Finn is the father – you'd have *guessed anyway – but I'm not telling anyone else. Not even my family. My parents would never understand why I don't want anything to do with him.' In an effort to lighten the atmosphere, I add: 'My father would probably go out and buy a shotgun.' Zelda doesn't laugh.*

'So what are you going to tell your parents when they ask who's knocked you up?' she says. 'Because they will. If not in those exact words.'

'I don't know. I'll think of something.' I fold my arms across my stomach. 'Promise me that you'll keep my secret.'

Zelda's eyes lock on mine. 'Nell, we've been best friends since the first day of high school. We've kept each other's secrets since we were teenagers. I think you're wrong not to tell Finn – but I'll keep your secret as long as you want me to . . .'

I reminded myself that, tonight, Savannah hadn't actually asked any questions about her father, but merely expressed an opinion about another child's parent. It was one insignificant remark in a constant stream of chatter, most likely forgotten as soon as uttered. There was no need for me to worry as yet, no need to regret the lie I'd told . . .

It's Christmas Day. I'm about to eat lunch with my mother, father and sister, the four of us sitting at my parents' dinner table, paper hats on our heads, our plates heaped with turkey. My father opens the wine.

'Not for me, Dad,' I say, placing my hand over my glass.

My father does a double take. 'Really? This is the good stuff I got specially for Christmas.'

My heart is racing. What an idiot I was to think I could put off this conversation until after the festivities.

'I can't,' I say. 'I-I'm pregnant.'

My mother gasps, the expression on her face passing rapidly from alarm to concern. With infinite care, my father puts the wine back down on the table. His face is expressionless.

'Are you sure?' *my mother says, eventually.* 'How far along are you?'

'Sixteen weeks,' I say. 'And, yes, I'm sure.'

'We didn't even know you had a boyfriend,' *my father says.*

'I don't right now,' I said.

'So who's the dad?' *Marianne pipes up.*

'Be quiet, Marianne,' *my mother says.* 'Nell, who is the baby's father?'

I've gone over this conversation with my parents so many times in my head, without deciding exactly what I'll say to them, but now, in this instant, I have to make a decision. I can tell them the truth and attempt to make them understand why I'm not even going to try to get in touch with my child's father. Or I can tell them a lie that'll ensure they'll believe contacting him is impossible.

'I don't know who the father is,' I say. 'I was in a club – I was drunk – I don't remember.'

'It's OK, Nell, we don't need the details,' *my father says hurriedly.*

Marianne opens her mouth to speak, but one look from our mother and she shuts it again.

'And you have absolutely no idea who –?' *my mother says to me.*

I feel so bad lying to my parents, but still I say, 'No, none at all.'

A look passes between my mother and father that I'm quite unable to interpret, but neither of them pursues the question of who impregnated their daughter.

'This is all a bit of a shock,' my mother says.

'I was shocked at first,' I admit, 'and I've had moments when I didn't see how I could go through with it, but I want this baby. I know it won't be easy doing it alone –'

'Oh, sweetheart, you won't be alone,' my mother says, leaping up from her seat and flinging her arms around me. 'We're always here for you . . .'

The ringing of my phone brought me back to the present, the screen informing me that the caller was Florence. Welcoming a distraction from my uneasy thoughts, I tapped the answer icon.

'Nell?' Florence said. 'I hope I'm not disturbing you?'

'Not at all,' I said. 'What's up?'

There was a pause, and then Florence blurted, 'I have to ask you about the cast curry. I was so drunk, I don't remember – My dad said a woman called Nell and two men brought me home –' I couldn't help wondering what else Mr Newton had said about us, but decided it was better not to inquire.

'That would be Justin and Matt,' I said.

'I'm so sorry. I didn't mean to ruin your night out – Nell, please tell me, did I do anything *terrible*?'

'No, you really didn't. The worst thing you did was sing in the street, and only me and the guys were there to hear it.'

Florence groaned. 'I feel so *stupid*. I don't even like the taste of tequila, but it seemed rude to refuse Leon when he was buying everyone shots, and I was fine until I stood up to leave the restaurant – at least I think I was. After that, it's all a blur.' She paused. 'Thank you for looking out for me.'

'That's OK,' I said. 'That's what friends do.' And then, because I was a responsible adult, whatever Florence's father might think, and because she was so much younger than me, I added, 'Listen, Florence, you're certainly not the first girl to have too much to drink on a Saturday night, and I'm not judging you, but I'd be a bad friend if I didn't say that you don't want to make a habit of it.'

'Oh, I'm never drinking again,' Florence said. 'I had such a ghastly headache all day today, and I still don't feel too good.' She sighed. 'My parents are being *so* annoying, telling me I've only myself to blame. And I know they're right. Which is even more annoying.'

'I recommend milk thistle, drinking lots of water and an early night,' I said. 'At least that's what I've found on the *extremely* rare occasions when I've had more wine than is strictly wise.'

Florence laughed at that. 'I think I will have an early night,' she said. 'Thanks, Nell. For getting me home and everything.'

'That's OK,' I said. 'See you at rehearsal.'

'See you tomorrow,' Florence said, and ended the call.

Poor Florence, I thought, having to suffer her obnoxious father's disapproval on top of a hangover. I was, I knew, very fortunate in my parents who, while they had at times expressed concern for my well-being and that of my fatherless child, had never uttered one word of disapproval, anger or even disappointment at what I'd done – or what I'd told them I'd done – even on that long ago Christmas Day. Of course, I'd been twenty-four and financially independent, not nineteen and still living in the parental abode, but even so . . .

My thoughts tumbled about my head. Savannah. The lie I'd told. *Finn.* Me and him last night, standing in the light from the restaurant window, the things we'd said and the promise in his lazy smile. My stomach clenched. He wanted me, I knew he did. And I wanted him. I hadn't felt like this about any other guy, not in years, not since him. *The father of my child.*

My mobile rang again: Zelda. The one person I hadn't lied to, and who'd kept my secret all this time. I snatched up the phone and stabbed at the screen.

'Hey, Nell,' Zelda said. 'The kids are asleep, and Martin's gone to the pub, so I thought I'd give you a quick call and you can tell me all the latest West End gossip.'

'Oh, Zelda, it's so good to hear from you.' I said. Suddenly, my chest felt tight. 'You're the only person I can talk to right now –'

There was a pause, and then Zelda said, 'Nell, is everything OK? Rehearsals going well?'

'Rehearsals are going great,' I said. 'It's just that –' I took a deep breath. 'It's Finn – seeing him every day – I don't know what to do.'

'Hey, slow up. What *exactly* are you telling me?'

'I *like* him, Zelda. And I'm sure he feels the same. I think something could happen between us. If I let it.'

There was a long silence, and then Zelda said, 'You need to think very carefully before you go there, Nell. Unless you want to stir up the past.'

'That's what I keep telling myself.'

'Just because you have the hots for a guy, you don't have to do anything about it.'

'I tell myself that too,' I said. 'Every time I see Finn. But I can't help what I feel.'

I heard Zelda sigh, and then she said, 'I'm not going to tell you what to do – or what *not* to do, but –' She broke off.

'What is it?' I said

'Sorry, but I have to go. Esme's woken up. I can hear her on the baby monitor. I'll call you back once she's settled.'

'No, it's OK, don't call back,' I said. 'It's late, and we've both got to get up for the school run tomorrow. Thanks for listening.'

'Anytime – but you know that.'

'Straight back at you,' I said.

'Take care, Nell. Seriously. I mean it.' She ended the call. I let my phone fall onto the sofa, and sank back against the cushions.

Even if she hadn't said it aloud, I knew that Zelda thought I should keep my distance from Finn. And *I* knew I had to end whatever was between us before it started.

Maybe if I told myself that enough times, I'd believe it.

Chapter Twelve

Olivia shouted, 'Hold it there.' The music crashed to a halt. I froze in position, as did the other dancers – the ensemble girls and Samantha – except for Florence and Marisa, who as I now saw in the mirrors, were both sprawled on the floor at the back of the performance space.

'All right, ladies?' Olivia asked, as they got back on their feet. Florence nodded.

'You were in the wrong place,' Marisa said, scowling at Florence. 'You barged right into me.'

Florence's face flushed bright red. 'I'm sorry,' she said.

Finn, who was sitting next to Olivia at the front of the studio, said, 'You were both in the wrong place. If you remember, we changed the spacing when we ran through the number this morning.' For the first time since the start of rehearsals, he sounded irritated when giving a correction, probably the result of the frustration he had to be feeling at the number of times this scene – Kitty and her friends getting ready for a night out at the speakeasy – had already been stopped and started.

'I *never* forget a dance,' Marisa said, her voice shrill. '*I* wasn't here when the choreography was changed. *I* was in a costume fitting. It wasn't *my* fault.'

I gasped, as did the girl standing next to me, and more gasps could be heard all around the studio. Samantha frowned, and then became very interested in the floor. Even Nicole gawped at her friend.

Finn didn't reply to Marisa, but his mouth tightened perceptibly. He leant towards Olivia and they held a brief muttered conversation. Then he got up from his chair, and walked to the edge of the performance space. His gaze travelled over his dancers, lingering on me longer than on anyone else, or so it seemed, and low in my stomach I felt the insistent tug of desire. His eyes met mine, and for an instant, it was as if he and I were the only people in the room, before his gaze moved on. For the last couple of weeks of rehearsal, while the show was put together, before we transferred to the theatre next week, I hadn't seen him to speak to outside the rehearsal room, but the attraction between us was still there.

Now, he said, 'Nell, Florence, Eleri and Nicole, you're out of this number and the rest of the scene. We'll take a break, and then we'll re-block.'

In any other production, I'd have been dismayed to be taken out of a dance, but at that moment all I felt was relief. Once *Speakeasy* was up and running, not being in this particular number would give me time to get my breath back after the previous one, and I wouldn't have a ridiculously quick costume change. In the mirrors, I saw Florence, her shoulders slumped, go and sit on the floor with Matt and

Justin who, like the rest of the cast not in the scene, were watching from the sidelines. She evidently cared rather more about this loss of stage time than I did.

Olivia said, 'I'd like to remind you all that if Wardrobe need you to go and try on costumes during rehearsals, it's your responsibility to catch up on anything you've missed.' She glanced at her watch. 'Everyone take ten.' Several of the cast left the studio; others headed straight for the coffee urn. I fetched a bottle of water from my bag, and joined Florence and the guys.

'I've really messed up, haven't I?' Florence said, as I sat down beside her. 'I was trying on costumes this morning at the same time as Marisa – I didn't think to ask if I'd missed anything – I thought all the dancing was set.'

'Not in stone,' Matt said. 'A number can be changed at any time – even after opening night, if the audience reaction isn't what the producers hoped for.'

'I've been in a couple of shows that were tweaked after they'd opened,' Justin said. 'It's a right pain when you have to rehearse new material during the day, while still performing the original version at night.'

'I wouldn't have thought to check if there'd been any changes,' I said to Florence, thankful that my own summons to Wardrobe – currently ensconced with their tape-measures and pins in a neighbouring studio – had been during a scene in which nothing had altered in my absence. I'd been so caught up in admiring myself in my 1920s flapper dress and diamante headband, it hadn't crossed my mind that I might miss anything important.

'I hope Finn doesn't cut me from any more dances,' Florence said. 'What if he thinks I can't pick up new choreography quickly enough?'

'He won't think that,' Matt said. 'After five weeks of rehearsal, he knows what you can do.'

'But why else would he cut me?' Florence said. It occurred to me to wonder why I – and Nicole and Eleri – had also been cut from of the dance.

'I was cut as well, don't forget,' I said, 'and I didn't make any mistakes.' I ran through the routine in my head. There were a lot of high kicks. Had I got my legs high enough?

'I honestly wouldn't worry, Florence.' Matt said. 'Marisa got the spacing wrong too, and he kept her in the number.'

Did I need to worry? Surely, if Finn thought I wasn't performing his choreography the way he wanted, he'd give me a correction.

'But Marisa explained *why* she didn't know it,' Florence said. 'Should I tell Finn I was trying on costumes, do you think?'

'I wouldn't,' Matt said. 'You're making far too much out of something that really isn't a big deal.'

My gaze drifted to Finn, who was now standing by the windows, alone, his hand resting on the sill, looking out over London . . .

I wake in a tangle of sheets to find that Finn has got out of bed, and is standing naked by the window, looking out over the night-time street, his hands resting on the high sill. I lie on my side, drinking him in, his tousled hair, his superbly toned body, burnished by the light of the full moon flooding into the bedroom. As if he senses that I'm awake, he turns around and smiles at me. I smile back at him. He walks slowly across the room, and sits on the side of the bed.

'Why did we never hook up when we were at college?' he says.

I sit up, allowing the sheet to fall to my waist. Finn's eyes glint appreciatively.

'I always thought of you as a friend,' I say. 'And having sex with a friend is not something that would have ever occurred to me. Until tonight.'

'Are you telling me that in all years we were training together, you never even considered *sleeping with me?' He sounds so incredulous that I laugh.*

''You are so up yourself, Finn Harris,' I say. 'Anyway, you never showed any interest in getting with me back then.'

'I did think about it, though,' he says. 'From time to time.'

'I thought about it too,' I admit. 'Once or twice.'

He cups my face in his hand, and traces my mouth with his thumb. 'If I'd known what I was missing . . . Nell, can I stay the rest of the night?'

'Yes, of course,' I say. He lies down next to me, pulls the sheet over both of us, and then rolls onto his side, with his back to me. In moments, I hear the sound of his regular breathing, and I know he's fallen asleep.

In the morning, I think, he'll walk away without a backward glance. Even if he wasn't leaving the country in a month's time, he'd walk away. And I'm fine with that . . .

We sit on a bench eating an al fresco lunch of supermarket sandwiches and crisps, and drinking wine from a screw-top bottle. All summer, the park has been crowded – only last week, sunbathing stretched out on the grass, we were startled by a wayward football and an over-friendly dog – but now that the schools have gone back, we have this small oasis of green amongst south London's grey expanse of terraced houses and flats to ourselves.

It's a bright sunny day, but there's a new crispness in the air, and a sudden gust of wind makes me shiver. Finn slides an arm around my shoulders. I lean against his hard muscular chest, and he drops a kiss on the top of my head.

'We've had a good time these last few weeks, haven't we?' he says. 'At least, I have.'

I twist around to face him. 'I have, too.' I was surprised when, a couple of days after he'd stayed over, Finn rang me and asked if I'd like to go with him to see a show, but I'd gone to the theatre with him, and we'd had a fun night out, ending up in a salsa club – neither of us had done salsa before, but being dancers, we picked up the steps very quickly. He slept at my side again that night, and has done every night since. Now, his suitcases are standing in my and Zelda's flat, packed and ready for his early morning flight to Berlin . . .

'You're good company when you want to be, Finn Harris,' I say. 'Oh, and by the way, in case you hadn't noticed, the sex was great.'

'Of course it was,' he says, with a grin, adding, 'Will you miss me when I'm far away?'

I look him straight in the eye. 'I'll miss having sex with you,' I say. He laughs.
'We do have one more night . . .'

'Nell?' Florence said. 'What do you think?'

'About what?' I said. 'Sorry, I didn't hear you.'

'I was talking about Finn,' Florence said.

'What do you think would be best thing to do?' Justin said.

'I don't know what to do about Finn,' I said. 'It's complicated.'

Justin raised one eyebrow. 'It's not that complicated. Florence is wondering if she should explain to Finn that she was trying on costumes like Marisa. Matt and I are of the opinion that she should let it go. What about you?'

'Ah. Sorry, I was thinking about something else.' Focus, Nell, I told myself, banishing the image of a naked Finn to the deepest recesses of my mind. To Florence, I said, 'My advice is to leave it. Finn wasn't impressed by Marisa's little outburst and if you bring it up again, you'll only annoy him.'

'Are you sure that –' Florence's voice broke off. 'Oh, no. He's coming over here.'

I swivelled around to see Finn walking towards us. His eyes met mine, and he smiled. My stomach clenched – just as it had ten years ago, when he'd smiled at me in the moonlight. I smiled back.

'Hey, Nell,' he said as he reached us. 'Can I have a word?'

'Sure,' I said, getting to my feet as rapidly as my tired legs would let me.

'Come with me,' he said, and headed for the door of the studio. Justin shot me a quizzical look. I shrugged, and hurried to catch up with Finn. He held the studio door open for me, and we went out into the corridor.

'So, Olivia has had a few thoughts about the show,' he said. 'And she's asked me to choreograph another number for Kitty and Nathan.' He hesitated. 'I know it's short notice, but are you free to come in to the studio tomorrow by any chance? I've got an idea of what I'm going to do, but it would really help me if you'd workshop it with me. I'll pay you, of course.'

My heart fluttered in my chest. Of all the dancers in Studio Four that he could have invited to work with him on a new dance, he'd asked me. I opened my mouth to say *yes*. Then I recalled how little time I'd spent with Savannah lately – and that my parents were expecting us to join them and Marianne for Sunday lunch.

'What time would you need me?' I asked.

'Ten 'til six.'

In other words, all day. I should tell him I couldn't do it. And yet . . . Helping a choreographer to create a dance would be fascinating. Savannah would be perfectly happy to be left with her grandparents and her aunt. It was just one Sunday. And it was for Finn.

'I'd love to workshop your dance,' I said, with only a smidgin of guilt.

'Good,' Finn said. 'Because there's no-one I'd rather workshop it with.' He stepped closer towards me, close enough that I could feel the heat radiating from his body. 'I'm looking forward to partnering you again . . . in my dance.'

I tilted up my face towards him. 'We used to dance so well together.' My legs felt decidedly weak, and not because I'd been dancing.

'We did, didn't we?' Finn said, his voice sounding hoarse. He cleared his throat. 'I should go back into Studio Four. I have to re-block *Just For Tonight*.'

'So you do,' I said. 'Finn, about that dance, can I ask why you took some of us out of it?'

'I've never been entirely happy with it,' Finn said, 'but I wasn't sure why. Then, today, when Florence and Marisa collided with each other, it occurred to me that what it needed was fewer dancers. I cut those of you who didn't have any solo singing lines so as not to make more work for Jonathan.' He hesitated. 'What I wanted to do was cut Marisa – preferably from the whole show. I never want to become one of those choreographers who yell at their dancers, but I nearly lost it with her today. Unfortunately, her ability to hit a high C, takes precedence over her personality – Oh, lord, she's not one of your best friends in the ensemble, is she?'

'No, she most definitely is *not* my friend,' I said.

Finn laughed. 'There's one like her in every cast,' he said, 'but their careers tend to be shorter than most. Anyway, I really do have to go and sort out that dance –'

Together, we went back into Studio Four, where half the cast immediately turned their heads in our direction. Seemingly oblivious to the interest provoked by our return to the studio, Finn strolled over to his assistant, Cameron, and Lucas, the Dance Captain, and plunged into conversation. Feeling more than a little self-conscious, I made myself walk slowly across the sprung floor, and rejoined my friends.

'What did our esteemed choreographer want?' Justin said, before I'd even sat down. 'Come on, Nell, you can tell us.'

I lowered myself to the floor. 'He's asked me to workshop a new dance for the show.'

'That's amazing!' Florence exclaimed.

'He must really rate your dancing,' Matt said.

Justin whistled. 'Either that or Marisa turned him down,' he said, with a grin.

I laughed. 'I'm not even going to pretend that I'm not excited – and flattered.' Turning to Florence, I said, 'I asked Finn why we were cut from *Just For Tonight* and he said it was because the routine needed fewer dancers.'

'Oh, I'm not worried about that anymore,' Florence said. 'Leon told me that shows get altered all the time. A star like him must know what he's talking about, right?'

'I'm sure he does,' Matt muttered.

'I'm going to get a coffee,' Florence said. 'Anyone else want one?'

'I'll come with you,' Matt said. They both got to their feet and went over to the coffee urn.

'Did I miss something?' I asked Justin.

Justin rolled his eyes. 'After you went off with Finn, Leon came over and asked Florence why she looked so sad. With the benefit of his vast theatrical experience – and his charming smile – he convinced her she had nothing to worry about. Florence has expressed her opinion that Leon is a really nice guy. I suspect young Matt's view of Leon is rather different.'

'I don't understand why Matt still hasn't asked Florence out,' I said.

'He told me he can't seem to find the right moment,' Justin said, adding, 'I can't believe she hasn't noticed the way he keeps looking at her. Almost as often as Finn looks at you. I was wondering why he couldn't take his eyes off you. And now I know. He really *really* rates your dancing.'

I caught Justin's gaze and held it. 'Yes, I rather think he does,' I said. I was far too old to blush, but my face grew warm even so.

Justin laughed softly, and looked away.

Chapter Thirteen

I walked into Studio Four to find Finn, dressed in cut-offs and a sleeveless vest, marking out a dance. He nodded at me, but continued what he was doing. I stowed my coat and bag next to his in a corner of the studio, took off the baggy sweatshirt that I was wearing over my calf-length leggings and strappy top, and without saying a word, started warming up, watching him surreptitiously in the wall mirrors. After a few minutes, he walked over to his bag, took out a notebook and wrote in it, and then turned his attention to me.

'Hey, Nell,' he said. 'Come and sit down. I want to talk to you about what we're going to be doing today.'

He walked to the centre of the studio and sat on the floor, stretching out his legs and leaning back on his hands, and I sat in front of him.

He said, 'I choreographed the dances already in the show long before we were in rehearsal. Today, we're going to be working on something entirely new. I know broadly what I want, but at this stage, it's just images in my head. I need you to help me make it real. You're going to have to be very patient, because I'm going to be asking you to repeat the choreography again and again. And then I'll probably change it because I've realised that what's in my head won't translate into actual steps. Are you OK with that?'

'Absolutely,' I said.

'So, towards the middle of Act II, Kitty and Nathan spend the night together. The dance shows Kitty's transformation from a virginal girl to a woman. At the beginning of the piece, she's shy and scared, but the dance shows her overcoming her shyness, abandoning herself to passion, and giving herself completely to the man she loves.' He grinned. 'Don't you just love it when a choreographer asks you to give him *passion* before you've even had your lunch?'

'I'll have to see what I can do,' I said, sounding rather more suggestive than I intended. I reminded myself that I was here to work with the guy, not flirt with him.

'OK, first of all we'll listen to the music,' Finn said. 'And then we'll make a dance.' He got up to switch on the sound system, and returned to sit with me.

Music filled the studio. Finn shut his eyes. I did the same, and let the music wash over me. It began slowly and quietly, a haunting tune, and then built and built until it ended in a crashing chord. It was glorious music that I could have listened to again, but more than anything else it made me want to dance. I opened my eyes.

'It's beautiful,' I said.

Finn was smiling.' I think so, too. Its title is *Dancing In The Moonlight*. And apart from Olivia, Jonathan, and the guy who wrote it, you and I are the only people to have heard it.' Holding out his hand, he hauled me to my feet. 'Let's get to work,' he said.

At first, as Finn's choreography was all in his mind, it was a matter of listening to a few bars of music and then doing my best to perform the steps as he described them, with many false starts, repetitions and adjustments – and breaks for Finn to make notes – but gradually, as we got used to working this way together, the arc of the dance took shape. It began with Finn and me – Nathan and Kitty – walking towards each other, from opposite sides of the stage. At this point we danced without touching, our movements mirroring each other's. When Finn reached towards me, I retreated from him, only to return to his embrace. The first time he put his arms around me, drawing me close, my body tensed – it felt strange, familiar yet unfamiliar to be held by him – but then my dancer's instincts took over and I lost myself in the dance, Finn no different to any other partner, his hands on my waist, supporting me as I raised my foot until it was resting on his shoulder, me knowing that he'd never let me fall. *He might not dance professionally any more,* I thought, *but he hasn't forgotten how.*

As the tempo of the music increased, the choreography became stronger and more dynamic, and the steps and the turns grew faster. There were a number of very demanding lifts for which I needed every bit of the technique I'd honed over the years. For the last sixteen counts of the music, my feet didn't touch the ground as Finn hoisted me behind his shoulders and down around his body. I locked my legs around his waist and bent backwards, and he spun me round, catching me as I let go of him and setting me on my feet. Holding my wrists, he lowered me to the floor and then sank down beside me. As the final chord faded, he bent over me, his face close to mine.

'At this point,' Finn said, 'Kitty and Nathan kiss. Then there's a black out.' He sat up. 'I think it should be pretty clear to the audience what Kitty and Nathan do next.'

'Ah, yes,' I said, suddenly very conscious of the sensual nature of Finn's choreography. Ridiculously – I was a professional dance, for goodness' sake, it was hardly the first time I'd danced a piece with erotic overtones – my face grew hot.

'Ready to go again?' Finn said.

'Is it OK if I drink some water first?' I said, hoping that if Finn noticed my red face, he'd think it was due to the physical demands of his choreography, not because I couldn't get the thought out of my head that he and I had just simulated making love.

'Oh, yeah, sorry,' Finn said. 'We should take a lunch break. When I'm working on something new like this, I forget that dancers need to eat and drink.'

After a quick trip to the canteen, we returned to the studio, and for the next few hours, worked on the dance. When Finn was satisfied that we were dancing it as he'd envisaged, he produced a camera and a fold-up tripod from his bag, and set it up so he could film us.

'We'll start off stage,' he said.

I walked to the side of the studio. Finn switched on the music and ran to the opposite side of the studio to me.

'From the top,' he said. 'Five, six, seven, eight.'

Kitty started to walk timidly towards Nathan. He reached for her, but she spun away from him, wanting him, yet fearful of his caress. He stepped closer, trailing his hand down her body, almost, but not quite touching her. When she did not draw away, he slid an arm around her waist. Desire overcoming all the reasons why she should make him keep his distance, Kitty melted into Nathan's embrace. His hands were on her waist, and then her thighs, her legs were wrapped around his body, and the rest of the world ceased to exist. Gently, he lowered her to the ground and lay down beside her, leaning over her, his face close to her. Kitty shut her eyes.

Finn kissed me. It was a gentle kiss at first, but then it deepened, and I kissed him back, sliding a hand around his neck, my body responding to his touch as he placed a hand on my hip, sliding it smoothly down to the top of my leg, lighting a flame of desire low in my stomach, fire spreading throughout my body. He raised his head from mine, caught my gaze and held it, his mouth lifting in his lazy smile. *That*, I thought, *was not a stage kiss.*

'And blackout,' Finn said. 'We've run out of time. I only booked the studio until six.' In one fluid movement, he got to his feet, went to the camera, switched it off, and began to dismantle the tripod.

I, too, stood up, my heart pounding in my chest. He had kissed me, and I had kissed him back. Going to my bag, with shaking hands I retrieved my sweatshirt and pulled it on, swopped my trainers for my boots, and put on my jacket. After a moment, Finn joined me in the corner of the studio, and put on his own street clothes. For an instant, as his head bent towards mine, I thought he was going to kiss me again. I willed him to kiss me again. Instead, he leant past me, picked up his holdall, and hoisted it onto his shoulder.

'Let's get out of here,' he said.

We left the studio, went downstairs and out into the street. Side by side, we walked to the station, Finn matching his long stride to my shorter one, me stealing glances at his handsome profile, and wondering what was going on in his head.

'You did a great job today,' he said, when we reached the bottom of the escalators.

'Thank you,' I said. 'I enjoyed it.'

'I'm glad.' He stepped towards me, so close that we were almost touching, and looked down at me through hooded eyes. 'Nell,' he said, softly, 'will you come back to my place? I have a bottle of white wine chilling in the fridge.'

'Oh – Finn –' I was not so naive as to think that he was inviting me back to his with the sole intention of our sharing a bottle of Chenin blanc. And, without any illusions that it would mean any more to either of us than it had the last time, I yearned to go with him, to have his strong arms around me, to feel him inside me. I wanted him. All I needed to do was make a phone call to say I'd be home later than I'd expected – Guilt hit me like a punch in the stomach. I was about go home with a guy for an evening of casual sex. Without sparing a thought for Savannah, who I'd hardly spent any time with all week. I took a step back, restoring the space between us. 'I can't Finn,' I said. 'I have to get back to my daughter. I hope you understand.' Finn's eyes widened in what I could only imagine was surprise. I guessed that he didn't get turned down very often.

'Of course, I understand,' he said. 'You have responsibilities that I can't imagine.'

No, you really can't, I thought. 'I-I'll see you tomorrow, Finn.'

'Yeah – our first rehearsal in the Nightingale Playhouse,' Finn said. 'Exciting, huh?'

'It is indeed,' I said. 'My first time rehearsing in a West End theatre.'

'And mine,' Finn said, with a smile. He headed off to catch his train, turning once to wave, before he was lost amongst a sudden flurry of other passengers. I let out a long breath, and, gathering myself together, started walking towards my platform.

I'd done the right thing tonight – the only thing I could do, and still call myself a good parent. I was no longer twenty-four years old, with no-one to think about but myself.

I raised a hand and touched my mouth. *Finn had kissed me.* He'd asked me to go home with him. Tonight, I'd had no choice but to turn him down.

I knew I was playing with fire, but I doubted I'd be able to make myself reject him a second time.

Chapter Fourteen

The following day, I caught a train to Leicester Square, in the heart of London's Theatreland.

Beyond the railings that encircled the gardens in the middle of the square, people were sitting on benches, enjoying the spring sunshine, drinking coffee, taking photos of the statue of Shakespeare or queueing at the booth that sold reduced-price theatre tickets. In a month's time, one of the shows they'd be buying tickets for would be *Speakeasy*. And one of the performers they'd be watching would be me!

Leaving Leicester Square, I turned onto Charring Cross Road, edging my way through the tourists clustered outside the secondhand bookshops, and then onto Shaftsbury Avenue, passing the theatres and restaurants that line this famous street, until I came to a halt outside the Nightingale Playhouse. I took a moment to look at the theatre's ornate, colonnaded façade, which had the words *ALL THE WORLD'S A STAGE* carved on a stone frieze above the main entrance, but what really caught my eye was a billboard listing the names of the *Speakeasy* cast, the stars, the minor roles, and then, in alphabetical order, the ensemble. I shivered with delight when I saw *Nell Avery* heading the list. Looking both ways along the street to make sure I wasn't observed by any of my fellow cast members, I quickly found my phone and took a photo. Maybe it wasn't the most sophisticated thing to do, but it had taken me fifteen years as a professional dancer to get to the West End, and I simply had to record the moment – and I did have the excuse that Savannah would be thrilled to see her mother's name outside a West End theatre.

Stowing away my phone, I walked around the theatre looking for the stage door, which I discovered down a narrow side-street at the back of the building, smiling when I saw another carved inscription on the lintel that read: *WE ARE SUCH STUFF THAT DREAMS ARE MADE ON*. I went inside and found myself in a small lobby, with another door opposite, and a counter, behind which a middle-aged stage-doorman sat drinking a cup of coffee and reading a newspaper. He looked up and smiled.

I took a deep breath. 'Good morning,' I said, 'I'm Nell Avery. I'm in the cast of *Speakeasy*.' Even after five weeks of rehearsal, what a thrill it was to say those words.

'And a good morning to you, Nell,' the doorman said. 'It's your first show here at the Nightingale, I think?'

'Yes,' I said, eagerly. 'Yes, it is.' I nearly told him how excited I was to be here, but managed to refrain myself.

The doorman turned around to consult a sheet of paper tacked to a notice board on the wall behind him. 'You're in Dressing Room Six,' he said. 'You need to sign in.' He indicated another sheet of paper with a column of printed names – a dozen or so already had signatures next to them

– attached to a clipboard on the counter, and I added my signature. 'Go through that door, which'll take you backstage,' he continued. 'Take the first right, second left, and first right again, and you'll come to the auditorium, where there's a meeting for the *Speakeasy* Company and the Theatre Management before rehearsal. And don't forget to introduce yourself to Miss Dene.'

'Miss Dene?' I said. 'Who is she?'

'You'll see her as soon as you're backstage,' the doorman said. 'You can't miss her.'

Bemused, I went through the door that led backstage, and found myself in a long, well-lit corridor. In front of me, several yards away, studying a picture on the wall, was Finn. For a moment I stood motionless, thinking how good he looked in his tight black T-shirt and jeans, drinking him in, while he was unaware of my presence, but then the door to the lobby thudded shut behind me, causing him to turn his face towards me. His smile made me want to break into a dance right there and then.

He said, 'Hey, Nell. Come and meet Lily Dene. As I expect the stage doorman informed you, she likes to meet everyone who performs on her stage.' I glanced up and down the corridor. It was empty apart from me and Finn.

'Where is she?' I asked.

'She's here,' Finn said. 'This is her portrait,'

'Ah – the way the doorman talked, I thought she was a real person.'

'She is,' Finn said. 'Or rather, she was.'

I went and stood next to him, and looked up at the picture in its gilt frame, which I now saw was an almost life-size oil painting of a woman standing in front of a red velvet curtain. She was dressed in an off-the shoulder, floor-length, ivory lace gown, with flounces around the neckline, a tiny waist, and a train, and her dark hair was pinned up under a broad-brimmed straw hat, trimmed with feathers and flowers. With her sparkling blue eyes and her laughing smile, she was, I thought, stunningly beautiful. Finn drew my attention to the words on a small bronze plaque on the bottom of the frame: *Miss Lily Dene ~ The Nightingale ~ 1872 - 1967.*

'I've not heard of her,' I said. 'Do you know why her portrait is hanging in the theatre?'

'Lily Dene, known as the Nightingale because of her exquisite singing voice,' Finn said, 'was a star of Edwardian musical comedies. She performed in this theatre – which at the time was simply called the Playhouse – throughout the 1890s, before she married a Lord Hillier who'd fallen in love with her when he saw her singing on stage.'

'Oh, my goodness, that's so romantic.'

'Once she became Lady Hillier, she gave up her career in the theatre – it wasn't a respectable profession for a woman in those days – but she came to the opening night of every show put on in the Playhouse, right up until she was in her nineties. When the theatre was refurbished in the 1980s, it was decided to re-name it after her – hence the Nightingale Playhouse.'

'That's a fascinating story,' I said. 'I'm impressed you know all this stuff.'

'Yeah, it's amazing what you can find out on the internet these days,' Finn said, with a grin. 'It's believed that Lily

Dene still attends every first night in her theatre, and a seat is reserved for her in the Grand Circle for the entire run of each show. She likes every performer to introduce themselves to her before they first step out onto her stage, and she's been known to play tricks – like hiding vital props – on those who don't. It's also customary for each member of the company to greet her portrait when they enter the theatre, and to say goodnight when they leave, to ensure the success of whatever show is currently playing in the Nightingale.'

Seriously? I gave him a long look.

'What?' he said. 'A lot of West End theatres are said to be haunted. The Lane has the Man In Grey; the Nightingale has Miss Lily Dene. Even when the final curtain has come down, some actors can't bear to leave the stage.'

'So have you introduced yourself to Miss Dene?' I asked.

'I have indeed,' Finn said. 'Not that I'm superstitious, but I'm not about to risk *Speakeasy* closing early because I disrespected a theatrical ghost.'

'I'm not superstitious either,' I began, but recalling the tiny ballerina, my good luck charm, who was still in my dance bag, I corrected myself. 'That is, I'm not *particularly* superstitious, and I'm not sure I believe in ghosts, but I wouldn't want to be impolite.' Feeling a little self-conscious, I addressed the portrait, 'Good morning, Miss Dene. I'm Nell Avery, and I'm in the *Speakeasy* ensemble. I've danced since I was four years old, professionally since I was nineteen, and this will be my first West End show.' To Finn, I said, 'I'm not sure what else to tell her.'

'I told her that I –' He broke off as the door to the lobby opened and shut. Looking back along the corridor, I saw Lucas, the Dance Captain, walking towards us.

'Good morning, Miss Dene,' he said, as he passed us. 'Morning, Finn. Nell.'

Finn and I chorused 'Morning, Lucas,' after him as he continued on his way.

The door opened again, and Florence came into the corridor, along with Matt and Leon Walsh. They joined us in front of the portrait.

'Morning Lily,' Leon said. To me and Finn, he added, 'She and I are old friends – I've performed in the Nightingale before. For Florence, however, it's her first time.' He smiled, a flash of dazzling white teeth. 'Go on Florence, introduce yourself.'

Florence stepped closer to the painting. 'Hi, I'm Florence Newton,' she said. 'This isn't only the first time I've performed in the Nightingale, it's the first time I've been in a West End musical, or any professional show –'

'Really?' Leon interrupted. 'You've never stood on a West End stage, looking out over the auditorium, and thinking of all the great actors who have stood in that very place where you are now?'

'No, I haven't,' Florence said.

'Then take it from me,' Leon said, 'for anyone in our profession, there's nothing like it. And I've worked in Hollywood, so I should know.'

Florence's eyes widened. 'But Hollywood must be amazing too,' she said.

'It has its moments,' Leon said. 'Walking along the red carpet at the Oscars was awesome – there's no other word for it.'

'Is acting in a movie very different to acting in a musical?' Florence said.

'Hell, yeah,' Leon said. 'What you have to remember when you get in front of the camera is that less is more –'

Finn cleared his throat. 'I've a few things I need to check in the auditorium before we begin rehearsal,' he said. 'Walk with me, Nell?'

'Sure,' I said. 'See you later guys.'

Leaving Leon explaining the differences between stage and screen acting to Florence under the benign gaze of Lily Dene, we headed off along the corridor, following the stage doorman's directions until we arrived at a fire-door with a sign that read: *Auditorium. No Entry during Performances*. I reached for the bar that would open it, but Finn put his hand on my arm, and drew me back.

'I wanted to thank you again for yesterday,' he said. 'It was only afterwards that it occurred to me that you'd given up the one day a week you get to spend with your daughter.' *Our daughter* – the thought came to me unbidden.

'It was only one Sunday,' I said, 'and Savannah spent it being spoilt rotten by her grandparents.'

'I didn't think about you having to sort out child-care when I asked you to workshop my dance,' Finn went on. 'It must be difficult for you, as a single parent, working the hours we do in the theatre.'

'It can be a bit of a juggling act,' I said, disquieted by the turn the conversation had taken – discussing child-care arrangements with Savannah's father in a West End theatre was not something I'd ever envisaged myself doing. Fortunately, Finn didn't pursue the subject, but opened the fire-door, and gestured for me to precede him through. The door led onto a side-aisle that ran from the back of the auditorium to the side of the stage, where we were now standing. My gaze swept over the auditorium, over the tiered stalls, with their rows of red velvet seats, where some members of the Company were already seated, past a wooden platform that had been constructed in the centre aisle, on which was a keyboard, up to the Royal Circle, and the Grand Circle, and then higher still to the Upper Circle, and the ceiling above, where painted gods cavorted among swirling clouds, and from which hung a magnificent chandelier.

'It's quite something, isn't it, this old theatre?' Finn said. 'I remember coming here when I was a student, queueing for cheap stand-by tickets up in the gods.'

'I did that a few times,' I said, 'but not in this theatre. Once I queued for a matinée, and when I didn't get in, I stayed in the queue for the evening performance.'

'You queued all afternoon?'

I laughed. 'I'm a musical theatre super-fan.' We walked further along the aisle, and both at the same time, turned to face the stage.

'Oh!' I gasped. 'Oh, Finn, it's spectacular.'

Although I'd seen pictures of the design, nothing had prepared me for the impact made by the stunning set for *Speakeasy's* opening scene, which had a bridge – recognizable as Brooklyn Bridge – spanning the stage against a backdrop of a New York skyline. At the beginning of each performance, the curtains would be closed, opening to reveal Kitty, down stage centre, her back to the audience, looking up at the bridge. She would then turn around and sing the first verse of the show's opening number, *Good Morning New York City*, on her own, before the ensemble ran on from the wings. Right now, the stage was occupied by Olivia, Jonathan, William the Company Manager, and a few other people, who I'd not seen before. Presumably they were some of the Nightingale's in-house team.

'*Speakeasy* is going to be a spectacular musical,' Finn said. He paused, and then he added, 'Nell, I get that you had to go straight home last night, but that bottle of wine is still in my fridge. I'm hoping I do get to share it with you sometime.' His grey eyes looked into mine, and I felt his fingers brush lightly against my arm. Without conscious thought, I smiled, but before I could frame a response, he walked off to the front of the auditorium, climbed the treads at the side of the stage and joined Olivia and Jonathan under the bright lights.

Ignoring an inconvenient fluttering in my stomach, and spotting Justin on the other side of the stalls, I made my way between two rows of seats and sat down next to him.

'Were you and Finn discussing his choreography again?' he said.

'Something like that,' I said. Finn's parting remark echoed around my head. I looked towards the stage, where he was now talking to Resident Choreographer Cameron, gesturing towards the spectacular bridge. Desire for Finn lanced through me, even as Zelda's words came back to me:

Just because you've got the hots for a guy you don't have to do anything about it. She was right, of course. I should take a step back, and end this thing before it got started. But what I should do and what I wanted to do were two different matters.

More of the Company drifted into the auditorium and took their seats in the stalls, including Matt, who flung himself down on the other side of Justin. A moment later, I saw Florence and Leon come in. Instead of finding a place to sit, Leon ushered her up the treads and out under the lights, downstage from Olivia and her entourage. He was speaking too quietly for me to hear what he was saying, but Florence was clearly hanging on his every word.

'Leon Walsh is so up himself,' Matt said. It seemed to me that expressing such an opinion of *Speakeasy's* leading man was not the best way for a young dancer to further his career in musical theatre, but fortunately Matt spoke in an undertone, and immediately slumped back in his seat, glowering at Leon on the brightly-lit stage from the relative gloom of the stalls. Justin raised his eyebrows, but like me, refrained from making any comment.

At that moment, I saw Olivia and her entourage moving downstage. With a smile for the Director, which she returned – presumably she didn't object to her star holding up her rehearsal – Leon led Florence off stage and back down the treads. He went and sat down in the front row of the stalls next to Samantha, while Florence trotted up the aisle and made her way along the row to sit next to me, oblivious to the attention she was attracting from a number of her fellow cast members.

'I can hardly believe that just happened,' she said. 'My first time stepping onto a West End stage, and it was with Leon Walsh.' She giggled. 'You must think I'm totally starstruck.'

I couldn't help smiling. 'Maybe just a little,' I said.

'It was so kind of Leon,' Florence went on. 'I told him I couldn't wait to get on stage, but I never imagined he'd insist on us going up there together.' She lowered her voice. 'I was worried that Olivia would be annoyed, but Leon said it would be fine if I was with him.' Matt muttered something under his breath.

Olivia, now standing near the edge of the stage, called out: 'If I could have everyone's attention –' The stalls fell silent. 'We have a lot to get through today.'

'When don't we have a lot to get through?' Justin whispered to me.

'First of all,' Olivia went on, 'I'll ask the Management Team here at the Nightingale to introduce themselves – I know you're all dying to know who you have to see to get cast tickets for Opening Night . . .'

An hour or so later, I was standing with Florence outside Dressing Room Six, five flights up from street level, reading an inscription, *THE PLAY'S THE THING*, painted above the door. I went inside, Florence following close behind, and found myself in a typical theatre dressing room, with mirrors surrounded by light-bulbs above a make-up counter that ran around the walls, swivel chairs, a kettle, a sink, a tannoy, and a noticeboard. The thought that this was *my* dressing room, that I was now one of the girls in Dressing Room Six at the Nightingale made me smile.

'Shall we grab places next to each other?' I placed my bag on the chair nearest the window – I knew how hot it could get in a dressing room – and Florence placed hers on the floor and sat down in the chair next to it. 'It's a theatrical tradition that you can't decorate the dressing rooms until opening night,' I said, 'so we can't put up any photos yet, but there's no reason why we can't have a coffee when we want it.' I produced a jar of coffee, powdered milk and two mugs from my bag – it had occurred to me that Florence might not realise that we had to bring in our own refreshments. 'Not that we'll be in here all that much during the show. With the number of quick changes we've got, for most of the time we'll be in the wardrobe village.'

'What's that?' Florence asked.

'It's an area behind the stage where the actors can change costume,' I said. 'Girls one side, boys the other. There won't be enough time between dances for us to run upstairs to the dressing rooms.'

'I'm a bit anxious about making my quick changes,' Florence said. 'What if I'm not ready in time for my next entrance?'

'Don't worry,' I said. 'On a show this size we'll have dressers.' It was, I reflected, going to be a luxurious experience for me to get changed in a wardrobe village, rather than struggle into a sequined leotard in the wings, as was usual for quick changes in smaller theatres – or in a restroom, as had happened at more than one of the less salubrious venues I'd performed in over the years.

The door to the dressing room opened and Hettie Parkes came in. 'Oh, good,' she said, taking the chair next to Florence. 'I was hoping I'd be in the same dressing room as you ladies. Do you know who else is in here?'

'No idea,' I said. Which was when the door opened again, and Marisa walked in, followed by Nicole. My heart sank. Sharing a dressing room with these two for six months was *not* what I'd have chosen – not that I had any choice in the matter.

'Hello,' Florence said, greeting the pair of them with a beaming smile. 'Isn't it awesome to be in the Nightingale at last ?'

'It is,' Nicole said, stepping out from behind her friend. 'I've performed in some wonderful theatres, but *Speakeasy* is my – and Marisa's – first time in the West End. I can't wait to get on stage.'

'Me neither,' Florence said. 'That is – I have been up on the stage – but I can't wait to dance on it.'

'Yes, Florence, we all saw you with Leon,' Marisa said. 'Unfortunately for you, his talent isn't contagious, however much you could do with some of it.' She laughed, as if she'd made a hilarious joke, and Nicole joined in. Florence laughed too, if a little uncertainly. Hettie frowned. As throwing Marisa out of dressing room wasn't an option, I turned away before I said something I'd regret, and started unpacking my bag, lining up hairpins, brush, comb and make-up wipes neatly on the counter. In my mirror, I saw Marisa go to the opposite side of the room, and also begin to unpack her bag, Nicole scuttling after her. I reminded myself that, as I'd said to Florence, once the show was up and running, the time we spent in Dressing Room Six

– and therefore in Marisa and her sidekick's company – would be limited.

The dressing room door opened yet again, this time to admit three women, one in her early twenties who I'd met before in Wardrobe and knew was named Annie, one around my age, and one several decades older. All were carrying large plastic boxes, which they placed on the counter.

'Hello all,' the elder women said. 'I'm Christina, Head Dresser. And here –' She indicated the box. 'I have your dressing gowns, tights, and mic belt.' She reached into her box and, with a flourish, produced a net bag containing the aforesaid items.

'I have your shoes for the opening number,' Annie said, holding up a shoe-box. A frisson of delight ran through me when I saw it had my name on it.

'And I have your stage make-up,' the third woman said. 'And a picture of how we want you to put it on.' She took a sheet of paper out of her box, and pinned it on the noticeboard – it was a drawing of a woman's face, with the bow-shaped lips characteristic of 1920s-style make-up. 'I'm Elle, by the way. Hairdresser and make-up artist by trade, in case you haven't guessed.'

Christina, Annie and Elle distributed the contents of their boxes, moving as fluidly around each other while they handed out shoes and make-up bags as if they were in one of Finn's dance routines.

'So, you girls need to get changed,' said Christina.

'And put on your dancing shoes,' said Annie.

'And do your make-up and put your hair in pin curls,' said Elle, 'and then come downstairs to the wig room.'

'And after that, I'll see you in the wardrobe village,' Christina said. The three women smiled in unison, spun around and left the room, reminding me so much of a well-drilled ensemble that I half-expected them to return for a curtain call.

'I didn't realise we'd have to do our own make-up,' Florence said. 'And what was the other thing? Pin curls?'

'You don't know what pin curls are?' Marisa exclaimed.

'No, I don't,' Florence said. '*Speakeasy* isn't only my first time in the West End, it's my ever first job.'

'But surely you learnt how to get yourself show-ready while you were in training?' Marisa said.

'I didn't go to performing arts college,' Florence said.

'So you didn't train *professionally*.' Marisa said. 'That explains a lot.'

The silence that followed this remark lasted long enough for Florence's face to turn scarlet. I glanced at Hettie, who shook her head as if to clear it. Nicole swivelled around in her chair and examined her stage-make-up.

'Ooh!' she exclaimed, 'Don't you just love the colour of this lipstick?' Either she was an exceptionally good actress, or she was completely unaware of the tension in the room caused by her friend – which, in my opinion, made her extremely stupid.

To Florence, I said, 'Don't worry, I'll show you how to do pin curls. The hairdressers will put a stocking over your pinned-up hair, one of the sound team will fit your head mic, and then your wig is pinned on top.'

'Listen, Florence,' Hettie said. 'I learnt as much about this glorious profession of ours in my first job as I did when

I was training. If there's anything you don't know, just ask any of us.' Her face grew thoughtful. 'The way I see it is, dancers, actors and singers compete for jobs at auditions, but once they're in the same cast, they're a *team*.'

'Absolutely,' I said. 'It takes the whole Company working together to make a show a success.' On impulse, I added, 'Don't you agree, Marisa?'

Marisa shrugged. 'We may all be in the same cast, but some of us will always be better dancers than others. Someone will always stand out.'

'I won't argue with that,' I said. 'And I'm not saying we shouldn't all aim to be the best dancer we can be, but we're not rivals.'

The disembodied voice of the Stage Manager crackling from the tannoy – 'This is your half hour call. Everyone on stage in full costume for a sound check in half an hour' – made us all jump, and also put an end to any more attempts to explain the concept of teamwork to Marisa.

'We need to get a shift on,' Hettie said, peeling off her T-shirt and jeans, and reaching for her dance tights.

'One thing you definitely need to know, Florence,' I said, as I began my transformation from twenty-first century West End dancer to 1920s New York chorine, 'is that it's *unthinkable* for a theatre performer to be late for the start of a show.'

'You'll do,' Christina said, zipping up my dress. 'Off you go.' I thanked the Head Dresser for her help, and checked my reflection – all of us, including Samantha, had our own allocated space in the wardrobe village, amongst the costume rails and shoe racks, and mine was luckily near a full-length mirror – deciding that in my drop-waisted dress, with a cloche hat pinned onto my chin-length wig, and my 1920s make-up I didn't look any older than the rest of the ensemble. Then I made my way to the stage, where the cast were assembling for the sound check.

Justin materialized at my side.

'You look very dapper,' I said, surveying his 1920s-style pin-striped suit. 'Quite the gangster about town.'

'You look cute in that hat,' he said.

I hoped that Finn, watching me – and everyone else, of course – from the stalls, thought the same.

'Are you absolutely sure we're allowed to watch the scenes we're not in?' Florence whispered to me, Matt, Justin and Hettie, as we crept up the side aisle and slid into seats on the end of a row, me and the girls in one row, the guys behind. Finn, I noticed was sitting a few rows in front of us on the other side of the aisle, next to Olivia.

'Yes, it's fine,' I said. 'We just need to keep our voices down or we'll be told to leave the auditorium.'

'You're expected to watch Kitty's scenes, Florence,' Hettie said. 'As a cover, it's your job to learn the role by watching the leads.'

'B-but surely I'll get rehearsals?' Florence squeaked.

'You will,' Hettie said, 'but not many and not until after the show's opened. You'll find it much less stressful if you know what you're doing beforehand.'

Until then the stage had been concealed behind a scrim painted with a street scene showing the boarding house where Kitty lived. Now, that became transparent to reveal an empty stage bathed in a pale blue light. There was no scenery, but the backdrop was a large casement window, through which could be seen a full moon above the New York skyline, and I knew I was about to see *Dancing In The Moonlight* – which Finn had today taught to Samantha and Leon in the theatre's rehearsal room, while the rest of us were on our lunch break. Florence leant forward in her seat, her brow furrowed in concentration.

The music I'd heard the day before filled the auditorium, now played by Jonathan on his keyboard. Leon, dressed in an open white shirt and loose black trousers, entered stage right, Samantha, wearing a white satin, knee-length slip, entered stage left, and they went into the dance. I watched them – sympathising when they messed up a lift; they hadn't, after all, had long to learn the dance – but in my head it was Finn and me up on the stage, his hands on my waist, Finn lifting me in his arms, lowering me to the floor, lying down beside me, his mouth on mine, his hands on my thighs . . .

The music stopped, and the stage was plunged into the pitch darkness of a blackout, jolting me back into the reality of the Nightingale's auditorium. I forced myself to breath evenly, but my body ached for Finn's touch.

'Hold it there,' Olivia said. 'Lights, please.'

The stage lights went up. Samantha and Leon untangled themselves and got up off the floor. Finn went to the front of the auditorium to talk to them. Giving them notes, I supposed.

'I feel quite emotional after watching that,' Hettie said.

'Mmm,' I said.

'It was beautiful,' Florence said, 'but the lifts look *impossible*. I don't know how I'm going to learn them.'

Pulling myself together, I said, 'I can go over them with you, if you like.' A thought struck me. I turned around in my seat and smiled at Matt. 'Maybe you could help too?'

'Me?' Matt said, staring at me blankly. Then his eyes widened. 'Oh. OK. Yeah. Er – happy to help you, Florence.' For a guy who'd presumably attended improvisation classes when he was in performing arts college, he was surprisingly slow on the uptake.

'Thanks,' Florence said. 'I'd appreciate it.'

Justin, sitting directly behind me leant forward and, put his mouth close to my ear. 'Am I right in thinking that extraordinarily erotic dance we just witnessed was the dance you workshopped yesterday with Finn? Was it just you and him working on it all alone in a dance studio?'

I twisted around in my seat, and locked my eyes on his.

'Yes, Justin,' I said. 'It was a wonderful opportunity for me to work one-on-one with a very talented choreographer.' I returned my attention on the stage. Finn, having finished whatever he was saying to Leon and Samantha, returned to his seat next to Olivia. Behind me, Justin chuckled.

Olivia spoke into her mic. 'From the blackout, please.' Again the stage was plunged into Stygian darkness. Then, gradually, the lights came back up, as, beyond the casement window, the sun rose, bathing the stage in the pink and gold of a new dawn. During the blackout, the empty stage had been transformed into Kitty's bedroom, and Kitty and

Nathan were lying entwined on her bed – both still in the costumes they'd danced in; this was, after all, a show for all the family. Nathan sat up, stretched, and swung himself off the mattress. Buttoning his shirt, he went to the window, and peered out. Kitty stirred, lifted her head from the pillow, and then she, too, sat up.

'I have to go,' Nathan said.

'I know,' Kitty said.

In that moment, it struck me forcibly that while I was almost sure that I was going to sleep with Finn, I'd given no thought to what might happen the morning after.

'I don't want to go,' Nathan said.

'You have to go,' Kitty said. 'If my landlady discovers you're here, she'll throw me out on the street.'

Ten years ago, even if I'd wanted a steady relationship with Finn, it wasn't on offer. But now, the thought of sleeping with him, and then watching him walk away, made my heart constrict.

'But I want to stay,' Nathan said.

I *liked* Finn. I wanted more from him than no-strings sex.

Kitty got out of bed, and went to Nathan. He folded her in his arms, and kissed her for a long time.

'When you kiss me like that,' Kitty said, 'I can't let you go.' Jonathan began to play the first notes of their next duet: *What Do You Want From Me*?

Hettie whispered, 'We'd better head backstage. There's only one more scene after this and then we're on.'

The five of us stood up, and filed quietly out of the auditorium.

I wanted Finn in my life, but what did he want from me? Did he feel anything for me – apart from the obvious? Now I came to think of it, I had absolutely no idea.

The last to leave Dressing Room Six, I walked slowly down the five flights of stairs to ground level, and turned into the corridor where Lily Dene's portrait hung. In front of me, two girls from Dressing Room Five and three boys from Dressing Room Seven paused a lively discussion of whether they had time to go for a drink before catching their respective trains, to call out 'Goodnight, Miss Dene,' before going through the door that led into the lobby.

Drawing level with the portrait, I came to a halt and stared up at the actress, wondering if she'd ever felt as tired after a rehearsal as I did right now. Not that we'd danced without a break the entire ten hours we were in the theatre, but all the stopping and starting and waiting around for the techies to sort out the lights, the impossibly quick costume changes, getting in each other's way as we made our numerous exits and entrances, and performing full-out when we were actually dancing – *and* keeping my mind on the choreography, not the choreographer – had proved challenging. At least to me.

Now, I looked up at Lily Dene and said, 'Rehearsal was tough today, Miss Dene.' Lily's serene smile didn't falter. 'It was only our first run in the theatre, there were lots of mistakes and hitches, and, wonderful though it is to dance on your stage, I don't mind admitting that I'm shattered. And I still don't know what I'm going to do about Finn. I *really* like him, but it's *so* complicated –'

The sound of voices approaching from the other end of the corridor told me that there were still other members of the cast about, and it occurred to me that while theatrical tradition held that performers in the Nightingale must introduce themselves to Lily Dene, discussing their love life with her might well be considered odd.

'Goodnight, Miss Dene,' I said, and made my exit.

Chapter Fifteen

Savannah ran up the front path to Zelda's house, and rang the bell. Almost immediately, Zelda opened the door, holding Esme, on her jeans-clad hip. The little girl beamed at us, while Theo and Charlie pushed past their mother, each of them seizing one of Savannah's hands.

'Come in the garden, Savannah,' Theo said. 'We're building a fort.'

'Come and see,' Charlie said.

'Savannah, you don't have to –' Zelda began.

'I don't mind, Auntie Zelda,' Savannah said, allowing the boys to tug her along the hallway in the direction of the backdoor that led into the garden.

'Oh, dear,' Zelda said. 'I did tell them Savannah might not be interested in construction work, and that Martin would help with the fort when he gets back from golf, but they seem to have forgotten.'

'It's fine,' I said. 'She'll enjoy playing the role of their big sister for a little while, and she'll have no hesitation in abandoning the fort in favour of the swing when she gets fed up with them.' Zelda laughed, and led the way along the hall to her large, sunlight-filled kitchen, setting her daughter down on a playmat, amidst a heap of stuffed animals, wooden bricks, a rag doll, and a large, empty cardboard box – which Esme proceeded to push contentedly around the floor.

'It's her favourite toy right now,' Zelda said.

'Well, it is a fabulous box,' I said. 'I remember Savannah having one just like it.' We exchanged smiles. I sat down at the scrubbed-pine kitchen table, and Zelda made us coffee. The sound of children's laughter floated in through the open window.

'So how are things, now that you're in the theatre?' Zelda asked, sitting down opposite me. 'I want to know *everything*.'

If I'd found the *Speakeasy* rehearsals at the Foundry tiring, it was nothing compared with the enervating exhaustion that came with two weeks of tech rehearsals in the Nightingale. Not that I was alone. After the first day, no-one was going home via the pub. I'd even spotted Florence yawning once or twice when we were all gathered on stage at the end of rehearsal for Olivia to give us our notes. There had been nights when, fearing that I'd sleep through my morning alarm on my phone, I'd set an alarm clock as well. And yet, as soon as I'd walked through the stage door the following day, my fatigue had vanished, to be replaced by the unique high that came from being in the cast of a West End musical, counting down the days to Opening Night.

To Zelda, I said, 'The sitzprobe was tremendously exciting – for everyone in the company, not just me!'

'The *sitzprobe*?' Zelda said.

'I'd not heard of it before either,' I said, 'but on a large-scale musical like *Speakeasy*, it's the first time the cast and the musicians get to rehearse together.'

The sitzprobe had taken place in the Circle Bar, with the cast standing together behind a row of microphones, ready to step up to a mic when it was their turn to sing. Everyone of importance attached to the show, including the producers, were watching from rows of chairs, with those of lesser importance perched on bar stools. It had been a little unnerving to walk up to the mic, knowing I was about to sing in front of some of the most powerful men and women in showbusiness – I was, after all, more of a dancer than a singer – but as soon as I launched into the now familiar *Good Morning New York City*, the music soaring and swirling about me, my only thought was how amazing it was to sing such fabulous show tunes accompanied by an orchestra.

'The sitzprobe was incredible,' I said to Zelda. 'but the dress rehearsal was a disaster. The leads missed an entrance, the villain's fake moustache fell off, a dancer couldn't find her tap shoes, lights failed to come on when they should, actors fluffed their lines . . . But everyone kept going, and we managed to run the entire show without one stoppage. And according to theatrical tradition, a bad dress rehearsal means a good first night, so no-one got shouted at by the director. Not that Olivia is one for shouting when things go wrong – she's far too professional.'

The only person who'd done any shouting at the dress rehearsal had been Marisa, who, amidst the chaos of ten dancers making a quick change in the wardrobe village, had accused Lizette, the youngest of our dressers, of losing her tap shoes, and threatened to report her to the Company Manager. The poor girl had been in tears, until Christina found the shoes – on the wrong shoe rack, admittedly, although Lizette swore she hadn't put them there – shoved them on Marisa's feet, and dispatched her unceremoniously to the wings. I'd resisted the temptation to ask Marisa if she'd remembered to greet Miss Dene that morning.

'And now,' I said to Zelda, 'we're half-way through the previews.'

In a speech to the entire company, Olivia had stressed that the week of nightly preview shows, with low-price tickets and only seats in the stalls available, were regarded by the creative team as a chance for Director, Choreographer and MD, having gauged the audience's reaction, to make last minute changes to any aspects of *Speakeasy* that weren't working, and no different to the rehearsals that continued during the day. For the cast, performing the show in front of a preview audience and hearing their applause – even when there weren't enough people in the auditorium to make much of a noise – was *wonderful.*

'Only four sleeps – and then we open!' I said to Zelda.

Four sleeps, and I could tell anyone who asked what I did for a living that I was in a show playing in the West End. I felt giddy at the thought.

'This is all very fascinating,' Zelda said, 'but how are things between you and Finn? That's what I want to know.'

'Ah,' I said. 'He – we –' I drank some coffee to calm a sudden quivering in my stomach.

Finn. Watching me from the stalls as I danced – even when I couldn't see him from the stage, I could feel the intensity of his gaze. The warmth of his smile each morning when I walked into the auditorium for the warm-up. Only yesterday when we'd broken for lunch, before I could follow the rest of the cast into the wings, he'd run up the treads, telling me he had some notes for me, the glint in his eyes making me think that whatever he was about to say to me, it had nothing to do with my interpretation of his choreography – and his barely concealed sigh when, before he got a word out, Olivia had called to him to come down from the stage and have a word with the Head of Lighting.

'I spent a day alone with Finn workshopping a dance,' I said. 'And we shared a kiss.'

Zelda's eyes widened. 'And?'

'And I'm pretty sure we'd have slept together, except I had to get home to Savannah.' I looked down at the table, tracing a knot in the wood with one finger. 'I really like him, Zelda. I want more than a casual fling with him this time around.'

'Is that what he wants?' Zelda said.

'I don't know.' I looked up at her. 'But I want the chance to find out.'

Zelda regarded me silently for a moment, resting her elbows on the table, and her chin on her steepled fingers. 'Just so we're clear, are you seriously considering *getting involved* with the man who doesn't know he's the father of your child?'

It shook me, hearing those words said aloud. My heart hammering in my chest, I got up from the table and went to stand by the sink, looking out of the window into the garden. Theo and Charlie were playing in their fort – a precarious arrangement of blankets draped over deck chairs and a clothes horse – but as I'd predicted, Savannah had left them to it, and was swinging slowly to and fro, gazing dreamily up at the clear blue sky. Zelda came and stood next to me.

'Nell, I know you don't want to hear this,' she said, her voice gentle, 'but if you're planning to have any sort of relationship with Finn outside a dance studio, you have to tell him he has a daughter. It's not fair on him to let him into your life and not tell him.' She hesitated, and then she said, 'And it's not fair on Savannah.'

At that moment, Savannah looked towards the window, and saw me standing there. She smiled at me and waved, before jumping off the swing and dancing across the lawn. I'd always thought she took after me, but watching her jump and turn so effortlessly, I was irresistibly reminded of Finn. Suddenly, the enormity of the lie I'd told, made my head reel.

'Nell?' Zelda said. 'If what I said has upset you, I'm sorry. But I felt it needed saying.'

'It's OK, Zelda.' If I'd made the wrong decision all those years ago, it was too late to undo it. Pulling myself together, I said, 'Maybe I will tell Finn someday. Whatever happens or doesn't happen between me and him. But not now. I can hardly spring something like that on him when there's only three more days before the show he's choreographed goes up in the West End. He has enough to think about at the moment.'

Zelda sighed, but nodded her head.

And then the children came bounding into the kitchen, and any further debate about whether or not I was going to tell Finn that he was a father, had to take a back seat to requests for ice cream and the more pressing decision as to whether we would be going to the park before or after lunch.

Chapter Sixteen

The door to Dressing Room Six was flung open, making me jump and almost drop my coffee mug – fortunately it was empty. Marisa stomped in, and threw herself down in her chair. Hettie caught my eye and mouthed, 'Now what?'

'I've just been to see Sebastian,' Marisa said. 'And he flatly refused to give me more than two tickets for Opening Night and the after-party. Can you believe it? Who does he think he is?'

Nicole, who had unexpectedly appeared in the dressing room alone after today's rehearsal, rather than sidling in with her friend – and equally unexpectedly produced a packet of biscuits from her bag and offered them to the rest of us – looked confused.

'He's the Box Office Manager –' she began.

'I am aware of that, Nicole,' Marisa snapped.

'Ah, yes, of course you are,' Nicole said, 'but I was going to say that it's probably not up to him how many tickets the ensemble get. It's more likely someone on the production team who decided we can only have two tickets each.'

'That's not the point,' Marisa said. 'I *need* four at least. For my agent and some other industry professionals.' She glared at me, Florence and Hettie, sitting in a row on the opposite side of the dressing room, as if her inadequate allocation of tickets was our fault. 'Do you need your Opening Night tickets?' she demanded. We all vigorously nodded our heads. Marisa gave an exasperated sigh. 'What about you, Nicole?'

'I've already invited Donald and my mother.'

'They can watch you dance any time,' Marisa said. 'It's showbiz industry professionals and influential theatre practitioners who you should invite to important events like a major show opening, not your boyfriend and your parent. Unless you don't know any useful industry people. In which case, it makes more sense to give your tickets to me.'

'I'm so sorry, Marisa,' Nicole said, 'but I can't do that. My mother has already booked her train ticket down from Leeds. And Donald has bought a new suit.'

Marisa raised her eyebrows, 'Well, all I can say is that you're wasting a valuable opportunity to get yourself noticed by the people who count in this business. You really should speak to me before you make decisions that affect your career.' With an exasperated sigh, she took her phone out of her bag, and began tapping away at the screen.

'I didn't think to give a ticket to my agent,' Nicole said to the dressing room at large. 'I hope he isn't offended.'

'I wouldn't worry, Nicole,' Hettie said. 'All the top theatrical agencies get a bunch of tickets sent to them for the opening of a West End musical, as do the most influential theatre critics, directors, producers, and playwrights. All the great and good of Theatreland will be in the Nightingale on *Speakeasy's* Opening Night watching us trip the light-fantastic on Lily Dene's stage.' She smiled. 'No pressure.'

'Evelyn Swann – my agent – called me to say that her agency has four tickets for Opening Night,' Florence said. 'She's coming with her husband and two of her junior agents. I've given my tickets to my parents.'

Making a mental note to avoid Florence's father at the after-party, I said, 'I think my agent is almost as excited about Opening Night as I am.' Amanda had left me a voice mail only that morning telling me how delighted she was to be seeing me make my West End debut. Having been on her books for so many years, it wouldn't have surprised me if she was also relieved that I'd got into a musical before she had to tell me that I was too old to carry on auditioning.

Her face deadpan, but her eyes glinting mischievously, Hettie said, 'It's a shame you didn't talk to me or Nell before you gave away that ticket to your agent, Marisa. We could have told you that they'd get one anyway, and you could have given yours to some other useful person.'

Marisa looked up from her phone. 'You say, that Hettie, but personally I find that an individual touch is important when forging professional relationships. I was, of course, aware that the theatrical agency to which I am signed would receive an allocation of tickets. I chose to give one to my agent regardless.' Her gaze went from Hettie to me. 'Who have you got coming to see you on Opening Night?'

'My nine-year-old daughter,' I said, 'and my mother. Much as my father would have liked to come too, he said that after all the running around my mother did when I was a girl, taking me to dance classes and festivals, she should be the first to see me on a West End stage.'

'I'd have thought you'd have better networking skills than to waste a ticket on a child,' Marisa said, 'what with your having been in the business for *such* a long time.' Her top lip curled, revealing her pointed teeth. 'I was only thinking the other day that it's a shame you have to work so much harder at your age, trying to keep up with the rest of us, but I'm sure you're doing your best.'

You bitch, I thought. I heard Hettie and Florence gasp. Even Nicole shifted uneasily in her chair.

'I would have thought that *everyone* in the Company would be working their hardest to ensure that the show was the best it could be,' I said. Fortunately, I was a good enough actress to make my voice sound a lot calmer than I felt. 'That's what I'm doing. Which is why I agreed to workshop a new dance for the show with Finn on my day off.'

'*What?*' Marisa said, her eyes narrowing.

'I was surprised he asked me rather than a younger dancer,' I said, 'but then I've so much dance experience that I pick up routines exceptionally quickly. Don't worry, Marisa, it's a skill that you'll develop eventually.'

Marisa scowled. 'I do pick up routines very quickly,' she said.

'No, you don't,' Nicole piped up.

'Yes, I do,' Marisa said.

'You don't.'

'I *do*.' Marisa returned her attention to her phone.

'All right, you do. Whatever.' Nicole shrugged, produced a magazine from her bag and began flicking though the pages. I looked at Marisa studiously ignoring her friend like a sulky child, and was angry with myself for once again letting her get to me. Using Finn's workshop to score points off her, was *not* one of my finer moments.

The uneasy silence that had fallen on the dressing room was broken by a knocking on the door. Florence sprang up to open it, revealing Justin and Matt outside in the corridor.

'Hey, Florence,' Matt said. 'We're going out to grab a bite to eat, if you'd like to join us? Nell? Hettie?'

Florence was straight out the door, Hettie fairly running after her. I'd already eaten the salad I'd made for myself at the same time I'd made Savannah's packed lunch, but there were still two hours before we had to start getting ready for tonight's preview, and as I had no desire to spend them breathing the same air as Marisa and her acolyte, I scooped up my bag and hurried after my friends.

An hour later, we arrived back at the Nightingale. I was about to follow Florence, Matt and Hettie through the stage door, but Justin drew me back into the street.

'So much for my cunning plan to get Florence to go to the pub with Matt and me, and then make some excuse why I had to go back to the theatre, leaving them alone,' he said. 'I suggested he invite her along, but then he goes and asks you and Hettie too.'

'He's too well brought up not to invite all of us,' I said.

'He's hopeless,' Justin sighed.

'Did you actually tell him what you were intending to do?'

'Not in so many words. I didn't want him to get stage fright.' Justin sighed again.

'I'll make sure I leave the two of them alone at some point when we work on the lifts for *Dancing In The Moonlight*.'

A male voice said, 'Working on *Dancing In The Moonlight*? Are you after a job as my assistant?' I spun around, quite unprepared for the pleasurable sensation that surged through me when I saw Finn standing directly behind me.

'Not at all,' I said. 'Just doing a bit of match-making.' Justin's gaze went from me to Finn and back to me again.

'Now is the perfect time for me to make my exit,' he said. 'I couldn't have planned it better. See you on stage, Nell.' He headed off through the stage door, leaving me alone with Finn.

'Match-making?' he said, raising his eyebrows.

'Matt and Florence,' I said.

'They do dance well together,' Finn said.

'Exactly.'

Finn smiled. 'So,' he said, 'only tonight and tomorrow and then we open. Exciting times.'

'Very exciting,' I said. Recalling the conversation in the dressing room, I added, 'Are any of your family coming on Opening Night?'

'Yeah, the whole Harris clan is descending on the Nightingale,' Finn said. 'My parents, my brother and sister-in-law, and my sister and her boyfriend. What about you?'

'Savannah and my mother,' I said.

'Not your father?'

'The ensemble only get two comps,' I said, hastily adding, 'Not that I'm complaining. I know tickets for Opening Night are like gold dust.'

'I could probably get your father a ticket, if you'd like me to. Although it might be up in the gods.'

'Oh, Finn that would be amazing,' I said.

'I'll see what I can do.' He glanced at his watch. 'I have to go – I'm meeting someone who's watching tonight's preview.'

'And I need to go and start putting on my make-up,' I said.

Finn made to leave, but then he turned back. 'That first day at the Nightingale – before you arrived, I told Lily Dene how glad I was to have met up again with a dancer who I'd last seen ten years ago. And that I don't want to lose touch with her once the show opens and I'm not coming into the theatre every day.'

'*Oh* –' It was as if he was standing in front of me and asking me to dance. And I knew without any doubt that I was going to let him take my hand and lead me out onto the dance floor. 'I don't want to lose touch with you again, either,' I said. Briefly, his fingers brushed against mine.

'I'll see you tomorrow, Nell.' He spun on his heel and headed off along the narrow street. I went inside the Nightingale.

I told myself to focus on the preview, to put Finn out of my mind at least until the show came down. But as I walked up the five flights of stairs to Dressing Room Six, I couldn't stop smiling.

I was just about to look in on Savannah, before going to bed myself, when my phone announced the arrival of a text: *I've got you three seats together in the Royal Circle. I've left them at the stage door for your parents to pick up tomorrow. No extra tickets available for the after-party. Finn x*

Three tickets in the Royal Circle!

I texted back: *Perfect. Savannah is too young for after-parties, and my parents don't like nightclubs!! Thank you so SO much :) xx*

He replied: *My pleasure. But please keep it to yourself, because I can't do it for everyone who wants more tickets. See you tomorrow xxx*

He done this especially for me. And sent me three Xs! My fingers tapped at my phone screen: *Goodnight, Finn xxxx*, and I pressed send before it occurred to me that counting the number of Xs in a text was the behaviour of a giddy teenager, not a thirty-four-year-old woman and mother.

Telling myself to get my head together, I went into Savannah's room. To my surprise, for she was usually sound asleep when I got in from the theatre, she sat up in bed.

'It's nearly midnight, Savannah,' I said. 'Why are you still awake?'

Savannah considered this for a moment. 'I think it's because I'm so excited about coming to see you in *Speakeasy* tomorrow,' she said.

'I suppose I can't be cross then,' I said, 'because I'm excited about you coming to see me too.' I sat down beside her. 'And I've some good news. I've been given three extra tickets, so Grandad can come with you and Grandma.' A thought struck me. 'And I can ask two more people if they'd like to come as well.'

'Who are you going to ask?' Savannah said.

'Auntie Marianne and Auntie Zelda,' I said, immediately.

'They'll be excited to watch you dancing too,' Savannah said.

'Do you think?' I said. 'It's hard to believe it, but some people don't like watching dancing!'

Savannah giggled. 'I know you're teasing me. Everyone is excited to watch a West End show.' Then she said, 'Who gave you the tickets?'

Your father. 'The Choreographer,' I said.

'That was nice of him.'

He's a nice guy. 'Time for you to go to sleep, Savannah,' I said. She lay down, and I tucked her duvet around her.

'What's his name?'

'The Choreographer?' I swallowed uneasily. 'His name's Finn. Now, you really must go to sleep.' I kissed her goodnight, and went to the door. 'See you in the morning.'

''Night, Mum.'

On shaking legs, I went to my room and sank down on the bed.

I reminded myself that Finn and Savannah would be nowhere near each other on *Speakeasy's* Opening Night. He would be seated with the important folk like Olivia and Jonathan in a box; Savannah would be in a different part of the theatre. It was a little surreal to think of them both watching me dance, but they were hardly likely to run across each other. And even if they did, Finn had no reason to suspect that he'd given me more than one little dancer all those years ago.

He wouldn't find out that Savannah was his until I told him – if I ever did.

Chapter Seventeen

The following morning, for the first time in an age, I woke up before my alarm. Flinging off my duvet, I sprang out of bed, and quickly showered and dressed. I'd packed my bag the night before, but I double checked that I hadn't forgotten something vital – like my shoes for the after-party or the Opening Night cards I'd got for the rest of the cast – and that my silver ballerina was still safely tucked away in the inside pocket.

My bedroom door opened and a pyjama-clad Savannah came in, holding a white envelope and a large, book-shaped parcel wrapped in brightly coloured paper.

'I've made you another good luck card,' she said, handing me the envelope, which I immediately tore open.

'Oh, it's fabulous,' I said, smiling at her drawing of a woman in a leotard dancing on stage, with red curtains on either side, decorated with copious amounts of glitter. The message inside – written in glitter pen – instructed me, in true theatrical tradition to *break a leg*. 'Thank you, Savannah.'

'I know you like glitter,' Savannah said. 'And I know you never wish a dancer *good luck* before a show.' Passing me the book-shaped parcel, she added, 'And this is your Opening Night present.'

I carefully unwrapped the parcel and found myself holding a scrapbook with a map of Theatreland on the cover.

'I love it,' I said. My heart brimmed – what a perfect gift. 'Thank you *so* much.'

'I went shopping with Grandma, and she said you'd probably take lots of photos of your friends in the cast while you're in *Speakeasy*, and I was going to give you a photo album, but you can stick your good luck cards in this as well.'

'And souvenirs like newspaper reviews,' I said. 'It's the best Opening Night present ever.' Savannah beamed. I gave her a hug.

'I wish I was in *Speakeasy*,' she said. 'It's my dream to be in a West End musical.' I did a double take. I'd said the same thing, so many times. Hopefully it wouldn't take her as long to get there as it had taken me.

'I expect you will be one day,' I said, 'if that's what you want when you're older, but for now you need to go and get ready for school.'

Savannah trotted off. I put her card in my bag, and went downstairs.

I might be about to have a life-long dream come true, but first I had to make a packed-lunch and do the school run.

Stepping out of the train carriage at Leicester Square station, the first thing I saw was a huge poster advertising

Speakeasy with the image of a line chorus girls – and one of them was me! With the rest of the passengers who'd alighted at the station streaming around me, I stood on the platform, grinning at the life-sized picture, and taking a photo – it was only with difficulty that I stopped myself informing my fellow travellers that it was me up there.

Travelling up the escalators, I saw more *Speakeasy* posters, and walking along Shaftesbury Avenue, I spotted another on the side of a double decker bus. Arriving at the Nightingale, I found Justin studying the billboards outside the theatre, the plain posters listing the names of the cast having been replaced with photos of scenes from the show. One was a life-size close up of Samantha and Leon. A quiver of delight ran through me when I saw Justin and me in our 1920s finery standing next to them.

'Selfie?' Justin said to me, holding up his phone.

'Ooh, yes, please,' I said. 'This is the day I make my West End debut. I need it recorded for posterity.' He draped an arm around my shoulders and took a picture of both of us with the Nightingale in the background. I took one on my phone as well, and we walked round to the stage door.

'After you,' Justin said, holding the door open for me. I took a deep breath, and went inside.

'Good afternoon, Nell,' the stage doorman said. 'These were left here for you.' Reaching under the counter, he produced a huge bouquet of coral-coloured roses.

'Oh, my goodness,' I said. 'How lovely.' With some difficulty, juggling flowers and my bag, I signed in, and Justin and I went into Lily Dene's corridor.

'Now who, I wonder, sent you such a massive bunch of flowers?' Justin said. 'Could it be that you have an admirer among our Company?'

I laughed. 'I expect they're from my parents,' I said, inhaling the roses' glorious scent. Spotting a cream-coloured envelope nestling among the blooms, I passed the bouquet to Justin to hold while I opened it. Inside was a card which read: *May tonight be everything you want it to be. Finn xxxx.* I couldn't be *sure* what he meant by that, but my heart fluttered in my chest.

'So, who are they from?' Justin asked.

I hesitated. If I told Justin, all the boys in Dressing Room Seven, if not the entire ensemble, would know – even before the Stage Manager called the half – that Finn Harris had given Nell Avery flowers. Having my fellow cast members gossiping about us before there even was an *us* would not be conducive to my giving my best performance.

'*Not* my parents,' I said. 'And that's all I'm saying.'

Justin didn't press the matter, but his mouth twitched with amusement. He handed me back the flowers, and we continued along the corridor – chorusing *good afternoon, Miss Dene,* as we passed Lily's portrait – and up the stairs.

When we reached the fifth floor, Justin said, 'Are you nervous, Nell?'

'Right now, I'm too excited to be nervous. Ask me again when we're waiting in the wings for the curtain to go up. What about you?'

'A few jitters, but I know I'll be fine once I hear the overture. I always am.' We exchanged smiles, and went to our respective dressing rooms.

In Dressing Room Six, I found Florence and Hettie exclaiming over the T-shirts with *Speakeasy* printed across the back, and a picture of a couple in silhouette dancing under a full moon on the front, that they – and every member of the ensemble – had received as Opening Night gifts from the producers, the hoodies with the same picture that they'd received from the creative team, the water-bottles they'd received from Samantha and the pens from Leon.

'I'd no idea we'd get such amazing presents,' Florence said, her eyes shining.

'It's a West End tradition that the producers, creatives and stars give the cast Opening Night gifts,' Hettie said. 'And I have to say, it's one I heartily approve of.' She added, 'What gorgeous flowers, Nell. Who are they from?'

'An old friend,' I said, which was true, after a fashion.

'There are some vases in the cupboard under the sink,' Hettie said.

I found a vase for Finn's roses and put them on my make-up desk, hung up the gorgeous, sparkly, ankle-length dress I was intending to wear to the after party, and delightedly examined my own gifts. The girls of Dressing Room Six had decided that rather than buy each other Opening Night presents, we'd club together to buy boxes of sweets for ourselves and as gifts for the other dressing rooms – I knew from Justin that the boys of Dressing Room Seven were doing the same – but I handed Florence and Hettie their cards. They both reciprocated, and I was touched to find that Florence had written *thank you so much for answering all my questions about the theatre and for being my friend* in the card she gave me. I stood the cards on my make-up desk, along with the several cards Savannah had made me over the weeks of rehearsal.

The door opened, and Marisa swanned into the dressing room, Nicole on her heels.

'I have news,' she proclaimed, as soon as she'd sat down. 'I've just had a most informative talk with Olivia – we happened to arrive at the stage door at exactly the same moment – and I was able to tell her that if *Speakeasy* isn't a success, it certainly won't be down to her. She is a very talented theatre practitioner.'

'She must be relieved to know that you approve of her skillset,' Hettie said, winking at me. I had to look away before I burst into laughter.

'I'm sure she is,' Marisa said, 'but that's not all that I wanted to tell you. Olivia informed me that Leigh Keaton himself will be in the audience tonight.'

'Who?' Florence said.

'Honestly, Florence, how can you not know who Leigh Keaton is?' Marisa said. 'What *are* we going to do with you? He's *only* one of the most influential producers working in musical theatre today. His presence in the Nightingale confirms everything I've ever said about an Opening Night being one of the best opportunities for a performer to further their career.'

'Well, I fully expect Leigh Keaton to spot me on stage tonight, pluck me out of the chorus and make me a star,' Hettie said.

'Such things do happen,' Marisa said, evidently not realising that Hettie wasn't serious, 'but I think making contact with him at the after-party and giving him a copy of my CV would be a better way forward than leaving it to chance. It's vital to be pro-active, if you want to get ahead.'

I'd auditioned for a Leigh Keaton musical only once, not long after I'd graduated, and I'd been cut first round, so I could hardly claim to know the best way to get into one of his productions. I did, however, suspect that thrusting a hard copy of a CV into the guy's hands at a party might not have the results Marisa was after.

'Cards!' Florence said, suddenly. Fishing two more envelopes out of her bag she gave them to Marisa and Nicole. Hettie and I did likewise, and Nicole produced cards for us. To my astonishment, Marisa handed each of us a signed photograph of herself.

'A keepsake for you of our time together at the Nightingale,' she said.

'Thank you, Marisa,' Florence said, without enthusiasm.

'I will treasure it always,' Hettie said, clasping the photo to her heart. 'What a lovely idea.' She was, I thought, an exceptionally good actress.

'Thanks, Marisa,' I said. 'This is very . . . unexpected. I don't know what to say.'

Fortunately, I was saved from having to come up with more fulsome thanks by the crackling of the tannoy, and the stage doorman's voice announcing: 'Flowers for Nicole Whitby and Marisa Cutler at the stage door.'

'Oh, I hope they're from Donald,' Nicole said, leaping to her feet, and heading out of the room.

'Bring mine up too, Nicole,' Marisa called after her.

The tannoy crackled again: 'Flowers for Florence Newton . . . Flowers for Hettie Parkes and Nell Avery . . .'

'I think we're going to need more vases,' Hettie said.

Her creative team and their assistants lined up on either side of her, Olivia stood at the front of the auditorium and surveyed the dancers and actors sitting in the stalls.

'First of all,' she said, 'I have some notes, well one note, and it's for Leon . . .'

My gaze went to Finn, standing next to Olivia. As if he was aware of me looking at him, he turned his head towards me and his eyes met mine. A smile flickered briefly about his mouth, before he returned his attention to what our director was saying about Nathan's entrance in the party scene in Act I – one of my favourite scenes as it led into *She Only Drinks Champagne,* a spectacular dance number, with some of Finn's finest choreography. My mind drifted back over the last few weeks. To say that I'd found rehearsals challenging was an understatement, but I'd got through them – enjoyed them even – and in just a few hours, the curtain would rise. My whole body tingled at the thought.

'Do you have anything to add, Finn?' Olivia said. 'Jonathan?' Both men shook their heads. 'In that case, everyone is free to go and have a late lunch, read their good luck messages, stroke their lucky rabbit's foot, meditate . . . or whatever else you choose to do before a show. If you leave the theatre, please ensure that you're back by 5.30, and ready for a warm up at 6.00.' She paused. 'And that's my job as *Speakeasy's* director done and dusted. All that remains is for me to thank you, on behalf of Finn, Jonathan and myself, for all your hard work throughout rehearsals. You are all immensely talented performers, and *Speakeasy* is going to be a great show. You've got this, guys. Have a good one.' With a gracious smile for her cast, Olivia led her entourage towards the door that would take them backstage, with Finn a little way behind the rest.

He'd sent me roses.

On impulse, I jumped up from my seat and went after him, touching his arm so that he turned around to face me.

'Hey, Nell,' he said. 'What can I do for you?'

'I just want to thank you for my flowers,' I said. 'They're beautiful, Finn.'

'I'm so glad you like them,' he said.

'I love them,' I said, smiling up at him. I was vaguely aware of other members of the cast filing past us as they left the auditorium, giving us speculative glances, but Finn made no move to go, so I too stayed where I was.

When everyone else had gone and we were alone, he said, 'Do you have plans for this afternoon?'

'Not right now,' I said, still smiling. 'There's something I have to do later – can't think what it is.' I shrugged. 'It'll come to me.'

Finn laughed. 'I have to make a couple of calls first, but I fancy getting out of the theatre for a bit. Will you have lunch with me?'

'I'd like that,' I said.

'Meet me outside the stage door in fifteen minutes?'

'It's a date –' I said, blushing as soon as the words were out of my mouth. 'I mean – I didn't mean –'

'But I did,' Finn said. 'Although, it'll only be sandwiches eaten on a bench.'

'Oh, Finn –' My heart soared.

'Is that OK with you?' he said.

'That is so OK,' I said.

We left the auditorium. Finn went off to make his calls. I went upstairs to Dressing Room Six, and discovered that while we were on stage, one of the front of house staff had left each of us a copy of *Speakeasy's* programme propped up against our make-up mirrors. Marisa was reading her biog aloud to an admiring Nicole, ignored by Florence and Hettie, who were exclaiming over a double-page-spread of rehearsal photos. I quickly leafed through my programme, before stowing it in my bag to look at properly later, ran a comb through my hair, and, saying vaguely that I was going out for some fresh air, went back downstairs, and out of the stage door.

Finn was there before me, and his smile when he saw me made me feel as if I was walking on air. Together, we strolled along the narrow street and turned onto Shaftesbury Avenue. Having dived into a coffee bar to buy take-away coffees and sandwiches, he led me down a side-road to a small square – a patch of grass, with wooden benches, flower beds and trees, surrounded by tall red-brick houses – far enough away from the main road for the sound of the traffic to be just a distant hum and for us to hear birdsong.

We sat on a bench, and ate our improvised lunch, chatting about the show. He told me that Olivia and Jonathan had both opined that *Speakeasy's* ensemble was one of the best they'd ever worked with. I assured him that the ensemble only had good things to say about the creative team – which was very unusual after such a tough rehearsal process. I thought how good it was to sit there with him in the spring sunshine, how easy he was to be with. I willed him to kiss me before we had to go back to the Nightingale.

A couple of hours later, hours during which we'd talked and laughed, and I longed for his kiss, Finn checked the time on his phone.

'We should head back,' he said. 'I'm sure Lily Dene wouldn't approve of a choreographer who made a dancer miss her call time.'

I was about to make my West End debut. It had taken me fifteen years to get to this point, but I still found myself wishing I could have just a few more minutes in the sunlit square alone with Finn. I reminded myself that I was a professional dancer, and whatever I was feeling now, as soon as I walked through the stage door, my focus had to be entirely on the show.

Finn rose to his feet. 'I keep thinking there's more I should have done during rehearsal,' he said, 'something I've forgotten to tell the cast –'

I stood up, studying his face, and seeing the tension in his jaw. 'You've done everything you can to make *Speakeasy* the best show it can be. It's up to us dancers now.'

'You're right,' Finn said. 'But it's so hard to let go.' He stepped towards me. 'I'm glad we came here, Nell, and not just because being with you has stopped me stressing about the show.' He reached up and pushed a stray strand of hair out of my eyes. Then he put his hands on either side of my face, and, at last, he kissed me on the lips. I melted against him, and he folded his arms around me, holding me close for an instant, before raising his head from mine. It was a chaste kiss – we were, after all, in a public place, even although at that precise moment we were alone except for an inquisitive pigeon – but it still caused desire to jolt through me, like an electric shock.

'We really do have to go back now,' Finn said.

He laced his fingers through mine, and we walked back to the Nightingale, hand in hand, only letting go of each other when we reached the stage door.

'The next time I see you, you'll be on Lily Dene's stage,' Finn said.

'I'll be dancing your choreography on Lily Dene's stage,' I said.

'And then we'll see each other at the after-party. And after that . . . Do you have to rush off?'

'No, I don't have to rush off anywhere tonight,' I said.

'In that case . . .' Finn broke into song, '*We can dance 'til dawn, and watch the sun rise.*'

That was a line from one of the songs in the show. I sang a line from the finale, '*On a night like this anything can happen.*'

Finn's mouth lifted in a lazy smile. 'Break a leg, Nell,' he said. 'Or, as they say in Germany: *Toi! Toi! Toi!*'

And then we went into the theatre.

Walking into Dressing Room Six, was like walking into a florists. Bouquets of flowers, some with balloons attached, now stood on every surface, along with cards, jars of sweets, boxes of chocolates and bottles of prosecco.

'There you are at last, Nell,' Marisa said. 'Everyone's been running up and down stairs all afternoon fetching your flowers from the stage door.'

'Sorry, guys,' I said. 'I – er – didn't realise I'd be gone so long.'

'No worries, Nell,' Hettie said. 'We've all had flowers to pick up. No-one had to make a special trip.'

Sitting down next to Florence, who was reading through her much-annotated copy of *Speakeasy's* script, I opened the cards which had come with the glorious array of roses, tulips, chrysanthemums, and other blooms I didn't know the names of, which now adorned my make-up desk. My parents, Zelda, Marianne, and my agent, Amanda, had all sent me bouquets, as had Miss Rachel, and there was a small posy from Savannah – she was staying the night with her grandparents, and they would take her to school in the morning – which my thoughtful mother must have arranged for her to send. I also had cards from my fellow dancers, saying things like how much they'd enjoyed working with me in rehearsal and were looking forward to the next six months. Reading all these kind messages left me glowing inside.

Remembering that I still had cards to deliver, I retrieved them from my bag, and took them to the other three ensemble dressing rooms – like ours, the other female dressing room was full of flowers, while a quick glimpse through the doorways of the male dressing rooms was enough to show me that the guys had accumulated an impressive number of Opening Night gifts of the alcoholic and confectionary variety.

I wasn't gone long, probably less than ten minutes, but when I walked back into Dressing Room Six, I was confronted with a pale-faced Florence slumped in her chair, with Hettie standing over her and fanning her with a programme, Nicole hovering a short distance away, wringing her hands, and Marisa regarding the three of them from the other side of the room, her mouth tightly pursed.

'What's happened?' I asked, hurrying across the room.

'I don't know,' Florence said. 'I was reading through the script one last time, and I started to feel dizzy. I thought I was going to pass out.'

'It was far too hot in here,' Hettie said, 'but I've opened the window now. You'll be fine in a minute.'

'You've not been at the prosecco already, have you, Florence?' Marisa said. 'We all know what happened the last time. I don't think our Company Manager would be too pleased to find out he has a lush in the ensemble.'

Florence looked stricken. 'I'm not – Is that what people think?'

'Nobody thinks that,' I said. 'Do they, Marisa?' I locked my eyes on hers. After a moment, she looked away.

'Honestly, Florence, can't you take a joke?' she said. 'You need to lighten up.'

I went to the sink, half-filled a cup with water and handed it to Florence.

'Just sit quietly and sip this,' I said. She did as I suggested, and I was relieved to see the colour gradually coming back into her face.

The Stage Manager's voice, interspersed with static, issued from the tannoy: 'All cast . . . stage . . . warm-up.'

'All right now, Florence?' I said.

She nodded, and got to her feet. 'I'm OK.'

We filed out of Dressing Room Six, meeting up with the other members of the ensemble in the corridor, the twenty of us clattering downstairs to the stage, where we joined the leads and the actors playing named parts in a vocal warm-up led by Jonathan – he told us we were all in great voice – and a dance warm-up led by Lucas. Florence had hidden herself behind the rest of the cast, and as we had only the empty auditorium in front of us, rather than the mirrors we'd have had in a dance studio, I couldn't see how she was doing, but I reckoned she must be fine or Lucas would have noticed and said something.

The warm-up over, with much calling out of 'break a leg' and 'see you on the other side,' – and *'merde'* from a girl who'd danced at the Lido in Paris – the ensemble trooped back up to the fifth floor and dispersed to their various dressing rooms.

Sitting in front of my mirror in my dressing gown, pinning up my hair, I cast surreptitious glances at Florence. Whatever had ailed her – whether it was an over-heated dressing room or, as I now suspected, a touch of pre-show nerves – she appeared to have got over it, deftly sticking on her false eyelashes and darkening her eyebrows. I decided I could stop worrying about her, and concentrated on applying my scarlet lipstick in a perfect Cupid's bow.

My make-up completed to my satisfaction, I slid my feet into my dance shoes and went to the window, looking out at the view of the theatres lining Shaftesbury Avenue in either direction, bathed in evening sunlight, enjoying the feel of a cool breeze on my face.

I was in Theatreland. In less than an hour, I would be dancing on Lily Dene's stage. This was really happening. I smiled delightedly.

The tannoy spluttered, and then a voice said: 'Nell Avery, Marisa Cutler, Hettie Parkes, Florence Newton and Nicole Whitby to the wig room, please. Dressing Room Six to the wig room.'

Marisa was straight out the door, Nicole scurrying after her. Hettie smiled at me and Florence, and followed them. Florence remained sitting in front of her mirror.

'Florence?' I said. 'We need to go.'

'I can't do it,' she said, her voice scarcely above a whisper. 'I can't remember the steps – I can't do the show –'

'*What*?' I turned her chair around so that she was facing me. Her forehead was filmed in sweat. In all my years of dancing, I'd never seen anyone have a full-on attack of stage fright, but I was pretty sure I was seeing it now.

'Florence, listen to me,' I said. 'You know the routines for *Speakeasy* so well you could dance them with your eyes shut –'

'I can't dance in front of all those important industry people,' Florence wailed. 'What if I mess up?' She was visibly shaking now, and breathing in rapid gasps. 'I can't go on stage – I can't –'

'You can and you will.' I took hold of her hands, which were cold and clammy. 'Look at me,' I said. 'Now breath in – slowly – hold it – and out. And again.'

Florence did as I said. After what seemed a long while – although it was likely only a few minutes – I saw that she'd stopped trembling and was breathing normally.

'Listen, Florence,' I said, in what I hoped was a calm yet firm voice. 'It's normal to feel nervous before a performance.' I decided against mentioning stage fright; best not to put the idea in her head. 'But once you start dancing, those nerves will vanish. Tonight, you're going to enjoy every moment you're on that stage, and you're going to make your parents – and Lily Dene – very proud. OK?'

Florence nodded. I let go of her hands.

'Off you go, then' I said, gesturing towards the door. Florence stood up, squared her shoulders, and headed out of the dressing room. I kept close by her side, ready to seize her arm and frog march her to the wig room if necessary, but we got there without incident. Fortunately, the hairdressers and the sound guy were busy with other dancers, so our late arrival went unremarked.

By the time we were in the wardrobe village, Florence was chattering away to her dresser, with no sign that she had ever been anything less than show-ready. As Christina fastened me into my costume for Act I, scene i, I felt confident that the only drama at the Nightingale that night would be taking place on stage. I took a moment to look at myself in the mirror, smiling at the reflection of a West End performer who looked back at me, and went into the wings.

Standing with my fellow dancers in the semi-darkness at the side of the stage, looking out onto the brightly-lit performance space, I could actually feel the adrenaline surging through me. I heard the voices of the audience as they took their seats, and, a little after that, I heard the musicians in the pit tuning their instruments. Justin came and stood next to me, taking hold of my hand. The cast moved aside to allow Samantha to walk to centre stage where, when the curtains opened, the audience would see Kitty in a New York street.

The stage manager announced, 'We have clearance.'
I am about to make my West End debut.
Justin gives my hand a squeeze. The orchestra plays the overture. My pulse beats faster, my stomach tightens, I shift from foot to foot. The curtains open, I hear the first notes of *Good Morning New York City*, my and Justin's cue to run onto the stage . . . Justin's hands on my waist as he lifts me, his voice blending with mine as we sing, the stage lights blindingly bright, staying in character and not looking at the audience but feeling their presence. Somewhere out there, Savannah is watching me, Finn is watching me, I am dancing on a West End stage . . .

Tonight, my dream is coming true.

Chapter Eighteen

'Five curtain calls,' Justin said, as we stood drinking champagne at the *Speakeasy* after-party, 'How good is that?'

'I thought the audience were never going to let us go,' I said. 'Not that I minded. I could have listened to that applause all night. I think we may have a hit on our hands.'

'You could be right,' Justin laughed. 'I always come off stage on a high, but right now, I'm higher than I've ever been before.'

'I'm floating in the sky,' I said. 'I may never come down to earth again.'

The applause had started even before the cast had left the stage after the finale, a ripple of clapping spreading throughout the auditorium, growing louder, pursuing us into the wings, a mighty torrent of noise rushing to meet us as we ran back on stage to take our bows. As arranged – although to the audience it would have appeared spontaneous – the orchestra struck up another tune, and we jumped into an accompanying tap dance. The audience had leapt to their feet in a standing ovation.

Running off stage and back on again, bowing, smiling, I'd let my gaze roam around the theatre. I couldn't see Savannah – she and my parents were sitting too far back – but I'd spotted Zelda and Marianne in the stalls, clapping so hard that their hands must have been stinging, and, in the Royal Box, I saw Finn, on his feet like the rest of the audience. As I looked at him, he looked at me and raised his hands and I knew for that moment it was only me he was applauding, and my heart soared as high as the back row of the gods. The applause had continued long after the curtains had closed.

Back in Dressing Room Six, we'd breathlessly opened a bottle of prosecco, drinking it from coffee mugs, while we got ourselves ready for the after-party, and admired each other's evening dresses. Giddy from the performance, I even found it in me to praise the dress with the neck-line that plunged almost to her navel and the skirt split to the top of her thigh, that Marisa was wearing, although it occurred to me that it would be a miracle if she didn't fall out of it before the end of the night. I listened to congratulations on voice mail from my proud mother and father, and a message from Savannah, from my mother's phone, saying I was the best dancer in the show, which made me happier than any number of curtain calls.

A knock on the door had announced the arrival of Justin and Matt, looking debonair in smart suits – an effect that was ruined when they'd let off party poppers all over our dressing room – and inviting us to walk with them to the nightclub near Leicester Square, that was the venue for the after-party. Marisa declined – she and Nicole would take a cab – although from the startled look on Justin's face, I suspected he hadn't intended to include them in the invitation. The other five of us had walked to the club through the crowded night-time streets of London – with Justin and Matt performing the occasional *grand jeté* to the bemusement of passing tourists – marvelling at how amazing it was to be a part of *Speakeasy*, how fortunate we were to have been cast, chosen out of all the hundreds of dancers who'd auditioned all those weeks ago. And all the while, my head was full of what might happen tonight between me and Finn. What I wanted to happen.

At the club, we'd found the party already underway, the five of us joining a milling throng of our fellow dancers, their friends and relatives, casting directors, agents, journalists, and celebrities – tickets to glamorous opening nights a perk of being famous – in the main bar, a cavernous room with low lighting and loud music. I'd looked for Finn, but couldn't see him or any of the creative team, and concluded that he'd yet to arrive at the party. Zelda and Marianne had materialised out of the crowd, enveloping me in hugs and congratulations. Seconds later, Justin's boyfriend, Philip, appeared, and amidst introductions, and more congratulations, we accepted the champagne offered to us by one of the circling waiters. As we raised our glasses, toasting *Speakeasy* and each other, I couldn't stop smiling.

Now, a burst of applause, beginning by the door and ricocheting across the club, signalled the arrival of *Speakeasy's* leading man and leading lady, along with Olivia, who tonight had swapped her plain black rehearsal clothes for a sequined evening dress, Jonathan, and two men who I recognised from the sitzprobe as producers. Surely, I thought, Finn should be with them. Where was he?

Yet more clapping made me swivel around, straining to see above the heads of people taller than me – and at last I saw him, walking towards me, looking extraordinarily handsome in a dark suit and collarless shirt. Desire lanced through me, and my stomach twisted almost painfully, as he saw me and smiled – just before he was surrounded by a horde of people wanting to shake the hand of *Speakeasy's* Choreographer, obscuring him from my sight. I drained my glass of champagne, and helped myself to another from a passing waiter.

The evening went on. My agent, Amanda, stopped by, congratulating me warmly on my performance – 'You were wonderful, Nell. Tonight was the best I've ever seen you dance' – before going off to talk to an up-and-coming movie director. Hettie, Florence and Matt went off to find their respective guests. Half-listening to what Philip, a musician, was saying about *Speakeasy's* music – Marianne was listening intently and voicing her own opinions – I watched as Finn emerged from the crowd of his admirers. He immediately fell into conversation with a guy a few years older than him, the resemblance between them making me think he must be his brother, and a grey-haired couple who I assumed were his parents. Not wanting to intrude on his time with his family, I resisted the urge to rush to his side.

'What does that woman think she's doing?' Justin said, suddenly. Tearing my attention away from Finn and his relatives, I followed the direction of Justin's gaze to see Marisa holding out a piece of A4 paper to a dark-haired man of about forty who I recognised as Leigh Keaton. Even as I watched, he shook his head.

'I think she's trying to give Leigh Keaton her CV,' I said, as Marisa stashed the paper in her bag, and the theatre impresario plunged into the crowd, 'but he doesn't seem to want it.' Marisa's gaze roamed around the club, as if she was planning who to pounce on next, and came to rest on me and my friends. To my surprise, she glided over to us.

'I'm making some extremely useful contacts tonight,' she said, by way of greeting. 'I was just speaking to Leigh Keaton, and he told me to have my agent send my details to his production office.'

'That's – er – wonderful, Marisa,' I said.

'It's annoying that he couldn't take the printed copy of my CV with him tonight,' Marisa said, 'but I assured him that an email will be with him first thing on Monday morning.' She sighed contentedly. 'Well, I'd love to stay talking with you, but there are so many important people here tonight that I really must speak to –' With a smile that could only be described as predatory, she dived back into the crowd.

'Do you think I should have told her that literally hundreds of actors send their details to Leigh Keaton Productions every week,' Justin said, with a grin. 'The email address is on the company website –' He broke off. 'I've just spotted my agent lurking by the bar. Although my networking skills are pitiful compared to Marisa's, I really should go and have a drink with him. See you guys later.' He and Philip strolled off.

'Shall we go for a wander?' I said, to Zelda and Marianne. 'I'd love you to meet the rest of *Speakeasy's* ensemble – who are nothing like Marisa, by the way.'

'I ought to think about going home –' Zelda's voice broke off, and she stared fixedly past my shoulder.

I turned my head, and saw Finn standing behind me.

'Hey, Nell.' Stepping closer to me, he kissed the side of my face. 'Well done,' he said. 'I've never seen you dance better.'

'Thanks, Finn.' I smiled up at him. 'So you don't have any notes for me?'

He laughed. 'Not tonight.'

Zelda said, 'Hello, Finn.'

'Zelda,' Finn said. 'How lovely to see you again after all this time.'

My heart began thumping against my chest. When I'd given an Opening Night ticket to my best friend so she could see me make my West End debut, it hadn't occurred to me that she and Finn might meet at the after-party. Now, seeing them together, all I could think was that Zelda knew Finn was Savannah's father, and that she thought he should know as well. I told myself that she hadn't kept my secret this long only to blurt it out now.

To Marianne, I said. 'This is Finn Harris, *Speakeasy's* Choreographer. Finn – Marianne. My sister.'

'Good to meet you,' Finn said. 'I'm sure you'll agree with me that Nell was terrific on stage tonight.'

'She was,' Marianne said. 'And your choreography is incredible. The dancing blew me away.'

'That's all down to the dancers, not me,' Finn said. 'I was very fortunate to have such a talented ensemble.'

'Have you and Nell worked together before?' Marianne said.

'No, but we've known each other a long time,' Finn said.

'We trained together,' I said. 'That's how we know each other.'

'And after we graduated, we went to the same auditions,' Finn said. 'But we were never cast in the same show.'

'And then we lost touch,' I said.

'Not entirely,' Finn said. 'Not until I went to Germany.' To Marianne, he added, 'I've spent the last ten years abroad. I didn't keep in contact with my friends in England, and I'd no idea if any of them were still dancing. When I walked into the first round of auditions for *Speakeasy* and saw Nell, it was quite a surprise.'

'It must have been quite a shock for Nell too,' Zelda said, to no-one in particular.

'It's always good to reconnect with old friends,' Marianne said. 'Although, ten years is a long time to be away. Now that you're back, you must have found so much that's changed.'

'Indeed,' Finn said. 'I've a lot of catching up to do.'

'I'll say,' Zelda muttered. In a louder voice, she added, 'It really is time I went home.'

I wasn't going to disagree with her. I wanted her away from Finn.

'I should get off too,' Marianne said, making a show of looking at her watch. 'I don't want to miss my last train. Enjoy the rest of the evening, you two. I expect you still have lots of . . . networking to do.' I shot her a look. She smiled blandly back at me.

'Goodnight, Marianne,' I said. ''Night Zelda.

Giving me a hug, chorusing their goodnights, my sister and my best friend headed off towards the club's exit, leaving me with Finn. He put a hand on my arm, turning me towards him, so that we were standing face to face, looking directly into each other's eyes. The noise of the party, the music, the chatter and the chink of glasses, receded, the other revellers became a blur, and all I could see was him.

'Was tonight all you dreamed it would be?' he said.

'I don't know yet,' I said. 'The night isn't over.' His mouth curved into a smile. I became aware of a delicious ache between my legs, spreading throughout my entire body.

'I think we've stayed long enough at this party,' Finn said.

'I'm ready to go when you are,' I said.

'Then let's get out of here,' Finn said, 'because I really want to kiss you, but I'd prefer not to have an audience.'

Through the thin fabric of my dress, I felt him place a hand on the small of my back, and he steered me across the club, through the still animatedly chattering crowd, to the exit. The thought came to me that for all Finn's discretion in not kissing me, our leaving the party together, and him helping me on with my jacket while we were still in the lobby, was quite enough to make us prime targets for backstage gossip, but I really didn't care.

I thought he might kiss me as soon as we were outside in the cool night air, but, taking my hand, a smile playing about his mouth, he led me along the pavement, and turned into a side-street.

'Where are we going?' I asked.

'Wait and see,' he said.

We continued walking, down one road and then another, crossing over the Strand – which was when I guessed where he was taking me – down a flight of steps, and along a narrow, empty street that brought us down to the Thames Embankment, the river silver in the light of the full moon. There was no-one else around.

I said, 'This is where we came that night . . .'

'That night ten years ago, when I kissed you for the first time.' Sliding an arm around my waist, Finn drew me to him. He said, 'Five, six, seven, eight,' and twirled me along the pavement, dancing with me in the silver moonlight. When we came to a halt, we were both laughing. Then we fell silent. My heart began to race. Finn bent his head over mine. I tilted up my face and looked directly into his eyes.

'Oh, Nell –' He did kiss me then, folding me gently in his arms, tasting of champagne and moonlight. We kissed for a long time, and both of us were breathless when he raised his face from mine. 'Nell, will you sleep with me tonight?' he said, his voice hoarse.

On a night like this, standing there with Finn, light-headed, my whole body tingling, his arms holding me close, the taste of him in my mouth, the full moon above our heads, there was only one answer I could give him.

Chapter Nineteen

We walked back to the Strand, and Finn hailed a cab, asking me which address he should give the driver, his or mine. The thought of travelling home the following day in an evening gown and strappy high heels, convinced me to say we'd go to my place. Half an hour or so later, the cab drew up outside my house. Finn paid the driver, and followed me up the short front path, reaching up and stroking the side of my face while, with shaking hands, I unlocked the door – I almost dropped my keys.

As soon as we were inside, and the door locked behind us, he kissed me again, crushing me against him, his mouth urgent and demanding, his tongue entwined with mine. I shrugged off my jacket, and he slid one of the straps of my dress off my shoulder, his fingers lingering, searing my bare skin with his touch.

'I want you, Nell,' he said. In answer, I took his hand, and led him upstairs and into my bedroom.

In the light of the moon shining in through the open curtains, he reached behind me and unzipped my dress. The flimsy material slid down my body and pooled at my feet. I peeled off my underwear. Finn groaned softly, and took off his clothes, pulling me to him, my breasts against his unyielding chest, kissing me hungrily, his erection pressing hard and hot into my stomach. He lifted me, and I wrapped my legs around him, and still kissing, he carried me across the room and lay me on the bed, lying down beside me, his hands stroking and caressing me, setting my blood on fire, my dancer's body remembering what he liked, the steps of our *pas de deux* ingrained in my muscle memory, kissing him, trailing my fingers along his spine, his superbly toned torso both familiar and unfamiliar, the scent of his skin, his mouth on my breasts, the revelation that in the last ten years, he had picked up a number of interesting new routines . . .

I opened my eyes to see sunlight streaming in through the bedroom windows. I was lying in my bed, with Finn's head beside mine on the pillow. He was already awake, and when he saw that I'd woken up also, his face creased into a smile.

'Morning, Nell,' he said. 'I was wondering if I should wake you, but I decided you could probably do with a lie in after all the dancing you did yesterday.'

I smiled drowsily back at him, my body pleasurably languid. Then, abruptly, I was wide awake, and sitting bolt upright. Last night, I'd fallen asleep in Finn's arms, with no thought of setting an alarm for the morning. With no show today, I was, for once, picking up Savannah from school, and I couldn't be late. To my immense relief, the clock-radio on my bedside table told me it was only just gone eleven.

'Is something wrong?' Finn said, sitting up also.

'No, everything's fine,' I said. 'It's just that I have to collect Savannah from school, but not until three o'clock.' I sank back on the bed. 'Panic over.'

Finn lay down next to me, on his side, bending one elbow and resting his head on his hand. His face grew serious.

'Nell,' he said, 'last night was great but – I'm not quite sure how to say this –'

My body went rigid. Was this when he told me that last night was great, but despite all he'd said about being glad I was back in his life, he wasn't looking to get *involved* with me – right before he got out of my bed and walked away. Ten years ago, I'd not expected anything more from him, but now, lying beside him, I wanted desperately for him to stay in my life – for *him* to want to stay.

'Why do I find it so much easier to express myself through dance?' Finn muttered. He ran his hand through his hair. 'What I'm trying to say to you, Nell, is that having you as a friend, and occasionally having mind-blowing sex with you, isn't enough for me. I'd like to cast myself in the role of your boyfriend.'

I felt as if I was melting inside. 'And I'd very much like to play opposite you as your girlfriend.'

Finn's smile lit up his whole face. 'Can we spend the rest of the morning together?'

'We most certainly can,' I said, liking that he'd asked me rather than simply assuming that he could stay. 'Would you like some brunch?'

'Brunch would be great,' Finn said. 'But first, I'd like to run out and pick up some newspapers so we can read *Speakeasy's* reviews. I know we could find them on-line, but that's not the same as reading them in the papers in true theatrical tradition.'

'Oh, I agree,' I said. 'Savannah gave me a scrapbook as an Opening Night present, and I'd much rather have newspaper cuttings to stick in it than a computer printout.'

'Your daughter giving you an Opening Night present is so cute,' Finn said.

'Er – yes,' I said. In that instant, it struck me forcibly that if Finn and I stayed together long-term, if our relationship became serious, he would at some point have to meet Savannah. But not today. It was far too soon. I didn't even have to think about how I'd deal with that today.

Finn's mind was still on the reviews, 'Is there somewhere near here that sells newspapers?' he said.

'There's a supermarket just around the corner,' I said.

'Right,' Finn said. 'Before I go out, can I use your shower?'

'Of course, you can,' I said. 'While you do, I'll make us tea. You don't take sugar, as I remember?'

'Could I have coffee?' Finn said. 'I got used to coffee first thing in the morning in Germany. You can get tea over there, but it never tastes the same as it does in England.'

I got out of bed, relishing the appreciative gleam in Finn's eyes as his gaze travelled up and down my naked body, showed him to the bathroom, found a couple of clean towels and a toothbrush still in its packet and left him to it. Ten years since I'd shared a bed with him, yet there was no morning-after awkwardness. Being with him felt *so* good.

Putting on a dressing gown, I went downstairs to the kitchen and made us drinks. Locating my evening bag on the floor in the hallway – I must have dropped it there while Finn and I were kissing – I went back to my bedroom, and, sitting on the bed, took out my phone and checked my messages.

There was a missed call from Zelda, and a text which read: *Call me.* That was one conversation I really didn't need to have right now. There was a text from Marianne: *Are you dating/shagging the choreographer? How long has this been going on? I expect a full disclosure asap xx PS Good for you – he's gorgeous!* And a text from Justin: *I know who sent you the flowers!! xx.* Both those texts made me smile, although I felt that neither of them required a reply.

Finn came back into the bedroom, the mere sight of him, with just a towel around his waist, making my stomach flip. Leaving him to get dressed and drink his coffee, I went and showered, and put on the dash of mascara and lip gloss that I wore when I wasn't on stage, returning to find him stretched out on the bed, listening to someone on his phone – he mouthed 'I won't be long.' After some thought – he'd seen me in rehearsal gear often enough, but now we were *seeing* each other, I felt a higher degree of sartorial elegance was appropriate – I put on a shirt dress, and a matching belt and sandals.

'Yeah, get back to me when you've set up a meeting,' Finn said to whoever was on the phone. 'Bye for now.' He ended the call, and sat up, swinging his legs over the side of the bed. 'That was my agent. He says that having watched *Speakeasy* last night, Leigh Keaton is very keen for me and him to meet to discuss the possibility of my working on his next project.'

'Oh, my gosh, that's *brilliant,*' I said. 'I'm so pleased for you, Finn.'

'Let's not get ahead of ourselves,' Finn said. 'It may never happen. But I won't pretend I'm not excited at the thought I might get to choreograph a Leigh Keaton musical.'

'Leigh Keaton's musicals are only as good as they are because he works with seriously talented choreographers,' I said. 'And that's you, Finn Harris.'

He laughed, self-depreciatingly. 'I'll go and get those newspapers and we can find out if the critics agree.'

While Finn made a sortie to the supermarket, I went to the kitchen and assembled the ingredients for potato omelettes – the morning after the first time we'd slept together we'd raided the fridge for cold pizza, but my culinary skills had improved over the last ten years. Finn returned with copies of every newspaper and magazine likely to contain a review, placing them in a tantalising pile on a worktop while we ate. He helped me clear away the debris of the meal, I made us both a coffee, and then we spread the papers out on the kitchen table.

'From the top,' Finn said. 'Five, six, seven, eight . . .' I laughed and reached for one of the nationals.

After the reaction of the audience, I'd never doubted that the reviews for *Speakeasy* would be good, but when I opened the newspaper to find a write up from one of the toughest critics in the business describing the show as a "triumph," and "the best musical to hit the West End in years," I gasped aloud. The review went on to praise the "exceptionally talented cast and outstanding ensemble," with the "spectacular dance numbers proving that we can only be grateful that choreographer Finn Harris has chosen to return to London and bring his exciting and impassioned choreography to the West End stage."

'You have to see this,' I said to Finn, passing him the paper. I watched him as he read, and saw his face break into a broad grin.

'Congratulations,' I said.

He looked up from the newspaper, his eyes shining. 'This is – I never expected –'. I felt such a rush of affection for him, that it made me dizzy.

'The stuff that dreams are made on,' I said.

We read the other reviews – all were effusive in their praise, with Finn's choreography receiving as much attention as Samantha and Leon's performances and Olivia's direction – and talked over the show. And then it was half past two in the afternoon. Time for me to stop smiling across the kitchen table at the hot choreographer who'd done such incredible things to my body last night, and come back to a world very different to the one I'd inhabited since making my West End debut.

Draining the last of my coffee, I said, 'Finn, I have to pick up Savannah now. I can drop you at the station on my way, if you like.'

'For sure,' Finn said, getting to his feet. 'I'll leave you the newspapers for your scrapbook.'

'Thank you,' I said, touched.

'I'm hoping you'll have dinner with me after the show tomorrow. And that you'll come back to my place and stay the night?'

'Sounds good to me . . .' My voice trailed off. I couldn't just agree to stay at his, however much I wanted to, not without first confirming that Savannah's grandparents were happy to have her yet again to stay with them. 'I'd love to have dinner with you tomorrow,' I said to Finn, 'but I'll have to check that my parents can have Savannah overnight.'

'Of course,' Finn said. He leant across the table and put his hand over mine. 'I get it, Nell. I know you can't just come and go as you please when you have children, even though I don't have kids of my own.'

I smiled weakly. Unknowingly, he'd provided the perfect introduction to a conversation where I informed him that he did have a child – but this was most certainly not the right time.

'Let's go, Finn,' I said. 'When you're a parent, one thing you cannot do is be late collecting your child from school.'

From the moment I met her at the school gates, Savannah chattered non-stop about *Speakeasy,* how she loved the dancing and the costumes, and how pretty Kitty was – although I was much prettier, apparently – continuing to voice her thoughts about the show for the entire car journey home, and after we went inside.

'I liked sitting high up so I could see the patterns the dancers made on the stage when you were all dancing together,' she said, following me along the hall to the kitchen, and sitting down at the kitchen table, while I poured her a glass of orange juice, made myself a mug of tea, and began preparing our evening meal, peeling potatoes and dicing carrots for a shepherd's pie.

'I prefer a circle seat too,' I said, 'but sometimes it's nice to sit right at the front of the stalls so that you get a close-up view of the stage, and the faces of the performers.'

Savannah put her head on one side and thought about this. 'I think it must be very hard to make up dances that everyone can see wherever they're sitting,' she said, eventually. 'The man who choreographed *Speakeasy* must be very clever.'

My pulse began to race. I was far from comfortable discussing Finn with Savannah, even if the conversation was limited to his undoubted talent as a choreographer.

'Would you fetch me another carrot, please, Savannah?' I said, in an effort to distract her.

She went to the larder, brought me a carrot, and sat down again. 'Auntie Marianne has a new boyfriend.'

'How do you know that?' I asked her.

'She was talking about him to Grandma and Grandad when she and Auntie Zelda met us in the bar in the interval, when she thought I wasn't listening,' Savannah said. 'Auntie Marianne does that a lot.'

I smothered a smile. I would have to alert my sister to her niece's precocious interest in gossip.

'Did you happen to hear his name?' I asked.

'It's Bradley,' Savannah said.

Sparing a moment to wonder what had happened to Anders – I was obviously long overdue a catch-up with my sister – I resumed cutting up vegetables.

'I think you should get a boyfriend,' Savannah said.

The knife slipped, and I almost sliced a finger.

'He would be company for you when I'm at the theatre,' Savannah said.

'I'm sorry, Savannah, you've lost me.'

'When I'm a dancer, I'll be out performing most nights. You'll need someone else to talk to.'

'Hmm,' I said. 'I'll have to see what I can do.'

After we'd eaten our shepherd's pie, and spent an hour or so cutting reviews out of newspapers and pasting them in my scrapbook, a yawning Savannah agreed to my suggestion that she have an early night. Having kissed her goodnight and switched off her light, I went back downstairs, took my phone into the living room, drew the red velvet curtains that I'd bought because they reminded me of stage curtains, sat down on the sofa, and considered how I might broach the subject of her staying overnight with my parents. Although I was a thirty-four-years-old autonomous adult, with a daughter and a mortgage, there was no way I could tell them outright that I was planning on having my own sleepover with *Speakeasy's* Choreographer – that would be excruciatingly embarrassing for all of us – but I reckoned that a vague mention of a date with a fellow company-member would be enough for them to get the picture and head off any awkward questions. Taking a deep breath, feeling like a teenager asking for permission to go to an all-night party, I rang my parents' land line. My mother answered, and for the first few minutes, I couldn't get a word in for her congratulations and compliments about *Speakeasy* in general and my dancing in particular. She put the phone on speaker, and my father added that I'd made him a very proud parent.

'I'm so glad you enjoyed it,' I said. 'And I'd love to hear more of your thoughts about it, but –'

'Before we talk more about the show,' my mother said, 'there's something I want to say to you. Don't take this the wrong way – on stage you looked great – but your father and I have both noticed how tired you've been when you've come in late at night after rehearsals. Having seen the dancing you're doing in *Speakeasy*, I can understand why.'

'I did find the rehearsals for *Speakeasy* tiring,' I said. 'And it's going to be tough for the next couple of weeks while we're still rehearsing during the day, putting in the covers and performing at night, but after that it'll get easier.'

'Maybe it will,' my mother said, 'but your father and I would like to make a suggestion. We think it would be a good idea, while you're in the show, if Savannah came and stayed with us at weekends. We could pick her up from school on Fridays – and take her to her dance classes on Saturdays – and you could come and join us for a meal on Sundays and take her home with you.'

I almost dropped my phone. My parents were offering to have Savannah to stay with them – I hadn't even had to ask.

'Nell?' my mother said. 'What do you say? It would give you a couple of days when you can sleep on a bit in the morning. In all honesty, I think you need it.'

With Savanah at her grandparents, I could be with Finn.

'It would be good for me to have days when I didn't have to get up quite so early,' I said, with only the smallest twinge of guilt. My parents' concern was for my health, not my love life, but with my busy schedule, how else was I to see Finn?

'That's settled then,' my mother said. 'Beginning tomorrow, we'll pick her up from dancing and have her stay overnight, and from next weekend we'll have her Friday to Sunday.'

'Thank you *so* much,' I said. 'And if ever something comes up and you need a weekend off you must promise to let me know.'

No sooner had I ended the call with my parents, than Marianne rang me. We had what was, for us, a very brief conversation, as Bradley was coming over, and she still needed to change the sheets on her bed – which was way too much information as far as I was concerned – but I was able to tell her that Finn and I had indeed 'hooked up,' as she put it, and that I was most definitely seeing him again. And to elicit her promise that, as it was very early days for us as a couple, and I hadn't told our parents that I was dating him, let alone Savannah, she'd keep it to herself.

There was one other phone call that I wanted to make that night, but before I did, I texted Finn: *All good for tomorrow night. Savannah staying with my parents. Nell xxxx.* Almost immediately, I got a text back: *See you at the stage door. Finn xxxx.* I allowed myself a few minutes to re-read the text several times, and think about what I might wear – not that I was going to go mad and buy a whole new outfit, but it was a long time since I'd dated anyone, and some new lingerie wouldn't go amiss. I went and made myself a coffee. And then, taking a deep breath, I phoned Zelda, who answered on the first ring.

'Can you talk?' I said to her.

'Hold on a sec,' Zelda said. I heard the shutting of a door. 'Martin is on bedtime story duty, so you have roughly ten minutes of my undivided attention.'

'Finn and I are in a relationship,' I said. 'I hope you can be happy for me.' If she couldn't, it was going to put a huge strain on our friendship.

'Are you telling me you're in a *steady* relationship with him?' Zelda said.

'I think we could be at the start of one,' I said.

'If you're getting *involved* with Finn, you have to tell him that Savannah is his,' Zelda said – which was exactly what I'd expected she'd say. 'I understand why you didn't tell him ten years ago – although I thought you should even then – and why you didn't tell him when you were rehearsing the show with him, but keeping it from him now is just plain *wrong*.'

Deep down inside me, I had to agree with her. If Finn and I were together, at some point I would have to tell him that Savannah was his daughter. I couldn't go on living a lie. But the thought of making such a momentous revelation, with no idea of how it might be received, sent icy shivers racing down my back. And it wasn't just about me and Finn. There was Savannah to consider. It had just been me and her for all her life. I couldn't just spring a father's presence on her. It would turn her little world upside down.

'I know that I have to tell Finn the truth,' I said to Zelda. 'But not yet. When the time is right.'

Zelda sighed. 'Make sure the right time is soon,' she said.

Chapter Twenty

I went through the door that led into Lily Dene's corridor and came to a halt in front of her portrait. She gazed serenely down at me.

'Good afternoon, Miss Dene,' I said. 'I hope you enjoyed watching *Speakeasy's* Opening Night. For me, that night was everything I dreamed it would be. And more.'

A male voice called, 'Hey, Nell.' I turned my head to see Matt strolling towards me.

'Good afternoon, Miss Dene,' he said. To me, he added, 'Were you having a conversation with her?'

'I was just telling her how much I like performing in the Nightingale,' I said. 'Which probably makes you think I'm very odd.'

'Not at all,' Matt said. 'I've heard she likes to know what's going on in her theatre.' He looked back at Lily. 'So, there's this girl in the ensemble that I partner in some of the dance numbers, and I really like her. I finally plucked up the courage to ask her out at the *Speakeasy* after-party. But she doesn't think of me that way. She told me she does like me – but as a friend.'

'Oh, Matt,' I said, 'I'm so sorry.'

'The show must go on, and all that,' he said. 'Isn't that right, Miss Dene?' He pushed his hair out of his eyes. 'I can't believe I'm actually talking to a painting.'

'She's a good listener,' I said. If he was heartbroken by Florence's rejection, he was doing a good job of hiding it. But then, he was a very good actor.

Leaving Lily Dene smiling benignly, we went upstairs to our respective dressing rooms.

Walking into Dressing Room Six, I was met by the glorious scent of the flowers, still blooming on every surface, and a chorus of greetings from Hettie and Nicole, while Marisa deigned to acknowledge my presence by looking up from her phone. I went and sat down in front of my make-up desk.

'Aren't you the sly one, Nell Avery?' Marisa said. 'I'm lost in admiration. I didn't know you had it in you.'

I spun my chair around so that I was facing her. Was she congratulating me on my performance on Opening Night? It seemed unlikely.

'I've no idea what you're talking about, Marisa,' I said.

'I'm talking about the after-party,' Marisa said. 'And who you left with.' Her smile made her look more than even like a hissing cat. 'I did wonder why Finn cast you. Now I know.'

For a moment, all I did was stare at her in stunned disbelief. Did she deliberately set out to be offensive? Did it give her some sort of warped pleasure? Anger flared up inside me – not that I was going to give Marisa the satisfaction of knowing how easily she'd riled me.

'Is that what you think?' I said, surprising myself at how calm I sounded. 'You really need to get a better grasp of the casting process. I'm amazed you know so little about it.' I swivelled my chair around so that my back was to her. In my mirror, I saw Marisa open her mouth and shut it again. Then she picked up her phone and began tapping away at the screen. Nicole looked from one of us to the other, before dropping her gaze and becoming absorbed in filing her nails. Hettie inclined her head towards Marisa, and rolled her eyes.

'Did you see the reviews, Nell?' she asked.

Pulling myself together – I couldn't allow Marisa to get under my skin like this – I said, 'I did. Weren't they fabulous?' just as Florence made her entrance, bounding into the dressing room with a beaming smile on her face.

'Hello, everyone,' she said, sitting down in her chair and spinning it around several times. 'Oooh – I can't wait to do the show again tonight.'

'Neither can I,' I laughed. Florence might now be a West End performer, but at that particular moment, her eyes shining, her face flushed, she looked and sounded much younger than her nineteen years.

'By the way,' Florence continued, 'about going over Kitty and Nathan's dance –'

The dance that was supposed to bring Matt and her together. Inwardly, I sighed.

'I really appreciate your offer to help me learn it,' Florence went on, 'but I was telling Leon how worried I am about the lifts and he's going to go over them with me on stage between today's performances.'

Marisa's head jerked up. 'Leon is doing what?'

'He's helping me learn *Dancing In The Moonlight*. I was talking to him about it at the after-party. It was so amazing – the party, I mean. I got to meet so many people that I've only ever seen on TV or read about in theatre programmes. I was talking to Sadie and her husband – did you know he's a casting director? – when Leigh Keaton came over and asked Sadie to introduce us.' Florence smiled guilelessly at Marisa. 'I wouldn't have known who he was if you hadn't told me. He's ever so nice and down to earth for someone so important.'

Marisa's eyes narrowed. 'What did Leigh Keaton say to you?' she demanded. 'Did he ask you to send him your CV?'

'No, he just asked me who my agent was, and when I told him I was with Evelyn Swann, he said she and him were old friends. A bit later, Evelyn came up to me and said Leigh had asked her to submit me the next time he was casting one of his shows. She was really pleased.'

'Well, I'd hate for you to be disappointed, Florence,' Marisa said, 'so I have to warn you that just because your agent submits you, it doesn't mean that Leigh Keaton is going to cast you. People say all sorts of things at parties.'

'It was still nice to be told that I show great promise as a musical theatre actress,' Florence said, tilting up her chin. 'Even if he was only being polite.'

Marisa looked as if she was about to spontaneously combust. 'I have to make a phone call,' she said, jumping to her feet. She marched out of the dressing room with Nicole scurrying after her.

Florence swivelled her chair around to face me and Hettie. 'I do know that a conversation at a party isn't enough to guarantee my next job in a musical,' she said. 'I'm not as stupid as Marisa seems to think.'

'Marisa,' I said, 'is a piece of work.'

Florence bit her lip. 'I feel awful saying this – I've tried to get along with her, really I have – but I don't think she's a very nice girl.'

'Let's be honest,' Hettie said, 'we all think Marisa is a complete bitch. There, I've said it.'

'I'm not arguing with you,' I said. 'Especially after what she said to me today.' To Florence, I added, 'Before you arrived, Marisa implied that I slept my way into *Speakeasy's* ensemble.'

Florence's eyes widened. 'What's wrong with her? Why would she say something like that?'

There was, I thought, no reason why my friends in the cast shouldn't know Finn and I were together. Backstage gossip being what it was, they'd find out soon enough. If I didn't tell them, Justin would.

'I imagine she guessed that I have more than a strictly professional relationship with *Speakeasy's* Choreographer and decided to make something of it,' I said.

Hettie smiled. 'So you and Finn are –?'

'It's early days,' I said, 'but we're seeing each other.'

'Oh my gosh, did he ask you out after watching you dance on stage on Opening Night?' Florence sighed, clasping her hands over her heart. 'That's so romantic. Just like Lily Dene and Lord Hillier.'

'Something like that,' I said, as the tannoy crackled into life summoning the cast to the stage.

We'd barely started the dance warm-up when Lucas Halliday stopped the music.

'Afternoon, Marisa and Nicole,' he said. 'Good of you to join us.' I wasn't the only dancer to turn their head to see Marisa strolling onto the stage, with Nicole half-hidden behind her.

'I'm not late, am I?' Marisa said. 'Unavoidable, I'm afraid. I had to take a call from my agent. You know how it is.'

Nicole's face flushed bright red. 'Sorry, Lucas,' she said.

Lucas frowned – possibly, like me, he doubted than anyone's agent would be calling a client on a Saturday – but he switched the music back on and resumed leading the warm-up.

'Looks like we're not the only ones Marisa has managed to annoy today,' Hettie whispered to me.

It occurred to me that while I had to put up with Marisa's obnoxious behaviour, the Dance Captain, part of whose job was to report any issues with the dancers to the Company Manager, did not.

'Will hearing that applause ever get any less wonderful?' I said to Justin, as we followed the rest of the ensemble upstairs after the evening performance.

'I don't think so,' Justin said. 'Ask me again in a couple of months.' He took the last flight of steps two at a time. Despite the protests from my leg muscles – two performances in one day were a *lot* of dancing – I did the same, but at a slower pace. By the time I reached the landing, our fellow performers had vanished into the dressing rooms.

'The gentlemen of Dressing Room Seven are intending to visit a local hostelry of good repute tonight,' Justin said. 'Would you care to join us, Miss Avery?'

'Thank you, Mr Ofabemi,' I said, 'but alas I must decline your invitation. I have other plans.'

'You have a hot date?' Justin said.

'I'm having supper with Finn,' I said. 'Does that count as a hot date?'

'That rather depends on what you do afterwards,' Justin said, with a grin.

'Could you talk a bit louder?' I said. 'There may be someone in the Nightingale who didn't hear you.'

'What does it matter if they did?' Justin said. 'Everyone loves a backstage romance.' Then his face grew serious. 'Matt said he told you about him and Florence. That's one backstage romance that isn't going to happen.'

'Poor Matt,' I said. 'Although, he seems to have left his troubles at the stage door.'

'Yeah, he's a trooper,' Justin said. 'It's a shame, though. Those two are made for each other. If they were characters in a musical, he'd have sung her a love song, she'd have joined in . . .'

'And by the time they got to the chorus, they'd have been dancing in each other's arms,' I said.

'Exactly,' Justin said. 'If only life was more like a musical.' He hummed the intro to *Dancing In The Moonlight*. 'See you on Monday, Nell.'

'See you, Justin.'

I went into Dressing Room Six, almost colliding with Marisa and Nicole in the doorway as they made their exit. Hettie was also ready to leave, exchanging 'goodnights' and 'see you next weeks' with me and Florence before she too was out the door. Sitting down in front of my mirror, I unpinned my hair, brushing it so that it tumbled around my shoulders in loose curls, and replaced my dark smoky eye-shadow and red lipstick with make-up that was a lot more subtle. I pictured Finn walking towards the Nightingale to meet me, and my heart fluttered in my chest.

Florence, sitting next to me, said, 'Dancing in the moonlight isn't as hard as I thought.'

'What?' I said. 'Oh, sorry, I was miles away. You're talking about *Dancing In The Moonlight* the show tune. Your rehearsal with Leon went well, then?'

'Er, yes, it did,' Florence said.

I took off my dressing gown and put on the floaty top and tight black jeans that, after trying on half my wardrobe, I'd decided to wear to for my date with Finn.

'Oh – I simply have to tell someone,' Florence blurted. 'After we'd gone through the lifts, Leon asked me to be his plus one for the premiere of *Road To Romance* in Leicester Square. I'll get to arrive in his limo, and walk along a red carpet!'

I gaped at her. *Dancing in the Moonlight* was supposed to bring her and *Matt* together, not her and *Leon*. I certainly hadn't seen this coming – and neither had Justin, or he would have been sure to tell me. My mind drifted back over the weeks of rehearsal. Leon had chatted with most of the cast at one time or other, but, as I recalled, he hadn't paid any particular attention to Florence. Not since our first day in the theatre, when he'd shown her the view from the stage, and I hadn't thought anything of that, other than, as an experienced actor, he was being kind to a starry-eyed newcomer.

'How exciting,' I said.

'I *know*,' Florence said, her eyes shining. 'It's in three weeks' time, and I wasn't sure if I'd be able to take a day off the show so early in the run, but I've checked with William and it's fine.' She swivelled her chair around and, in the mirror, I saw her smile dreamily at her reflection. 'I won't deny that I'm excited about going to a premiere – who wouldn't be? But that's not why I agreed to go on a date with Leon. I like *him*, the guy I danced with this afternoon, just me, him and that beautiful music, not the *star*. Leon is so nice.'

Poor Matt, I thought. With the charming, generous, ridiculously good-looking Leon – who also happened to be a genuinely nice guy – as a rival, he never stood a chance.

My thoughts drifted to another really nice guy, who by now would be standing outside the stage door, waiting for me to appear. My stomach clenched.

'See you, Monday, Florence,' I said. 'Enjoy the rest of the weekend.'

Leaving Florence taking off her stage-make-up, I headed off downstairs, calling out 'goodnight' to Lily Dene as I trotted past, wondering if she'd felt as giddy when she knew that Lord Hillier was waiting for her outside the theatre, as I felt right now.

Coming out of the stage door, I walked straight into a small crowd of people, many of them holding programmes, others carrying mobile phones, accosting members of the cast with requests for autographs and selfies. Dancers in an ensemble lacking the fan-base of stars like Leon or Samantha – both of whom were signing autograph books and chatting to their admirers – I made my way through the throng without any musical theatre aficionado asking for my signature, and spotted Finn standing a little way along the narrow street in the glow of one of the lamps on the theatre wall. For a moment I just stood there watching him, thinking how glad I was that he was back in my life, and then a wave of affection swept me towards him. He looked up and saw me, and smiled. I covered the last few metres between us at a run, and he put his hands on my waist, lifting me off my feet, and kissing me lightly on the mouth, before setting me back down on the ground.

'The show well tonight,' he said.

'You were watching?' I said.

'Yeah, I can get a house seat at any time during *Speakeasy's* run. I say the show went well, but I only saw parts of it. When you were on stage, I couldn't take my eyes off you.'

My stomach tightened deliciously. 'Do you have any notes for me?'

He shook his head. 'I wouldn't presume to do Cameron's job for him.'

A deep male voice called out: 'Hey, Finn. I didn't expect to see you here again so soon.'

Finn and I both turned our heads to see Donte, standing a short distance behind us, regarding us with an indulgent smile.

'I find I can't keep away,' Finn called back – just as the boys of Dressing Room Seven, along with a boy from Dressing Room Eight and a couple of the girls of Dressing Room Five emerged from the crowd of autograph hunters. Under their unabashedly inquisitive gaze, Finn steered me along the street, and into Shaftesbury Avenue.

'I've booked us a table at a little Italian place in Covent Garden,' he said.

'Lovely,' I said. 'Italian is my favourite type of food.'

Finn smiled. 'I remember.'

It occurred to me, as we walked hand in hand to the restaurant, that if Justin hadn't already informed the rest of the ensemble that Finn Harris and Nell Avery were an item, they would know now. The thought that we were *Speakeasy's* first backstage romance made me smile.

'Oh, Nell . . .' Finn kissed me gently, just a brush of his lips on mine. For a brief moment, he stayed lying on top of me, still inside me, his weight on his elbows, before raising himself off me, and lying down next to me on his bed, in his rented house in Camden. I rolled onto my side to face him, and he rested his head on one hand, brushing a strand of hair back from my face with the other. I smiled at him, my body languorous, a delectable ache between my thighs. He sat up, reaching for the half-drunk glass of wine on his nightstand. I also sat up, leaning back against the bedstead, and picked up my glass.

'I'm so glad I finally got to open this wine,' he said.

'So am I,' I said. 'The promise of drinking the wine that's been in your fridge all this time is the reason why I came here.'

'The only reason?'

'Well, I can't think of any other reason right now,' I said.

He laughed softly. 'How long can you stay tomorrow? I thought maybe we could visit Camden Market and get lunch from one of the food stalls – any type of street food you like, there's sure to be someone selling it.'

'Sounds good to me,' I said. 'As long as I'm on the train home by four-thirty. Savannah is expecting me to pick her up from her grandparents by six.'

Finn's face grew thoughtful. 'Have you told Savannah about me?'

'No, I haven't.' I placed my glass very carefully down on the nightstand on my side of the bed. 'I will tell her,' I said. 'I do want to tell her. But not yet. It's been just me and her for so long. When I've told her, you can meet her – if you'd like to.'

'Nell, we're in a relationship,' Finn said. 'Of course, I'd like to meet your daughter – when you're ready to introduce us.' With a smile, he flicked a switch on the wall that turned off the overhead light and lay back down on the bed, pulling up the duvet so that it covered both of us. Very soon, his regular breathing told me he'd fallen asleep.

I lay next to him, this lovely, extraordinarily talented man who had come back into my life so unexpectedly, the man who, although he didn't know it, was the father of my child, and I experienced such a powerful lightning strike of emotion that it made me dizzy.

Beside me Finn stirred, but didn't wake up. I watched him as he slept, his chest rising and falling.

The desire I'd had for him from the moment I'd walked into the first *Speakeasy* audition, all the feelings I'd had ten years ago flooding back, had been undeniable, impossible to resist. But what I felt for him now was so much more than that.

Somehow, despite all the reasons I'd told myself why I shouldn't let myself get involved with him, I'd fallen in love with Finn Harris.

Chapter Twenty-One

'Good afternoon, Miss Dene,' I said, smiling up at Lily's portrait. 'It's three weeks since *Speakeasy* opened, and we're playing to full houses every night. So many fans are coming round to the stage door that the Theatre Manager has had to put up crush barriers so that Samantha and Leon can sign autographs without being mobbed. Miss Rachel, my first dance teacher, came to see the show last week, and she loved it. I met her afterwards, and she told me that I'd made her very proud, which made me very happy. She performed here at the Nightingale many years ago, in a variety show, when she was one of the famous high-kicking Sunflower Girls – you may have seen her.'

I glanced up and down Lily Dene's corridor. No sign of any of my fellow cast members.

'But what I really wanted to tell you, Miss Dene, is that I'm in love with Finn. I haven't told him. I may be a modern, independent woman, but I'm enough of an old-fashioned girl to want him to say it first. I still haven't told him that he's Savannah's father either. I know I'll have to tell him at some point – my friend Zelda's right about that, although I wish she'd stop going on at me about it. Anyway, enough about me. The rehearsals to put the covers and the swings into the show went very smoothly. My friend Florence was great as Kitty. Not that there's much chance of her ever having to go on for a performance, what with her being the second cover.'

It occurred to me that this time last year, Florence would have been revising for her impending 'A' Levels. Now she was performing in the West End, covering a lead – and going on a date with Leon Walsh. Tonight was the premiere of *Road to Romance,* and when I'd come out of the station at just after 5.00 o'clock, Leicester Square had already been swarming with movie fans hoping to catch a glimpse of the stars of the film and other celebrities – such as Leon – as they made their way along the red carpet and into the cinema. So far as I knew, apart from Florence and Leon themselves, Hettie – who had been informed in a whispered conversation only the day before – and I were the only members of the cast who were aware of the identity of Leon's plus one for the event. Although, I doubted that would be the case for much longer, given the number of press photographers already gathered outside the cinema, and the speed with which backstage gossip spread at the Nightingale.

'So that's all the news I have for you, Miss Dene,' I said. 'It's time I went and started getting ready for the tonight's performance.'

Leaving Lily Dene presiding over her corridor, her smile unwavering as always, whatever I said to her, I went upstairs to Dressing Room Six.

Chapter Twenty-Two

'So, how did your date go last night, Florence?' I said, as she, Hettie and I sat in a café on Shaftesbury Avenue, between the Saturday matinée and evening shows, eating paninis and drinking coffee.

Naturally, I'd asked Florence more or less the same question as soon as she'd bounced into Dressing Room Six earlier that day, and she'd got as far as saying that she had *so much* to tell me, when Marisa and Nicole had made their entrance – Marisa complaining that she couldn't take the holiday she wanted because another member of the ensemble already had holiday booked and was selfishly refusing to swop. Florence had immediately fallen silent. Not that I blamed her; I'd avoided any mention of Finn in front of Marisa ever since she'd made her vile accusation. When Hettie had suggested that the three of us went out to get something to eat between the two performances both Florence and I had been quick to agree. Glancing at the other customers, I'd seen several people reading theatre programmes. The café, it seemed, was popular with audiences who'd just come out of an afternoon show.

Now, Florence said, 'It was awesome – there's no other word for it. The way the crowds were screaming when Leon and I walked along the red carpet – they were even louder than our audiences – I felt like I was a star myself, even although I knew that really it was the celebrities they were shouting for, and that the photographers with their flashing cameras were trying to get a shot of Leon, not me. Once we were inside the cinema, we were escorted to our seats and given a programme.'

'A bit different from my local multiplex,' Hettie said. 'I'm guessing you didn't get given popcorn?'

'Just as well, as I was way too excited to have eaten anything,' Florence laughed. 'Not long after Leon and I were in our seats, the stars of the film arrived. They and the director made speeches about how pleased they were to have worked together. And then we watched the movie.'

'Was it any good?' Hettie asked.

'Oh, yes,' Florence said. 'It was a very funny rom com.'

'Never mind the movie,' I said. 'What we really want to know, is how did it go with Leon?'

'It went just fine,' Florence said. 'Better than fine.'

'This sounds interesting,' Hettie said. 'Did he ask you for another date?'

'Not yet, but I'm sure he's going to,' Florence said.

'Aw,' Hettie said. 'I'm happy for you, Florence.' She checked her watch, and then hastily swallowed her last piece of panini and drained her coffee. 'I have to go – I need to ask Sebastian about cast-discount tickets for Monday's performance. I'll see you two back at the theatre.' She hurried out of the café.

Florence said, 'I had such an amazing time last night. When me and Leon left the film's after-party, it was already getting light. We were both starving, so he had his driver take us to this all-night café that he – Leon – used to go to when he was a drama student, and we had breakfast together.' She sighed happily. 'Then he took me home. I thought he'd just drop me off, but he got out of the limo and walked me up to the front door and – and then he asked me if he could kiss me. I said *yes*, of course.' A faint blush appeared on her face. 'He kissed me and told me I was beautiful – and then he waited until I was inside the house before he went back to the car.'

I reminded myself that however young Florence seemed to me, she was in fact nineteen – plenty old enough to kiss a guy, if she wanted to. All the same, I was very thankful that I had a good few years before Savannah would be of an age to go around kissing movie stars – even well-behaved ones like Leon, who saw a girl home safely after a date.

Florence leant forward. 'I *really* like him,' she said. 'I-I've never felt this way about a guy before.' Her smile lit up her whole face. I smiled back at her.

'Excuse me,' a female voice said. 'Are you girls in the cast of in *Speakeasy?*'

I turned my head to see two thirty-something women standing by our table. They were both holding *Speakeasy* programmes.

'Yes, we are,' I said.

'My friend Gillian and I have just watched the show,' one of the women said, somewhat breathlessly. 'We were reading our programmes, and we saw your photos –' She held open her programme at the page with the cast's headshots. 'I said to Gillian, those girls are in the show.'

'You did, Meera,' Gillian said, adding, 'I loved, loved, loved *Speakeasy*. I don't think I've ever seen such a spectacular musical. And the dancing was amazing.'

'Thank you,' I said, her words giving me a warm glow. 'I'm so glad you enjoyed it.'

'Thank you so much,' Florence said.

'Would you mind signing our programmes?' Meera asked. 'I know it's a bit cheeky to ask you when you're off duty, as it were, but it would really make our day.'

Never before, in all my years of performing, had anyone asked for my autograph. Realising that my mouth had fallen open, I hurriedly shut it, and held out my hand for Meera's programme.

'It would be my very great pleasure,' I said. Meera produced a pen, I signed her and Gillian's programmes, and Florence did the same.

'Ooh, this is so exciting,' Gillian said. 'Well, we mustn't take up any more of your time.'

'Thank you again,' Meera said.

'You're very welcome,' I said.

Chorusing their thanks one more time, Meera and Gillian stowed their programmes in their handbags, and, with broad smiles on their faces, left the café.

'Oh, my goodness,' I said. 'When I got into *Speakeasy*, I never thought I'd be asked for my autograph. But I must admit that I rather enjoyed it.'

'So did I,' Florence said. 'Leon told me that he's always happy to sign autographs. He feels he owes it to his fans to 'stage door,' even when he's tired after doing the show and would rather be straight off home. He is such a nice guy – Oh, look at the time! We need to get back to the Nightingale or we'll miss the half.'

It occurred to me, as we headed back to the theatre, that being nice did not necessarily preclude a guy from taking a girl out, making her feel really special, and then *not* asking her for another date, but I kept my thoughts to myself.

Chapter Twenty-Three

I awoke with a start to find myself lying spooned against Finn, his arm draped over my waist.

'What was that noise?' he said, sitting up.

'I don't know,' I said. 'I was asleep.'

'It sounded like your front door,' Finn said. 'I think there's someone else in your house.'

'What?' I, too, sat up. My bedroom door was shut, but I heard the sound of footsteps running upstairs.

My mother's voice came to me, faintly: 'Don't go in your Mum's room, Savannah, I think she's still asleep.'

There was a silence that lasted at least two minutes, during which time I held my breath clutching the duvet around me, and then I heard more footsteps, this time retreating down the stairs. The clock on my bedside table showed me that it was gone midday.

'Oh, no,' I said, 'I forgot to set my alarm again last night.' The one Sunday my parents were going out and couldn't hang on to Savannah until the evening – last night I'd told Finn he had to be gone by 10.00 a.m. 'We have to put our clothes on, Finn. Savannah may come back.' Leaping out of bed, I yanked open a couple of drawers, pulled out underwear and a T-shirt, and started to get dressed. Finn yawned and swung his legs over the side of the mattress. 'Here –' I picked his boxers and jeans up off the floor and threw them to him. My heart began to race. 'What are we going to do? Savannah doesn't know anything about you. She can't find you here in my bedroom.'

'Shall I hide in the wardrobe?' Finn said, with a grin. 'Or would you rather I made my escape by shinning down a drainpipe?'

'Don't joke, Finn. This isn't funny.' I struggled into the tight jeans I'd worn the previous evening.

'Alternatively,' Finn said, buttoning his shirt, 'I could come downstairs with you and you could introduce me to Savannah and your mother – I assume that was your mother I heard?'

This threw me. I hadn't made any decision about exactly when, how or where I'd introduce Finn to Savannah, but I'd had it in my head that I'd have told him that she was his before they came face to face.

'I think it's about time I met my girlfriend's daughter,' he said. 'Unless you think it's still too soon.'

I swallowed uneasily. It was so important that I got this right. Perhaps, after all, it was better for Finn to meet my daughter – his daughter – and for them to get to know each other before I revealed the truth about her parentage, rather than afterwards. I certainly wasn't about to leave him skulking in my bedroom while I went downstairs. I'd never had any inclination to star in a farce.

'No, I don't think it's too soon,' I said, surprised at how steady my voice sounded. 'I'd love you to meet her.'

'OK, then, let's do this,' Finn said.

With Finn close on my heels, I walked out of my bedroom and down the stairs. In the hallway I stopped and listened. Savannah's laughter was coming from the living room.

'Ready?' I said to Finn.

He ran his hand through his hair. 'Suddenly, I feel like I'm about to go into an audition.'

You are, I thought. *Although you don't know it, this could be the most important audition of your life.* 'I'll count us in,' I said, reaching for the door handle. 'Five, six seven, eight . . .' I opened the door, and we went into the room.

My mother was sitting in an armchair, scrolling through her phone. Savannah was sitting cross-legged on the floor, watching the TV. Seeing me hovering just inside the doorway, she jumped up and ran a few steps towards me, coming to a halt when she realised that I was not alone.

'Ah, there you are, Nell,' my mother said. 'I was just saying to Savannah that we'd give you another ten minutes and then we'd have to wake you up –' She broke off as she, too, caught sight of Finn. Her eyes widened and her mouth formed an 'O.' Locating the remote on the dining table, I switched off the TV.

'Morning,' I said. 'Er, this is Finn. Finn, this is my daughter Savannah, and my mother, Judith.'

'Good to meet you, Judith,' Finn said. 'Hey, Savannah.'

Recovering herself, my mother managed a smile. 'Hello, Finn. Lovely to meet you, too.'

I glanced at Savannah, who was regarding Finn with an expression that could only be described as suspicious. My stomach churned.

'Are you in *Speakeasy*?' she asked.

If Finn was surprised by the question, he managed not to show it. 'I'm not in the cast,' he said. 'I'm the Choreographer.'

Savannah continued to stare at him. 'Your choreography is very clever,' she said, eventually.

'Why, thank you, Savannah,' Finn said. 'It's always good to hear that someone likes my work. Especially when they're a dancer.' Savannah smiled. I let out a breath I hadn't realised I was holding.

'Have a seat, Finn,' I said, giving him a gentle push in the direction of the sofa. He sat down, leaning back against the cushions and resting his ankle on his opposite knee. I thought, *now what?* 'Would anyone like a coffee?' I said, before the silence that had fallen on the room could grow awkward.

'Not for me,' my mother said. 'I'd love to stay and chat, but your father and I are expected at your Aunt Carol's.' She smiled again at Finn. 'Sorry I have to rush off. I'm so pleased to have met you.'

'Likewise,' Finn said, half-rising from the sofa.

'No need to get up,' my mother said, waving him back to a sitting position. 'Nell – I'll let myself out. See you tomorrow.'

'See you, Mum,' I said.

With a spring in her step – probably brought on by the discovery that her chronically single elder daughter had a man in life – my mother made her exit.

'How do you know I'm a dancer?' Savannah asked Finn.

'Your Mum told me.'

Savannah's eyes went from Finn to me and back to Finn again. 'Are you my Mum's boyfriend?'

'Savannah!' My face grew hot, but Finn appeared unperturbed.

'Yes, I am,' he said.

Savannah considered this for a moment, and then she said, 'I'm not really a dancer. I'm only learning.'

'You're not a *professional* dancer,' Finn said, coping admirably with Savannah's abrupt changes of subject. 'But if you dance, I'd say that makes you a dancer.' Savannah beamed at him.

'Would you like to see the solo I'm doing in my dancing school show?' she said.

'I most certainly would,' Finn said. I flashed him a grateful smile. I was happy to watch Savannah dance anytime, but I'd have forgiven Finn if he viewed the prospect of seeing a nine-year-old dancing around her living room with less enthusiasm. Especially as he hadn't had any breakfast.

'I'll go and put on my ballet shoes,' Savannah said. She trotted out of the room and bounded upstairs. I found my phone, checked that Miss Rachel had emailed me Savannah's music – as she usually did when Savannah had a solo, so I could rehearse her at home – and sat down on the sofa next to Finn.

'How am I doing?' he said. 'I hope you don't mind my telling Savannah that I'm your boyfriend.'

'No, I don't mind.' It was, I realised, a relief to have my relationship status out in the open, although I suspected Savannah might have more questions about it later. 'And you're doing fine. Saying you'd like to see her dance was a very good move on your part.' I smiled. 'So far, this audition is going really well. You've made it past the first cut and you're through to the next round.' Finn visibly relaxed, which made me relax as well. 'After we've seen Savannah's solo, how about I make us some lunch?' I said. 'And, if you like, you could spend the rest of the day with us.' Now that he'd met her, Finn might as well start to get to know her.

'Sounds good to me,' Finn said.

Savannah, who took Miss Rachel's maxim that dancers should always wear the correct shoes and clothes for dancing very seriously, came back into the room wearing her ballet shoes, and a leotard and tights.

'I start on stage,' she said, taking up a position in the middle of the carpet.

Finn smiled. I started the music, and a lively tune filled the living room. Savannah began her solo – not a dance that I'd seen her perform before. I looked from her to Finn, and saw him lean forward, his brows drawing together in concentration, as his gaze followed her around the room. I looked back at her, just as she leapt from one side of the carpet to the other, ending her dance with a series of turns which brought her to the front of her performance space. She wobbled slightly on the last turn, but corrected herself, smiling at her audience, as the music ended with a crash of cymbals. *That's my girl*, I thought, as she performed an elaborate curtsey, the full *reverence* that Miss Rachel always expected from her students at the end of a ballet class or performance, done out of respect for teacher and pianist, and for the art of dance. Finn clapped, and I hurriedly joined in.

'Well done, Savannah,' I said. 'Good job.'

'I wobbled when I came out of the turn,' Savannah said.

'That doesn't matter,' Finn said. 'You made an excellent recovery. It's important that you can do that, because if something goes wrong on stage, you have to cover it up so the audience don't notice. You danced very well.'

Savannah gave him a shy smile. 'Do you have any notes for me?'

'Savannah!' I exclaimed. 'You should be saying 'thank you' to Finn for telling you that you danced well, not asking him for notes.'

'It's fine,' Finn said, amused. 'Savannah, the reason you wobbled was because your weight wasn't quite in the right place. Do the turns again, but keep your weight forward.'

Savannah did as he said, executing the turns perfectly – no mean feat as our living room carpet was hardly the ideal surface to dance on.

'Well done,' Finn said. 'Would you do something for me? Would you stand in third position? And developé your leg to second?'

That was a way of testing a dancer's turnout, strength, and flexibility. I shot Finn a quizzical look, but his attention was all on Savannah.

She skipped to the middle of the room, stood in third position, effortlessly raising her knee and then unfolding her leg so that her foot was above her head.

Finn let her stay there for half a minute, and then he said, 'And close.' Savannah lowered her foot to the floor. He said, 'Do you know why I asked you to do that?' She shook her head. 'Well,' Finn went on, 'it shows me that you could become a very good dancer. If you want to, of course. And if you work very hard.'

'I am going to be a dancer,' Savannah said. 'But not a ballerina. I love ballet, but I want to be in musicals so I can do tap and jazz as well. And singing and acting.'

'Oh, I think musicals are much more fun,' Finn said.

My stomach rumbled, reminding me that Finn and I hadn't eaten since last night.

'Right, enough dancing for now,' I said. 'It's time I made us some lunch. Are you hungry, Savannah?'

'I'm starving,' Savannah said.

'I'm not surprised after all that dancing,' Finn laughed.

'Go and put your T-shirt and leggings back on, Savannah,' I said.

'OK.' She skipped out of the room.

Finn stared after her. 'She's incredible,' he said. He turned his head towards me. 'But I'm sure you don't need me to tell you that.'

'I do think she's talented,' I said. 'Not that I'm biased.'

'You must be so proud of her.'

My heart swelled. He would be proud, too, if he knew she was his. All at once, I was overwhelmed with a longing to tell him that Savannah was his daughter – but I resisted it. When I told him, it had to be when we were alone, not when Savannah was around. That was only common sense.

Aloud, I said, 'I am proud of her, and I'd love it if she chooses dance as a career. But, like you said, only if she wants to. I'm not a pushy Stage Mother.'

'You're an amazing mother,' Finn said. 'As well as being an extremely beautiful woman.' He leant towards me, as if to kiss me – only to jump away from me, as Savannah's footsteps thumped down the stairs.

'To be continued another time,' he said, with a smile that promised a lot more than a kiss.

I threw together a quick lunch of pasta with pesto sauce – not my most impressive dish, but we were all too hungry to wait for a more elaborate meal – which we ate around the dining table. Savannah, apparently unfazed by our new dining companion, chattered away about her dancing school show – fortuitously, it was due to take place on a Sunday, so there would be no problem in my watching it – and listened fascinated to the stories Finn told her about the shows he'd choreographed in Germany. He even made her giggle with a story about a show where everything that could go wrong did. *So far, so good*, I thought.

After lunch, we went for a walk by the nearby canal, which passed through our leafy neighbourhood in North London on its way to the Midlands, Finn and I hand in hand – he'd checked with me in an undertone if it was OK for him to hold my hand in front of Savannah, which I thought was sweet of him – Savannah dancing ahead of us along the towpath. It was a bright sunny day, and there were a lot of people about, cyclists, fishermen, dog-walkers, couples enjoying a romantic stroll and admiring the brightly-painted house-boats, and families throwing bread to the ducks, moorhens and swans. It occurred to me, with a *frisson* of delight, that to an outsider, Finn, Savannah and I must look like a family, the three of us out for a walk on a warm spring afternoon. I wasn't under any illusion that this was what our life would have been like if I'd made a different decision ten years ago, but it was what our life could be now. I stole a glance at Finn's handsome profile, noticing the way his eyes creased at the corners as he smiled at Savannah, and it came to me that what I wanted more than anything was for me, Finn and our daughter to have a future together.

And, for the first time, I allowed myself to believe that the man I loved might want it too.

Chapter Twenty-Four

'So I didn't need to panic after all,' I said to Zelda on the phone the next day, after Finn had left, and I was sitting on my still unmade bed, Savannah safely out of earshot in the garden. 'Finn's first meeting with Savannah couldn't have gone any better, and the three of us had a lovely afternoon together. It turns out that Finn is great with children – or, at least, children who dance. I was a bit apprehensive as to how Savannah might react to finding him still in our house this morning, but she didn't even seem surprised, and with it being half-term, we were able to have breakfast together. After he went home, Savannah told me that she likes him, and that she doesn't mind that he doesn't do magic tricks like her friend Amy's dad, because he knows about dancing and that's better.' I couldn't help smiling at the thought of how earnestly Savannah had assured me that Finn was a good boyfriend for me because we had such a lot in common – presumably she had gained her opinion of the qualities necessary for a successful relationship from another overheard conversation between her Grandma and her Auntie Marianne.

'It's great that Finn and Savannah got along,' Zelda said, 'but – well, you know what I'm going to say.'

So don't say it, I thought, irritated. The big advantage in talking to Lily Dene was that she kept her opinions to herself.

'The longer you leave it, the harder it's going to be to tell Finn the truth,' Zelda said. 'Not to mention confusing for Savannah.' She paused, as if allowing time for her words to sink in, and then went on, 'So, what are you and Savannah up to this half-term? We're off to Cornwall this afternoon, once Martin gets back from work.'

'Ooh, Cornwall,' I said, relieved to switch to a non-contentious subject. 'How lovely. I haven't decided what Savannah and I are going to do yet.' As I spoke, I was hit by a veritable torrent of parental guilt. I might have slightly more spare time now that I wasn't rehearsing during the day, but I was still leaving for the theatre by five o'clock in the afternoon, doing a demanding show, and not getting home until after midnight. Planning exciting half-term activities hadn't been as high on my agenda as catching up on sleep. 'I'm thinking we'll take it easy this half-term,' I said. My gaze fell on my scrapbook, which was on my dressing table. 'Maybe we'll do some crafting. Savannah enjoys that sort of thing.'

We chatted a while longer, and then Zelda went off to finish her holiday packing. I got up off the bed, plumping up the pillows, still indented from where Finn had lain his head next to mine, and straightening the duvet. Before embarking on the rest of my household chores, I went and stood by the window, looking down at the garden, smiling at the sight of the daffodils that I'd planted last autumn dancing in the breeze – and at the sight of Savannah, absorbed in playing with her skipping rope. My thoughts drifted back to Finn. Seeing him getting along so well with Savannah had made my heart sing. But what would his reaction be if I told him that my talented little dancer was his daughter? Would he be pleased or would he be so shocked at my deception that he'd be straight out the door? And would Savannah accept Finn as a father as easily as she appeared to have accepted him as my boyfriend? *No*, I thought, *I'm not saying anything to either of them yet. I'll give them more time to get to know each other first.*

Having tackled my most pressing household chores, I made lunch for me and Savannah. Now that she'd had a whole morning to think about it, I thought that she might come up with all sorts of questions about Finn, but apart from saying that she wondered if he'd like to watch her dancing school show – having no idea of Finn's views on children's dance shows, I told her we'd ask him nearer the time – she didn't mention him, and I was again reassured that she'd taken the change in my relationship status in her stride.

Savannah was back outside in the garden and I was in the kitchen, filling my water-bottle to take to the theatre, when my phone rang. Somewhat to my surprise, as my parents were due at my house to look after their granddaughter, the caller ID showed me it was my mother. I hit the answer icon.

'Hi, Mum –' I began.

'Nell, listen,' my mother interrupted, her voice high and urgent. 'Your father and I were driving back from your Aunt Carol's, when the car started making the most horrendous noise. We made it to the nearest motorway services, but then we saw smoke coming out from under the bonnet, so your father had to turn off the engine. We called our breakdown people straight away, but we're still waiting for them, and now they say they can't be here for another two hours – we're an hour away from you – and we can't get back in time to look after Savannah.'

In less than an hour, I had to be on a train – and my parents were stranded somewhere on the M1. I told myself very firmly to stay calm.

'Please don't worry about Savannah, Mum,' I said. 'I'll sort something out.'

'I'm so sorry to let you down. I thought we'd left Carol's in plenty of time.'

'It's not your fault. These things happen. Let's hope the breakdown people can fix the car.'

'Oh, no, my phone's about to –' my mother wailed, as the call cut out.

I looked at my watch, and my heart plummeted. I had forty-five minutes to arrange child care for my daughter. Ordinarily, I'd have asked Zelda to have Savannah, but even if they hadn't already left, I could hardly expect her to postpone her family's journey to Cornwall. Instead, I tried Amy's mother, Donna – whose her phone went straight to voicemail – followed by some other 'school mums,' but no-one picked up. Surely everyone I knew hadn't gone off on a half-term holiday? Checking the time again, I saw that

I now only had thirty minutes before I had to leave the house. I always hesitated to call anyone at their workplace, but decided this was enough of an emergency to phone Marianne, only to be informed by her assistant that she was away at a conference.

I thought, *now what*? Briefly, I toyed with the idea of taking Savannah with me to the Nightingale, but I was fairly sure that leaving my nine-year-old alone in a dressing room while I danced on stage would contravene any number of theatrical regulations. With reluctance, I decided my only option was to phone William and explain that I couldn't perform tonight because my child care arrangements had fallen apart. He wouldn't be pleased, but there wasn't anything I could do about that.

And then it struck me that there was someone else I could ask to look after Savannah that evening: Finn. I called him, relief flooding through me when he answered his phone on the first ring.

'I have a huge favour to ask you,' I said to him. I explained about my parents' car, and the lack of available child-sitters. 'Is there any way you could step in and keep an eye on Savannah tonight? No worries if you have other plans.'

'I'd be delighted,' Finn said, immediately. 'No problem at all.'

'Oh, thank you *so* much.' Crisis averted, I found I was shaking. Pulling myself together, I said, 'Can I drop her at your place on my way to the theatre and pick her up on my way home?'

'You'll be pushed to get to the Nightingale on time if you come to me first,' Finn said. 'Why don't you and Savannah go straight to the theatre, and I'll meet you at the stage door? I'll get her and me tickets for tonight's show. Do you think she'd like to sit in the Royal Box, if it's available?'

'Oh, Finn, she'd love that,' I said. 'Thank you.'

'My pleasure,' Finn said. 'I'll be interested to hear her notes on your performance.'

I laughed. 'I'd better go,' I said, 'or I'll make myself late – not a good example for a child who wants to be a dancer.'

'See you soon,' Finn said, and ended the call.

I flew out into the garden and told Savannah that she had an unexpected half-term treat of a trip to the theatre. Her smile when I added that it was Finn who would be taking her made me feel as if I was dancing.

'There's Finn,' Savannah said, as we turned into the narrow street alongside the Nightingale. She ran along the pavement to meet him, with me walking quickly after her, catching up with her at the stage door. Finn greeted me with a kiss on the side of my face – usually, he'd have planted a kiss on my mouth, and I appreciated his restraint in front of Savannah.

'The tickets are waiting for us at the box office,' he said to me, 'but before we collect them, I thought Savannah and I might watch the cast warm-up. Would you like that, Savannah?'

'Ooh, yes, please,' Savannah said.

The three of us went inside the theatre. I signed in, as did Finn, adding his and Savannah's name to the stage doorman's list, and showing her where to sign her name, which she did very carefully in her large, round hand-writing. We went through the door that led back stage and into Lily Dene's corridor, coming to a halt in front of her portrait.

'Good afternoon, Miss Dene,' I said. To Savannah, I added, 'Do you remember what I told you about Miss Lily Dene?'

Savannah nodded solemnly. 'Can I talk to her?'

'Of course.' Standing behind Savannah with my hands on her shoulders, I said, 'Miss Dene, this is my daughter, Savannah.'

'Hello Miss Dene,' Savannah said. 'I'm watching *Speakeasy* tonight with Finn. He's my Mum's boyfriend.' She thought for a moment. 'I'm a dancer and when I'm grown up I'd like to dance on your stage, please.'

'Now that,' Finn said, 'is exactly what Miss Dene likes to hear.' He smiled at me over Savannah's head. 'Come on, Savannah, let's go and find a good place to sit to watch the warm-up.'

'I'll see you in a bit, Savanah,' I said.

I watched the pair of them as they headed off towards the auditorium, amused to see Finn adjust his long stride so that Savannah didn't have to run to keep up with him. Then, having checked the time and realised it was later than I'd thought, I walked quickly up the stairs to the fifth floor.

In Dressing Room Six, I found Florence, Hettie and Nicole.

'I thought you might not be coming in today,' Hettie said. 'You're usually the first to get here.'

'I have cut it a bit fine,' I said. 'I had to ring around at the last minute to find a child-sitter. Luckily, Finn was available to play the role at short notice. He and Savannah are watching tonight's show.'

'Marisa's off today,' Nicole said. 'She asked me to tell everyone she's not well.'

'I'm sorry to hear that,' I said, hoping I sounded more sincere than I felt. 'She must be so disappointed to miss a performance.'

'I doubt it,' Nicole said.

'How so?' Hettie asked.

Nicole's face blanched. 'I-I shouldn't have said that,' she stuttered. Then, taking a deep breath, she added, 'Oh, I can't keep it to myself, I just can't. The truth is, Marisa isn't ill. She's been seeing this guy – he's very well-connected – and he wanted to meet up with her tonight, but it was too short notice for her to get holiday, so she rang in sick.'

'But that's so unprofessional,' Florence said.

'Please don't tell anyone,' Nicole said. 'If word gets around – if William finds out – Marisa will know it could only have come from me.'

'I'm sure none of us would go telling tales to the Company Manager,' I said. Florence and Hettie murmured their agreement.

'Thank you,' Nicole said. 'What makes it worse is that he's married, but Marisa doesn't care.'

The appalled silence that followed Nicole's revelation was broken by the tannoy bursting into crackling life, summoning *Speakeasy's* cast to the stage. Nicole got to her feet.

'Marisa made a bad choice today,' she said, and left the dressing room.

'Am I imagining it,' Hettie said, 'or is Nicole not best pleased with her best friend Marisa right now?'

I shrugged. 'That's one friendship I'll never understand.'

The three of us went out of the dressing room, joining the rest of the ensemble trooping down the stairs and along the labyrinthine corridors that led to wings. Walking out onto the stage, I immediately spotted Finn and Savannah sitting in the third row of the stalls. I waved to them, before positioning myself at the front of the assembled cast, where Savannah could easily see me, aware that their presence was the cause of a stir of curiosity and whispers among my fellow performers.

After half a minute or so, Gwen Marsh, accompanied by Jonathan Gower, came onto the stage, and I saw Finn pointing at them and talking to Savannah – I guessed he was explaining to her they were the Resident Director, and MD. Gwen gave out a couple of notes, before informing the cast that Donte Travis was on holiday, so the part of Spenser Henderson IV, would, today, be played by his understudy, and that Marisa Cutler was off sick, and her track would be danced by a swing. Once Gwen had left the stage, Jonathan took us a through the vocal warm-up, before he, too, made his exit, and Lucas stepped out of the ranks to lead the dance warm-up.

'OK, guys, have a good one,' he said, once he was satisfied that none of us were going to pull a muscle on his watch. I waved to Savannah, and was about to follow my fellow the cast members into the wings, when Finn got to his feet and indicated that I should stay where I was.

'Hold on a sec, Nell,' he called. Ushering Savannah to the front of the stalls, he took her hand and led her up the treads and onto the stage.

'*Oooh*,' Savannah said, gazing out at the auditorium. 'It looks so big from here.'

'Your first time on a West End stage, Savannah,' Finn said. 'I think we need a photo for your Mum's scrapbook, don't you?' He took his phone out of the pocket of his jeans. 'How about you with your Mum?' A huge smile on her face, Savannah stood next to me, and Finn took several photographs.

Florence and Hettie, who had been watching the photography session from the side of the stage, now came over to us.

'Hi, Savannah,' Hettie said. 'I'm Hettie. I'm a friend of your Mum's.'

'And I'm Florence,' Florence added.

'You're dancers,' Savannah said, her eyes shining. 'I saw you on Opening Night.'

'Would you like a photo of you with the dancers, Savannah?' Finn asked.

'Yes please,' she said.

Another female voice said, 'Please may I be in the photo too?'

I spun around to see a smiling Samantha Ellis – to my surprise, as I thought she'd already returned to her dressing room.

'Of course,' I said. To Savannah, I added, 'This is Samantha.'

'Kitty!' Savannah said, hopping from foot to foot with excitement. 'I want to star in a musical like you, when I'm grown up.'

'Well, once you're old enough to leave school, you should go to performing arts college,' Samantha said. 'That's what your Mum told me to do if I wanted to work in musical theatre – and she was right.' We exchanged smiles.

'I know I'm not your choreographer any more,' Finn said, 'but can I ask you to group yourselves around Savannah and Nell so I can get a good shot of all of you?'

The dancers arranged themselves on either side of me and Savannah, and Finn took a photo.

'Perfect,' he said.

'Now let me take one of you with Nell and Savannah,' Samantha said, holding out her hand for Finn's phone. He handed it to her, and positioned himself next to me, his arm around my waist, with Savannah in front of us.

'Five, six, seven, eight – and smile,' Samantha said. 'That was great.' She passed Finn back his phone.

'And now, Savannah,' he said, 'we'd better let these ladies go and get ready for tonight's show.'

'Oh, yes, my Mum says you mustn't ever be late for a performance,' Savannah said.

'Quite right,' Hettie said.

'Enjoy the show, Savannah,' I said, a sentiment echoed by my friends.

Finn ushered Savannah downstage right, once again taking her hand to steady her as they walked down the treads, and they went out of the auditorium through the exit at the back of the stalls. Seeing him so caring of her made my heart brim – if I wasn't in love with him already, I'd have fallen in love with him right there and then.

'Savannah is so cute,' Florence said.

'She looks so like you, Nell,' Hettie said.

'And she wants to be a dancer like you,' Samantha said. 'It must be in her genes. It's interesting how a talent for dancing or acting is so often passed down the generations from parent to child.'

'Mmm,' I said, my smile a little weak.

At that moment – before Samantha could make any further speculations about the genetic basis of Savannah's dancing talent – the main tabs swished shut, and Jerome, the Stage Manager, walked out of the wings and onto the stage.

'What are you lot still doing here?' he said.

'We've been passing down our love of musical theatre to the younger generation,' Samantha said.

'Very admirable, I'm sure,' Jerome said, 'but if you stay here much longer, you won't have time to get back upstairs before you have to come down again.'

We exited the stage at a run.

Chapter Twenty-Five

I came out of the Nightingale, and, making my way past a crowd of autograph-hunters, spotted Finn and Savannah standing by a lamp post on the opposite side of the street. I ran over to them, hugged Savannah, and without thinking, hugged Finn and kissed him on his mouth. Fortunately, Savannah appeared unperturbed by my public display of affection for my boyfriend.

'I saw you waving at me when you took your bow,' she said. 'Did you see me and Finn wave back?'

'I did,' I said. 'Did you like watching *Speakeasy* from the Royal Box?'

'It was brilliant,' she said. 'I liked being so close to the stage. And I liked seeing a different actor play the villain, but he wasn't as good at acting as the man I saw last time.'

'I agree with you,' Finn said, with a grin. 'Few actors can twirl a moustache like Donte Travis.' Savannah giggled, and then yawned, reminding me how late it was for her to be out.

'I should get Savannah home,' I said to Finn. He nodded, his eyes gleaming in the lamplight. I felt a quivering in my stomach. Although I was tired, I didn't want this evening to end just yet. 'Are you coming with us?' I asked.

'Oh, yes,' Finn said.

For most of the way home, while we were on the train, Savannah talked non-stop about how much she'd liked watching *Speakeasy* again, and going up on the stage and meeting Samantha and the dancers – and the sweets and ice cream Finn had bought her in the interval – but by the time we'd walked the short distance from the station to our house, she was yawning again, and made no objections to going straight up to bed as soon as we were inside. Finn and I went into the living room. I crossed to the windows to draw the curtains, and he came and stood behind me, brushing aside my hair so that he could kiss my neck, sending a delicious tingling all the way down my back. I turned around, and tilted up my face towards him. He leant in for a kiss, putting arms around me and holding me close – which was just as well for, by the time we broke apart, my knees were feeling distinctly weak. I sank down on the sofa and he sat beside me.

'Thank you so much for tonight,' I said. 'Savannah had such a good time.'

'So did I,' Finn said. 'She's a great kid. I was surprised at some of the things she said about my choreography.'

'Oh, dear,' I said.

Finn chuckled. 'No, it was all good. She noticed that some dance tracks are more challenging than others – some of the dancers *do harder steps* was how she put it. I wouldn't have expected a child to pick up on things like that. I sent the photos to your phone, by the way. And

Savannah told me that she wants you to get her a phone for her birthday. Just so you know.'

I groaned. 'I was hoping she'd forgotten about that. I think nine is way too young for her to have her own phone.'

'When is her birthday?' Finn asked.

'20th June.'

'Ah – you've not got long to persuade her that she'd prefer something else.'

'Quite,' I said, adding, 'I must go up and check she's in bed, and say goodnight. Would you like to help yourself to a glass of wine from that bottle of red on the dining table – and pour one for me?'

'For sure.'

Leaving Finn to perform the role of *sommelier*, I went upstairs to Savannah, and wasn't too surprised to find that she was already asleep. I kissed her softly on her forehead, crept out of her bedroom, and headed back downstairs to the living room.

Finn was still sitting on the sofa, staring into space, the wine unpoured.

'Did you change your mind about a drink?' I said.

He started as though unaware that I'd come back into the room. 'No, I – Nell, there's something I have to say to you. Come and sit down.'

'OK.' What could be so important that he had to ask me to sit down before he said it? Was he about to tell me that he loved me? Trying to ignore the fluttering in my unruly stomach, I sat down next to him, and twisted around so that I was facing him. 'What is it?' I said, willing him to say the three words that would tell me felt the same way about me as I felt about him.

'You mentioned that Savannah's birthday is in June.'

'Er, yes, that's right,' I said, bemused. As a declaration of love, this was not a promising start.

'And she's turning ten,' he said, a statement not a question. 'Ten years ago, in the September, I went to Berlin. And Savannah was born the following June.'

'What of it?' My mouth went dry.

'Is she mine?' His eyes bored into me.

'She – I –' Now, the blood was pounding in my head.

'I know how to count, Nell. Is Savannah my child?'

'Yes,' I said, my voice scarcely above a whisper. 'She's yours.'

All Finn did was stare at me, his mouth slightly open, as though he'd lost the power of speech.

'Finn,' I said. 'Please say something.' My whole body was trembling.

'Why didn't you tell me you were pregnant?'

'I didn't know until after you'd left for Germany,' I said.

'You couldn't have picked up a phone?'

'Why would I do that? You and me were over.'

'It didn't occur to you that I might want to know I had a child?' Finn sounded incredulous.

'Would you, though?' I said. 'Ten years ago, you made it very clear to me that you didn't do relationships, that you wouldn't be tied down. Strictly no strings, you said. If I had told you about Savannah, you wouldn't have wanted anything to do with her.' My voice sounded more strident than I'd intended.

Finn rose to his feet and paced about the room. 'Maybe you're right, but you denied me the choice.' He came to a halt in front of me. 'Who else knows that Savannah is my child?'

'No-one except for Zelda,' I said. 'Other friends were too polite to ask me about her father – back then, if you remember, hardly anyone knew we were sleeping together – and I told my family that she was the result of a drunken encounter with a stranger in a club.'

'*Seriously*?' Finn said. 'Why would you do that?'

'At the time, it was the only thing I could think of to stop my parents putting pressure on me to get in touch with my baby's father.'

'And you've kept up this fiction for *ten years*?' Finn said, shaking his head.

'It wasn't so hard,' I said. 'Not with you being hundreds of miles away, and never coming back to England.'

'I could have come back at any time.'

'But you didn't,' I pointed out, not unreasonably it seemed to me. Finn pulled out a dining chair and sat astride it, facing me, resting his arms on the back.

'I can't get my head around this,' he said. 'We see each other every day in rehearsal for weeks, we begin a relationship, I meet Savannah – and yet you fail to mention she's my daughter.'

'I was going to tell you –'

'When?'

'I don't know. Soon.'

Finn ran a hand through his hair. 'And what about Savannah? I assume you haven't told her about her mother's fictitious drunken one-night-stand, so what have you said to her about the identity of her father?'

'Nothing,' I said. 'For Savannah, it's always been just the two of us. She's never asked me any questions about – about you.' When Finn made no comment, I went on, 'It's really not so unusual for a child to live with just one parent. These days, families come in all shapes and sizes.' To my annoyance, I sounded defensive. Which I had no need to be. I wasn't going to regret the lie I'd told all those years ago. At the time it had been my only option.

'So, what happens now?' Finn said. 'Do you intend to tell Savannah that she's my daughter?'

'I think I have to . . .' My voice trailed off. Suddenly my heart was thumping so hard that I thought Finn must be able to hear it. I said, 'I would very much like to tell Savannah the truth. And for you to be a dad to her. But is that what you want, Finn? To be a permanent figure in her life? Can you make that commitment?'

'Oh, Nell –' Abruptly, Finn stood up, knocking over the chair. In two strides, he crossed the room, and placed his hands on the table, with his back to me.

'Finn?' I said. 'You need to decide what you want.'

'Give me a frickin' minute,' he snapped. 'Sorry, I –' He turned to face me, and when he spoke again, his voice was gentle. 'I can't do this. It's too much. I need to take some space and time apart from you – and Savannah.'

'So what you're saying is that you won't make a commitment to your child,' I said. He hadn't changed. He was the same feckless guy that he was ten years ago.

'I can't,' Finn's eyes were stricken. 'You want more from me than I can give.'

'Then I think it's best that Savannah never knows who her father is,' I said. 'You can't opt in and out of a child's life as you like, Finn, being a parent doesn't work like that.' I should never have let myself get involved with him. He was the man I loved, but I couldn't be with him if he wasn't prepared to make a commitment to Savannah. It wasn't fair to let her get fond of him, and call him *Dad,* only for him to vanish out of her life. A leaden weight settled in my chest. I said, 'You and me are over.'

For a long moment, Finn regarded me in silence, but then he gave a brief nod of his head and said, 'I'm sorry, Nell.' To my dismay, tears stung my eyes. I blinked them away.

'It's late,' I said, getting slowly to my feet. 'I'm going to bed. I won't ask you to leave in the middle of the night when the trains aren't running – you can sleep on the sofa – but I want you gone before Savannah wakes up in the morning. It's going to be hard enough for me to explain to her that I've broken up with my boyfriend, without you still being here when she comes downstairs for breakfast.'

'I'll go now,' Finn said. 'I'll call a cab.'

'Up to you.' I righted the toppled chair, went to the door and reached for the handle.

'Nell, I really am sorry,' Finn said.

I paused in the doorway. 'So am I.'

I left the room, closing the door behind me.

Chapter Twenty-Six

For a long while I lay in bed staring dry-eyed into the darkness, hearing the front door open and close as Finn left, the strip of sky visible in the narrow gap between my bedroom curtains gradually growing lighter. I felt both exhausted and beyond sleep, but at some point, I did drift off, waking up with a pounding headache, disorientated, not knowing where I was or what had happened. Then it all came rushing back to me: I'd confessed to Finn that he was Savannah's father and he'd walked away, out of my life, and out of our daughter's life. A tight ball of misery formed in my throat, and my eyes welled over with tears. All I wanted to do at that moment was pull my duvet over my head and howl. But I couldn't do that – not when Savannah would soon be waking up. Instead, I wiped my eyes with the heel of my hand, forced myself to get out of bed, and dragged myself along the landing to the bathroom. Wincing at my reflection in the bathroom mirror – I'd managed to smudge the mascara I hadn't bothered to remove the night before over most of my face – I took an aspirin, stripped off my pyjamas and stepped into the shower, standing under the hot water until it ran cold, telling myself over and over that I was not going to cry.

By the time I was dressed, the throbbing pain in my head had receded to a dull ache behind my eyes, and, reasonably confident that I'd got my tear ducts under control, I went downstairs to the kitchen. I made myself a large mug of tea and sat at the kitchen table to drink it, wondering how best to explain a break-up with a boyfriend to a nine-year-old. A short while later, Savannah trotted into the kitchen.

'Morning, Savannah,' I said. 'What would you like for breakfast?' My voice sounded abnormally bright, but Savannah didn't appear to notice. 'Toast or cereal.'

'Cereal, please,' she said, sitting down at the table. 'Where's Finn?'

The kitchen lurched around me. Very carefully, with a shaking hand, I put down my mug.

'Finn went home,' I said. What could I say to explain his absence? Wishing I'd taken more improvisation classes when I was in training, I stood up, a little unsteadily, retrieved a bowl and a packet of cereal from a cupboard, along with a bottle of milk from the fridge, and put them in front of Savannah. The thought of eating anything turned my stomach, but I made myself another mug of tea and sat back down again.

'I like this cereal,' Savannah said, 'but I prefer the chocolate one.'

'Ah,' I said. 'Right. OK. I'll get the chocolate one next time I go shopping.'

'Can we stick the photos of me on the stage into your scrapbook today?

The photos that Finn had taken. The photo that Samantha had taken of the three of us.

'Maybe another day,' I said. 'Listen, Savannah, last night Finn and I . . . had a talk and we decided that he isn't going to be my boyfriend anymore.'

'Did you have an argument like Kitty and Nathan?' Savannah said, through a mouthful of cereal.

'What?'

'Like in *Speakeasy* when Kitty thinks Nathan is a gangster and she's cross with him. She sings *A Jar of Moonshine* so that the audience know she's angry.'

'No, nothing like that,' I said, quickly, before Savannah got it into her head that scenes as dramatic as she'd seen on the Nightingale's stage had been taking place in our living room. 'Finn and I won't be – er – making-up like Kitty and Nathan do, either.' I steeled myself for more questions, but it seemed that musical theatre had the power to explain away the complexities of adult relationships in a song and dance routine – at least to Savannah's satisfaction, for she resumed eating her cereal.

When she'd finished, she said, 'I expect you'll get another boyfriend.'

'What if I don't want one?' I said. I loved Finn, he was the only man I wanted, but I couldn't have him. There would be no more dancing in the moonlight for me.

'Auntie Marianne has lots of boyfriends,' Savannah said.

'But I have you,' I said.

Chapter Twenty-Seven

I stood on the Nightingale's stage, next to Justin, and bowed, while the audience roared their appreciation for *Speakeasy's* dancers. As the ensemble stepped back, and the actors playing named characters ran onto the stage from the wings, the cheers became louder, only to become louder still when, hand-in-hand, the stars appeared, Samantha curtseying while Leon applauded his leading lady, Leon bowing while she applauded him. My gaze strayed to the Royal Box, which tonight had only a single occupant, a blonde woman in a sparkly dress, who, as I watched, got to her feet and waved to someone on stage. Only a short time ago – five days to be precise, not that I was counting – Finn had sat in that box and watched the show with Savannah, the child he'd rejected. Feeling my smile beginning to slip, I bowed once more, waved at the audience, and made my exit ahead of the rest of the cast.

In the wings, having taken a moment to get myself together while my fellow cast members streamed past me, I was about to head to the wardrobe village, when Justin planted himself in front of me.

'Fancy going for a drink with me and Matt in the Troubadour?' he said.

'Not tonight, Justin,' I said.

'Why not? Do you have somewhere else you have to be?'

'No, I don't –' There was, I realised no reason why I shouldn't go for a drink with Justin, other than the fatigue that lay in wait for me every time I came off the Nightingale's stage. Suddenly, the thought of going home to my empty house was unbearable. 'Actually, I will come to the Troubadour with you,' I said. 'I could do with some company tonight.'

'You miss him, don't you?' Justin said.

I didn't have to ask him who he was talking about.

The day after Finn had walked out of my life, knowing that my parents would be eager to find out more about the man my mother had met so unexpectedly, I'd forestalled any awkward conversations by informing them that we weren't an item, and they were unlikely to meet him again, almost as soon as they'd walked through my front door. If they suspected that I wasn't quite as blasé about Finn's exit as I made out, they kept it to themselves, and I'd left for the theatre confident that if Savannah mentioned him, they would change the subject, their daughter's love life – or lack of it – surely not a topic for discussion with their granddaughter.

At the Nightingale, the demise of my relationship with *Speakeasy's* Choreographer had so far gone unremarked by the show's cast – although, my fellow cast members would no doubt work it out once they noticed that he was no longer hanging around the stage door. I'd told Florence and Hettie, and Justin and Matt – and Lily Dene, of course – but I'd managed to sound regretful rather than heartbroken, and I'd thought that none of the friends telling me how sorry they were, knew that my acting abilities were stretched to the limit by my efforts not to cry. Each night, I danced my ex-boyfriend's choreography with a smile on my face – and I'd no notes from Cameron to suggest that I'd made any mistakes. I had, I hoped, remained the consummate professional dancer, even when there were moments when I felt I was falling apart inside.

Now, I said to Justin, 'And there was me thinking I'd done a good job of leaving my troubles at the stage door.'

'You have,' Justin assured me. 'But I've been dancing with you long enough to feel the tension in your body when you're not OK.'

'I'm not OK right now,' I said, 'but I'll get there.'

'And in the meantime, the show must go on,' Justin said. 'But if you ever feel the need to talk, I'm ready to listen. And, I promise you, I can keep a confidence. When I want to.' I smiled at that. He was my dance partner, who I could always trust never to let me fall, and my friend. But that didn't mean I'd be sharing the truth about my and Finn's relationship with him.

'Thanks, Justin,' I said, 'but I don't want to talk about Finn – I want him out of my head.' A thought occurred to me. 'Shall I ask Florence and Hettie if they want to come out tonight as well?'

'Yeah, good idea,' Justin said. 'Our Florence could do with the distraction.'

Florence's appearance at the *Road to Romance* premiere on Leon's arm, had *not* gone unremarked by our fellow cast members, several of whom had stopped in Leicester Square on their way home from the theatre to see the celebrities coming out of the cinema – even West End performers have the occasional starstruck moment – and had spotted Florence and Leon climbing into a limo. Word of their liaison had spread backstage in whispers, sidelong glances and speculative rumours, encouraged by Florence's gazing at Leon adoringly from the wings when he was on stage and she wasn't, and jostling past other dancers to stand next to him in the warm-up. In Dressing Room Six, she continued to talk about the premiere – exclaiming over a photo of Leon at the event that she found on line, even although she wasn't in it, and recounting how he had introduced her to the film's director – oblivious to the effect this was having on Marisa, who looked daggers at her whenever she mentioned Leon's name. Leon, meanwhile, smiled charmingly at Florence if they chanced to meet in a backstage corridor, and said 'good morning' and 'good night' to her – just as he did to every other member of the Company – and carried on his way, whether that be to his dressing room before the show or out of the stage door and into his car afterwards.

'Florence is still convinced Leon's going to ask her for a second date,' I said to Justin, 'but I don't think he's on the same page of the script.'

'I have to agree with you,' Justin sighed. 'Anyway, the Troubadour it is. Matt and I'll meet you in Lily Dene's corridor.'

The two of us hurried off to transform ourselves from frequenters of a speakeasy in 1920s New York to twenty-first century Londoners, able to wind down in a bar after a show with a glass of wine and no fear that we'd be raided for breaking the laws of Prohibition.

In Dressing Room Six, I passed on Justin's invitation to Hettie and Florence. Hettie was already going out with friends who'd watched the show that night, but Florence immediately said she'd love to join us, and the two of us left the dressing room together.

We'd clattered downstairs as far as the ground floor, and had just walked past Leon's dressing room, when Florence came to a halt.

'I'm going to ask Leon if he'd like to come with us,' she said. My heart sank. Florence's chasing after Leon when he was clearly not interested in pursuing a relationship was definitely not something to be encouraged.

'I wouldn't do that, Florence,' I said. Thinking rapidly, I added, 'He's *Speakeasy's* leading man. He won't want to slum it with Justin, Matt and me.'

'Leon's not like that,' Florence said. 'He's totally down to earth. Really, he's just like any other guy.' She smiled and blushed. 'I should know.' With that, she raised her hand, rapped lightly on Leon's dressing room door, and without waiting for a response from within, turned the handle.

The door swung open. Inside, sitting on the bed that was provided should the star of the show need to rest between matinée and evening performances, were Leon and the blonde woman I'd seen earlier in the Royal Box. And he was kissing her, on the mouth, passionately, his hands roving over her. She threw back her head, and he kissed her on the neck, his hand going to her thigh and sliding under the hem of her dress. Florence made a sound that was something between a gasp and a moan, and then she quietly closed the dressing room door, before the two within became aware of our presence. For a moment, she stood there motionless, and then she set off at a fast-paced walk, breaking into a run as she turned into Lily Dene's corridor, rushing past a startled Justin and Matt, and Lily's portrait, and through the door that led into the lobby. Beckoning to Justin and Matt to follow, calling out a hasty 'Goodnight, Miss Dene,' I hurried after her.

In the lobby, Toby and Annelise were signing out, but there was no sight of Florence. Hastily, I scribbled my signature, and darted through the stage door. Outside, there seemed to be more people waiting for a glimpse of the actors than ever before, with the queue of ardent fans stretching halfway to Shaftesbury Avenue. Samantha was already working her way along the crush barrier, signing programmes, as was Donte. From my elevated position on the stage-door steps, I scanned the street, but couldn't see Florence. Justin and Matt came and stood beside me.

'What's happened?' Matt demanded. 'Why did Florence run off like that?'

'She went to Leon's dressing room and saw him in a clinch with another woman,' I said.

Matt swore under his breath.

Justin raised his eyebrows. 'Another member of the cast?'

'No – I've no idea who she is. She was watching the show tonight – I saw her in the Royal Box.' Suddenly, I spotted Florence's slight figure standing in a doorway on the other side of the street. 'There she is –' I jumped down the steps, and crossed the road. There were a few fans here, too, but I skirted past them and ran up to Florence, who was staring fixedly at the stage door.

'Did you see them?' she said to me. 'In the dressing room.'

I nodded. Justin and Matt arrived, and hovered at my shoulder.

'Hey, Florence,' Justin said. 'How about we get out of here?'

'You go,' Florence said. 'I'm not in the mood for the Troubadour.'

'We can find a quieter bar,' Justin said.

'I'm not going anywhere,' Florence said. 'I have to see if Leon and Kelsey come out of the Nightingale together.'

'Leon has *Kelsey Dickson* in his dressing room?' Justin said, raising his eyebrows.

'That blonde woman is Leon's ex?' I said. 'The soap star?' No wonder she'd looked familiar. 'I thought they broke up months ago.'

'They did,' Justin said.

'Oh – he's coming out –' Florence said, her voice catching in her throat.

Across the road, Leon emerged from the stage door, Kelsey Dickson at his side, both of them smiling. He raised his arm to wave at the fans, who began cheering and chanting his name, and Kelsey waved also. Then, placing his arm around Kelsey's waist, Leon ushered her into his waiting limousine. The car pulled away from the kerb, and drove past us, its passengers hidden behind its blacked-out windows.

Florence gave a strangulated cry. Pushing past me and the boys, she headed off along the narrow street. The three of us exchanged startled glances and then as one, followed after her, catching up with her as she turned the corner.

'Wait, Florence,' I said. 'Where are you going?' She swung around to face us.

'I'm going home,' she said, sounding surprised to be asked.

'I think I'll head home too,' Matt said. 'We can travel together.' I recalled that he lived just one stop away on the tube from Florence.

'I'd rather be on my own,' Florence said. 'You three go and have a drink in the Troubadour. I'll see you Monday.' Her lower lip was trembling and her face was abnormally pale.

'Listen, Florence,' Matt began, 'You're obviously upset and –'

'Just leave me alone,' Florence said. '*Please.*' She resumed walking, her head down and her shoulders slumped.

'She should have her friends with her,' Matt said, gazing after her, his forehead creased with concern. To think that Florence ought not to be trudging around London on her own after the shock of walking in on the object of her affections kissing his ex, did not strike me as being over-protective.

'I agree,' I said. 'I'm going after her.' Matt made as if to follow me, but Justin put a hand on his arm.

'Florence won't appreciate all of us chasing her through the West End,' he said. 'Nell can text us, when she knows she's safely home.'

Leaving the guys on the corner, I set off along Shaftesbury Avenue, anxious to reach Florence before she became lost to sight among the audiences still pouring out of the theatres after the evening performances. She hadn't got very far, and by elbowing my way through the theatre-goers, I drew level with her before we were half-way to Charing Cross Road.

'I don't need an escort, Nell,' she said, coming to a halt. 'I'm not going off to drink myself senseless, if that's what you think.'

'Well, no,' I said, 'if you were going to do that, you might as well have come to the Troubadour. But I can see you're upset, and I'd like to know that you got home all right.'

To my dismay, Florence burst into tears.

'Oh, don't cry,' I was about to add the proverbial *he's not worth it,* but on second thoughts, decided she wouldn't believe me. I found a tissue in my jacket pocket and handed it to her. After a few more gulping sobs, she wiped her eyes, and blew her nose.

'Sorry,' she said, adding, 'I've changed my mind. I don't want to go home just yet. Not until I know my parents will be asleep. If they're still up, and they see me like this, they'll start asking questions, and I can't face that tonight. Could we maybe go and get a coffee?'

'Absolutely,' I said, quiet understanding why Florence might want to avoid a parental interrogation – at least from her father. A thought struck me. 'Would you like to stay at my house tonight? I can only offer you instant coffee, but I have chocolate biscuits to go with it.'

'Oh, yes, please,' Florence said. 'If you're sure you don't mind. I've already messed up your plans for this evening. I don't want to be any more trouble.'

'It isn't any trouble, Florence,' I said. 'As long as you don't mind sleeping in a bedroom with a *lot* of pink in it, and ballet-shoe-patterned curtains.'

'Ooh – that sounds wonderful,' Florence said.

Chapter Twenty-Eight

I switched on the light in the living room. 'Have a seat,' I said to Florence, gesturing towards the sofa. 'I won't be long.' I went to the kitchen and quickly texted Justin and Matt with an update about Florence's whereabouts, returning to the living room with two coffees and a plate of biscuits. Florence was sitting in the corner of the sofa with her legs tucked up under her. I placed her coffee and the biscuits on the side-table where she could easily reach them, and sat down in an armchair.

On the journey home, she'd barely spoken, staring ahead of her, with unseeing eyes, but now she said, 'How could Leon do this to me?' A single tear ran down her face, and then, suddenly she was crying in earnest, half-lying on the sofa, burying her face in her hands, her body racked with sobs. Leaping up and across the room, I sat next to her while she wept, occasionally patting her shoulder. Eventually, she stopped crying, and sat up.

'I-I thought Leon liked me,' she said. 'H-how c-could he cheat on me like that?' She wiped her eyes with the palm of her hand.

I wasn't entirely sure that Leon's hooking up with his ex-live-in girlfriend could be defined as cheating on a girl he'd taken out on just one date. But I was certain it wouldn't make Florence feel any better if I pointed that out to her.

'I thought we were going to be a couple,' Florence went on.

'Is that what he told you?' Fury reared up inside me as I re-cast Leon as a heartless womaniser, toying with Florence's affections.

Florence bit her lower lip. 'No, he didn't say anything like that.'

With relief, I gave Leon back his role as a nice guy, who likely had no idea of the havoc he had caused by one kiss. He and Florence had been reading from a different script; wretched for her, but, sadly, it happened.

'But – after he kissed me – he told me that I was a sweet girl and I should never change.' Florence's eyes became suspiciously bright. She blinked several times.

'A guy can like a girl, and take her out, and make her feel special,' I said, gently, 'but that doesn't mean that he wants an on-going relationship with her. Or even another date.'

Florence looked down at her hands. When she looked up again, her face was stricken.

'I've got this all wrong, haven't I?' she said. 'Leon never wanted us to be together. It was all in my head. How can I have been so *stupid*?'

'You're not stupid, Florence,' I said. 'Wanting a relationship with a guy who doesn't feel the same doesn't make you stupid.'

'I've made a complete fool of myself,' Florence said, 'and everyone in *Speakeasy* has seen it. They're all talking about me and Leon, I know they are.' Her hands fluttered about her face. 'I can't possibly go into work on Monday. I can't face Leon – or the rest of the cast – I just *can't*. It's too mortifying. I'll have to pull out of the show.'

Oh no you won't, I thought, *because I'm not going to let that happen.* 'Now *that* would be stupid,' I said, 'because if you break your contract, it'll mean the end of your theatrical career. Even a top agent like yours won't be able to get someone like Leigh Keaton to audition you if you've got a reputation for dropping out of West End musicals.'

Florence looked as if she might be about to cry again, but she got herself under control. 'You really think leaving *Speakeasy* might wreck my career?'

'Yes, I really do.' Deciding just the tiniest bit of emotional blackmail might be forgiven, in the circumstances, I said, 'And if you walk out, you'll be letting down all your friends in the ensemble who've worked so hard to bring *Speakeasy* to the stage. It's not easy to put a new dancer into an existing cast – it would mean more daytime rehearsals for all of us. And you know how exhausting that is.' Florence sank back into the sofa. Her eyebrows drew together in a worried frown. I felt somewhat guilty at that point – even if my manipulation was for her own good – but sensing I was close to winning her around, I decided to give her more time for my words to sink in, and concentrated on drinking my coffee.

'I wouldn't want to let anyone down,' Florence said, eventually.

'Then no more talk about quitting *Speakeasy*,' I said. 'It sounds harsh, but the show must go on, whatever you're feeling inside. That's what it means to be a professional dancer.'

Florence slowly nodded her head. 'I can't bear the thought of never appearing on a West End stage ever again,' she said. 'I guess I'll have to carry on dancing in *Speakeasy*. However idiotic people think I am, I won't have them saying I'm unprofessional.'

Relief flooded through me. It seemed that while Florence was understandably upset to discover that she wouldn't be playing the role of Leon's girlfriend, she was more embarrassed by her own behaviour than devasted by his indifference. And, thankfully, she wasn't about to throw away what promised to be a brilliant career because of a kiss.

'I can't help wondering if Leon and Kelsey are back together for good,' Florence said.

I shrugged. 'I'm sure it won't take long before someone in the cast finds out and passes it on.'

Florence sighed, and fished her phone out of her bag, which she'd left on the floor next to the sofa. 'I need to send a text.'

I almost spilt my coffee. 'Please tell me that you're not about to text Leon,' I spluttered.

'Of course not,' Florence said. 'I have to text my parents to let them know I'm staying at a friend's house. They insist on it, if I stay out overnight unexpectedly, so they don't worry when they discover my bed's not been slept in.'

Quite right too, I thought, mentally filing what seemed a perfectly reasonable parental demand away for use in ten years' time, when Savannah would be nineteen.

Florence returned her phone to her bag, picked up a chocolate biscuit, ate it, and reached for another.

'It's going to be so awkward seeing Leon next week,' she said.

'It'll get easier,' I said. 'You won't want to hear this, but you will get over him.'

'Yeah, I'll be OK.' To my astonishment, Florence's mouth lifted in a smile. 'Leon might not want to be my leading man, but I did have the most wonderful night.'

Evidently, Florence was going to be fine. As for me . . .

'Would you like some more coffee?' I asked.

'Please,' Florence said, holding out her empty mug.

I hurried out to the kitchen, made two more coffees, and stood by the sink, gazing through the window, past my pale reflection, into the darkness beyond, until the in-coming tide of misery that threatened to drown me had receded.

'It's showtime,' I said to my reflection, raising my hands in a basic jazz hands position. Then I picked up the coffee mugs and went back to the living room.

Chapter Twenty-Nine

On Monday, having done a major supermarket shop, I was staggering up my front path laden with carrier bags, when my mobile rang. What with the shopping and rummaging for my phone in the subterranean depths of my shoulder bag, it stopped ringing before I could answer it. I let myself in – after another hunt through my bag for my front door key – put away my provisions, made myself a much-needed post-shopping coffee, and, sitting at my kitchen table, checked my phone. The missed call was from Rachel Mullings – who never rang any of her students' parents unless she had an important reason. Hastily, I called her back.

'Hello, Rachel,' I said.

Now in her seventies, Rachel Mullings' formerly dark hair, always worn in a bun, was white, but she still carried herself like the dancer she'd been in her twenties, her back ram-rod straight, her body enviably trim. A brilliant teacher, she not only passed on her knowledge and expertise to her students, but also her love of dance in all its forms – and she'd turned me into a good enough dancer to get accepted for professional training. It was an effort for me not to call her Miss Rachel when I spoke to her, as I'd done when I was Savannah's age.

'Good morning, Nell,' Rachel said. 'Thank you for getting back to me so quickly. I trust I didn't wake you?'

'Oh, no. I've been up for hours.'

'I guess the lifestyle of a dancer has changed a great deal since I trod the boards at the Nightingale,' Rachel said. 'Back then, chorus girls like me rarely had a night when we didn't have a young man waiting at the stage door to wine and dine us after the show or take us somewhere thrilling like Paris or Monte Carlo. We rarely got up before noon . . . But I digress.'

'Oh, please go on,' I said. 'It all sounds so glamorous.'

Rachel laughed. 'Another time, perhaps,' she said. 'I do have a reason for calling you other than reminiscing about the past. I have a favour to ask you. As you know, there are only eight weeks until the Rachel Mullings School of Dance Annual Summer Show, and we've so much left to do that I don't see how we're possibly going to be show-ready. How would you feel about choreographing a number for the advanced tap class? They're aged fifteen and sixteen – six boys and eight girls – and many of them want to pursue a career in the theatre.'

'Me?' I said. 'But I've never choreographed a dance – apart from a few short routines for Savannah.'

'Exactly,' Rachel said. 'I've seen Savannah perform your choreography, and I'm sure you'd be able to come up with something that would challenge my advanced students without it being too much for them. It would, however, mean that I'd need you to be able to teach it to them and rehearse them on a Saturday morning, before you go to the theatre.'

My first thought was to tell Rachel I couldn't do it – if I did, for the next eight weeks, I'd only have Sundays when I didn't have to get up early. Then, out of nowhere, it struck me that teaching and inspiring the next generation of dancers – handing on the torch, as it were – just as Rachel had taught me, was something for me to seriously consider as a new career when I could no longer dance professionally.

'I do understand if you feel it would be too much for you to take on while you're in *Speakeasy*,' Rachel continued. 'You don't need to give me an immediate answer. Why don't you sleep on it and let me know tomorrow?' She paused, and then she said, 'It would be a marvellous opportunity for the students to learn from a West End dancer.'

A West End dancer. That was *me*, Rachel was talking about. An idea for a dance I could make with teenage students – and sort of the music they could dance it to – began to form in my mind.

'I don't need to think about it, Rachel,' I said. 'I'd love to choreograph a dance for your Summer Show. Actually, this has come at a good time for me. I – I've realised that, as a dancer, I'm no longer exactly in my prime, and I need to think about my future. What I'm going to do next. When I can no longer earn my living by dancing.'

'I see,' Rachel said, softly. 'It comes to us all, Nell. Every dancer who has ever turned a triple pirouette or star-jumped higher than their head wakes up one morning and realises they can no longer turn as fast or jump as high.' She hesitated, and then she added, 'I can't tell you what to do with your life, once you've stopped dancing, but one thing I will say to you: not everyone who is a performer has the ability to teach others to become the same. Teaching full time is something you have to *want* to do, not just something you fall back on when the dance work dries up. But teaching your choreography to my advanced students will give you a chance to find out if enjoy working with young people.'

'Absolutely,' I said.

We talked a while longer, me agreeing that I'd have a dance ready to begin teaching it by Saturday, Rachel telling me more about her plans for the Summer Show, and then, with a wish for me to *have a good one* that evening, she rang off.

I placed my phone on the table. Pushing back my chair, I danced a few tap steps around the kitchen – before my way was blocked by the fridge. I pictured fourteen teenagers dancing those same steps on the community centre stage. This could be fun, I thought. Of course, it could be awful – I might turn out to be hopeless at choreographing for anyone older than nine, or the students might prefer their usual teacher, even if I did have a West End credit. But if nothing else, it would help me discover if I was cut out to teach dance. And it wasn't as if I had anything else to do on a Saturday morning, nowhere else I had to be, no-one to be with –

Finn.

I hadn't wanted to disturb Zelda's Cornish holiday with my woes, but suddenly I felt the need to talk to my best friend. I sat back down at the kitchen table and called her.

'So how was the Cornwall?' I asked, after we'd exchanged the usual greetings.

'It was amazing,' Zelda said. 'Everything you've heard about the beaches, the picturesque villages, the dramatic scenery – it's all true. We had such a good time.' She continued talking about the delights of Cornwall – Martin teaching the boys to swim while she and Esme looked for crabs in rock pools, cream teas and boat trips – for several minutes before asking, 'And what did you and Savannah get up to at half-term?'

'Finn worked out that Savannah is his daughter,' I said. 'He doesn't want to be a father to her. He – we broke up.'

There was a long silence, and then Zelda said, 'I'm so sorry, Nell.'

'I should never have let him back into my life.' My heart constricted. 'I-I'm in love with him.'

'Oh, Nell –'

'I love him, but I can never be with him. I thought he'd changed, but he hasn't. Ten years later and he still can't make a commitment.'

'Maybe if you gave him some time?'

'No,' I said. 'He doesn't want anything to do with me – or our daughter. He made that abundantly clear.'

'I really am sorry that he took it that way.'

'I should have told him. Not ten years ago, but now, before I let myself fall for him –' My voice caught in my throat.

'Nell? Are you OK?'

'No, not really,' I said. 'But the show goes on. Speaking of which, I'm going to have to go, or I'll miss the half.'

'Before you go, would you and Savannah like to come to lunch on Sunday?'

'That would be lovely,' I said. 'It'll be so good to see you all.'

'And please, *please*, call me if you need a proverbial shoulder before then. Any time. Even if it's the middle of the night.'

'Thank you,' I said, quietly. 'You're the best friend *ever*.'

'Straight back at you,' Zelda said. 'But I've known that ever since you made sure I got home safely when I drank too much punch at that party when we were sixteen. Now off you go before you make yourself late for curtain up, or whatever you theatre folk call it. Break a leg.' She ended the call.

I rested my elbows on the kitchen table, my chin in my hands. It would be good to spend some time with my best friend and her family this coming weekend, just as if Finn hadn't come back into my life. Of course, if things had worked out differently, it would be me and Finn and our daughter visiting *our* friends Zelda and Martin and their children. I pictured how it would have been: Finn and Martin kicking a ball around the garden with Theo and Charlie, me and Zelda sitting in deck chairs, glass of wine in hand, Savannah making a daisy chain for Esme. My eyes stung, and before I could get a hold of myself, a tear ran down my face. I jumped up from the table, wiping the tear away with my hand.

I couldn't allow myself to cry over Finn, because once I started, I knew I wouldn't be able to stop.

Chapter Thirty

I walked along Lily Dene's corridor and came to a halt in front of her portrait. Other than to wish her *good morning* or *goodnight*, I realised, I hadn't spoken to her in over a month. We really were due a catch up.

'Good afternoon, Miss Dene,' I said. 'It's been an eventful few weeks. Backstage, and in the showbiz gossip magazines, the headline news is that Leon Walsh and Kelsey Dickson are engaged. Leon announced it the Monday after he and Kelsey got back together, when the cast were all gathered on stage for notes, and he got a huge round of applause. I did have a slight worry that Florence might be less than thrilled, but she was as delighted as everyone else. Never underestimate the restorative power of chocolate biscuits.'

When Edward from Dressing Room Seven had come to Dressing Room Six with a card for Leon and Kelsey that all the ensemble were signing, Florence had written a really sweet message saying that she was *so delighted to hear that you are to be married* and that she hoped *you will always be as happy as you are now*. Not many men, I suspected, would have received such warm wishes on their engagement from a girl whose affections they'd spurned. My own offering of *Congratulations and Best Wishes from Nell xx* had seemed paltry in comparison.

'In other news, Marisa has now had two warnings from *Speakeasy's* Company Manager. The first one was because she missed a warm-up. I doubt she'd have broadcast it to Dressing Room Six the way she did if she hadn't been so furious with Lucas for reporting her to William. Not that Lucas had any choice. It's his job as Dance Captain on the line if a dancer injures themselves on stage because they can't be bothered to warm up before a performance. The second warning was because she wore her costume up to the dressing room during the interval, and spilt coffee on it. The dressers tried their best to get it out, but despite their best efforts – and Marisa screeching at them – it looked awful under the stage lights. William was furious – Toby from Dressing Room Eight heard him giving Marisa a right telling off through the door of his office.'

Marisa, I thought, *needs to watch herself*. Another warning and her contract could be terminated – barely half way through the run.

'As for me . . . Last weekend, my daughter turned ten. She had a sleepover party, although stay-awake-all-night party would be a better name for it!'

The noise made by half a dozen excited nine-and-ten-year-old girls – even at two in the morning – had to be heard to be believed, and the amount of crisps that I was still hoovering out of the living room carpet a week later was extraordinary. But it was worth every bit of parental exhaustion to see Savannah's smiling face as she and her friends danced around to pop music, and demolished pizza and birthday cake, washed down with copious amounts of fizzy drinks. To my surprise, Savannah had asked for and received roller boots for her birthday present from me – apparently *everyone* in her class was in possession of a pair. I was only glad that I hadn't given in and bought her a mobile phone.

'What else can I tell you?' I said to Lily. 'Well, I've now done five sessions of teaching my choreography to teenage dancers. I'm dubious as to whether I'd have the patience to teach full time, but it's been extremely satisfying to watch 'my' students performing a dance that I've created. It's only now that I fully understand how Finn must have felt seeing the cast of *Speakeasy* dancing his choreography.'

Finn. A tight ball of misery formed in my chest. I was getting on with my life without him. There were whole days when I didn't think of him. But then something – like discussing choreography with Lily Dene – reminded me of him, and the hurt was back. I still woke in the night with my body aching for his touch. I still loved him.

'I *will* get over him,' I said, aloud, knowing that I was talking to myself as much as Lily. I took a moment to get myself together and went on, 'So, tomorrow night is the Hillier Charity Gala Performance, and I'll be dancing in the presence of Lord and Lady Hillier.'

When I'd first heard about it back in the spring, I'd not realised that the Gala Performance, which took place annually on a Saturday in July, was such a prestigious event, with tickets selling for hundreds of pounds, the proceeds going to the Hillier Foundation, a charity set up by Lily

Dene's many-times great grandson, and a very good cause. If I was honest, my heart had sunk just a little when I'd learned that the cast were expected to come in for daytime rehearsals again in the week leading up to the Gala, but I'd made sure to dance full out and hide my yawns.

The sound of someone clearing their throat jerked me out of my thoughts, and made me spin around to see our Company Manager regarding me intently from only a few feet away. My face flooded with heat as I realised he'd likely overheard me talking to the portrait.

'Hey, William,' I said. 'I was just – er – bringing Miss Dene up to date with – er – a few things. It's a theatrical tradition.'

William smiled. 'Yeah, I know,' he said. 'I do that too.'

My face grew hotter. Naturally, the Company Manager would be familiar with all the traditions at the Nightingale.

'That's why I'm here,' William said. 'I can't have her playing tricks on the cast because she feels neglected, especially not tomorrow night.' Tilting his face up towards the portrait, he went on, 'Hello, Miss Dene. I'm afraid Samantha Ellis is unable to perform in tomorrow's Gala show. She woke up this morning with laryngitis, and has completely lost her voice.'

'Oh, no. Poor Samantha.' I shuddered. This was every singer's nightmare.

William nodded. 'She's devastated to miss one of the most important nights in the theatrical calendar. Fortunately, we have a very experienced understudy in Sadie Price. Although, with the rave reviews that Samantha's been getting, Sadie is going to be under a lot of pressure, both tonight when she plays the part for the first time, and even more so at the Gala. It takes guts to walk out on stage knowing that the audience bought tickets to see a particular star, and you are very much a second choice. Anyway, Nell, I'll leave you and Lily to finish your conversation. Goodbye, Miss Dene.'

William headed off into the depths of the theatre.

Performers got sick. And had their hearts broken. But the show went on.

Chapter Thirty-One

On the day of the Hillier Charity Gala Performance, the first thing I did on arriving in Dressing Room Six was to throw open the windows to let in some air. Not that it made any difference; on this hot summer afternoon, the dressing room was stifling. Taking off my sunhat and the sleeveless T-shirt I'd worn over a crop top and knee-length leggings to travel into central London, I sat down in front of my mirror, and pushed strands of wet hair back from my forehead. Dancing in temperatures like this, it would be easy to get dehydrated. I made a mental note to drink plenty of water, and could only be glad that with the front of house staff preparing for the Gala, there was no matinée performance.

Hettie and Florence came into the room, Hettie collapsing onto her chair, and Florence making straight for the sink to splash water on her face.

'I swear it's hotter outside than under the stage lights,' she said – just as Marisa made her entrance, Nicole sidling in after her.

'I have just had a very informative conversation with our Box Office Manager,' Marisa announced, settling herself on her chair, and spinning around to face the rest of us. 'You won't believe some of the people who've bought tickets for the Gala.'

'Are they useful, well-connected people?' Hettie said, winking at me. To my surprise, Nicole gave a short laugh which she immediately turned into a cough.

'Most of them are well-known theatre practitioners,' Marisa said.

Nicole piped up, 'Sebastian was a bit short with you, wasn't he, Marisa? I did tell you that front of house staff have enough to do on a big occasion like the Gala without you pestering them to find out if Leigh Keaton is going to be in the audience again.'

'I can assure you that I know when or when not it's appropriate to talk to the theatre management team,' Marisa said.

Nicole muttered something inaudible, and became intent on re-arranging the make-up on her worktop.

'I also discovered that someone very well-known to the cast is returning to the Nightingale tonight,' Marisa went on. 'Did you know that Finn Harris is attending the Gala, Nell? I guess not, since you and he are no longer together.'

Finn. My body went rigid.

'No, I didn't know Finn would be here.' My heart began to pound against the wall of my chest. I fought to keep my breathing even, in and out, in and out.

'I hope it won't throw you, knowing he's somewhere out there in the auditorium,' Marisa said.

I took another breath and consciously made my body relax. Finn's presence would *not* affect my performance.

Once I was on stage, nothing was going to stop me dancing to the best of my ability – certainly not anything Marisa Cutler might say to me.

'Leave it, Marisa,' I said. 'This song of yours has been reprised too many times. I'm bored of it now.'

'What are you talking about?' Marisa said. 'I'm giving you a heads up. It would be awful if you messed up a routine in the Gala Performance.'

'Oh, do shut up, Marisa!' Nicole snapped, springing to her feet. 'You couldn't care less if Nell fell flat on her face tonight. You don't care about anyone in *Speakeasy's* cast apart from yourself.'

I gasped, as did Hettie. Florence put a hand over her mouth. Marisa almost fell off her chair.

'I think you like making other dancers feel bad about themselves, Marisa,' Nicole said. 'I don't know why. Maybe it's because you're jealous of anyone who is blatantly more talented or successful than you are.'

'How dare you?' Marisa's eyes blazed, and she, too stood up. 'After all the help and advice I've given you –'

'Your advice about not bothering with the warm-up could have got me fired,' Nicole said, 'And while we're having this conversation, I haven't forgotten how you stole my idea for my character's backstory on the first day of rehearsal. All that stuff you said about being a nurse in the First World War was what I'd told you I was going to say, almost word for word.'

'Now you're being ridiculous,' Marisa said. 'If you want to go on renting a room in my flat, you'll take that back.'

'Is that so?' Nicole said, squaring her shoulders. 'Well, I've no intention of taking anything back, so I guess I'll be moving out.'

'Fine,' Marisa said, her mouth curling into a sneer. 'Whatever.' Turning her back on Nicole, she flounced across the dressing room and opened the door. Looking over her shoulder, she said, 'You won't survive in show-business without my help, Nicole. You just don't have what it takes.' With that, she left the dressing room, slamming the door shut behind her.

'As you've told me so many times,' Nicole said to the empty air. 'But I don't believe you. Not anymore.' While Florence, Hettie and I gaped at her, she went to the sink, filled a glass with water, and drank. 'Sorry about that. I lost it for a moment there, but I've calmed down now.' She did appear calm. Her face was a little red, but that could have been down to the heat in the dressing room.

There was a long, uncomfortable silence, which Hettie broke by saying, 'Marisa is enough to make anyone mad.'

'I've known her since college,' Nicole said. 'She was always ambitious, but she never used to be so . . .'

'Manipulative?' I offered. 'Toxic?'

Nicole's eyes widened, and I thought I'd gone too far, but she nodded her head. 'I-I thought she was my friend, but she's played me for a fool. Or rather, I let her.'

I was fortunate in my friends. I couldn't help but feel sympathy for a girl who'd been so mistaken in hers.

The tannoy sputtered into life. Amongst the static, I could only make out a few words: 'Cast . . . stage . . . All cast . . .'

'They really ought to fix that,' Hettie said. 'Come on, ladies, we can't be late for Lucas's warm-up.' I saw Nicole wince.

'May *I* give you some advice, Nicole?' I said. 'You can beat yourself up later all you want, but right now you need to focus on *Speakeasy*. Whatever is happening in your life off-stage, the show goes on.'

Nicole nodded, and followed after Hettie and Florence who were already out the door. The four of us walked downstairs.

We'd got as far as the second landing when we heard the screams echoing up the stairwell.

Chapter Thirty-Two

I ran down the stairs, freezing on the spot when I reached the ground floor and was confronted by Sadie Price, lying prone on her back, no longer screaming, but moaning in pain, her right leg bent at a hideously unnatural angle. Justin was kneeling beside her, holding her hand, telling her to stay still, reassuring her that she'd be all right, and that Donte was fetching help. Matt and a couple more boys from Dressing Room Seven, stood nearby, eyes wide with shock. I heard exclamations from the other girls of Dressing Room Six, and then I heard Jerome's voice telling everyone to 'stand back, and let me through' – the Stage Manager, I knew, was trained in first aid. He was accompanied by Donte, who came and stood beside me.

'She fell down the whole flight,' he said, his face ashen. 'I saw her. My God, the way she screamed –'

Jerome, meanwhile, was bent over Sadie. 'Anyone got a phone on them?' he said. No-one answered. Jerome looked up, his gaze coming to rest on me. 'Go to William's office,' he said. 'Tell him to call an ambulance.'

'My leg,' Sadie cried. 'My leg –'

My heart pounding, I ran through the warren of corridors that led to the Company Manager's office, bursting through the door and skidding to a halt in front of William, who was seated behind his desk. I was dimly aware that there was another person in the room, but such was the urgency of the situation, that they were merely a blur on the edge of my vision.

'What the –?' William began.

'Sadie has fallen down a flight of stairs,' I said, breathlessly. 'You need to call an ambulance.'

To William's credit, he immediately picked up his desk phone, and made the call, giving clear and concise instructions to the emergency call handler to have the ambulance come to the stage door.

'Where is she?' he asked me, as soon as the call had ended.

'At the foot of the stairs on the ground floor,' I said. 'Jerome is with her.' Now that I'd delivered my message, I realised that I was shaking. I put my hands on William's desk to steady myself. He strode past me and out of the door.

A male voice, heart-wrenchingly familiar, said, 'Nell.' I spun around, and found myself standing face to face with Finn, dressed in a dinner jacket, the ends of a bow tie hanging loose at his neck.

'Ah – you're here,' I said, stupidly. Why he was in the Company Manger's office, I couldn't imagine – his being there made no sense. 'I – I have to – go back –' With his grey eyes on me, I was finding it hard to string a coherent sentence together.

'I'll come with you,' Finn said. I'd much rather he stayed where he was, but it wasn't up to me. He was free to come and go in the Nightingale as he pleased.

I walked out of the office, and he fell into step beside me, his long stride easily keeping pace with me.

'How are you, Nell?' he said.

'A bit shaken up, to be honest.' My head was all over the place, which had as much to do with him as poor Sadie's fall.

Finn put his hand on my arm, drawing me to a halt. 'It's weeks since I saw you. How are you doing?'

What could I say to him? I'm broken inside. I feel hollow and empty. My heart aches for you . . .

'Can we not have this conversation?' I said.

Finn nodded. 'You're right – this isn't the time.'

We turned into Lily Dene's corridor, where we saw a number of the cast, coming towards us Justin, Matt, Florence and Hettie among them. If they were surprised to see me with Finn, they gave no sign.

'How's Sadie?' I asked Justin, as they drew level.

'Still in a lot of pain,' Justin said, acknowledging Finn's presence with a nod.

'The ambulance is on its way,' I said.

'Yeah, William told us,' Justin said. 'He's waiting for it outside the theatre. Jerome and another first aider are with Sadie. Meanwhile, the cast are instructed to go to the auditorium.' He and the other performers continued walking along the corridor.

'Listen, Nell –' Finn began.

'I'd better go too,' I said. 'You're not cast so there's no reason for you to come with me any further.' I darted away from him before he had a chance to protest, coming to a halt once I was around the corner and out of his sight, leaning against the wall until my heart had stopped racing and I'd more or less pulled myself together, before going after my friends.

In the auditorium – thankfully airconditioned – most of the cast were already scattered along the first few rows of the stalls, their conversation subdued, everyone horribly aware that Sadie's career might have just ended that afternoon at the foot of the stairs. I joined Florence, Hettie, Matt and Justin, sliding into a seat on the aisle. Letting my gaze travel around the auditorium, I spotted Nicole sitting on the end of one row of seats, with Marisa sitting at the other, next to Leon, talking animatedly. From the set of Leon's shoulders, he did not look as if he appreciated her conversation, and after a minute or so he stood up, and went and sat next to Donte. I thought, *that woman never knows when to stop.*

Justin, sitting next to me, whispered, 'Nell, are you and Finn back together?'

'No, we're not,' I whispered back.

'When I saw you just now, I thought you looked like a couple.'

'Well, you're wrong,' I said. 'I've no idea why Finn's parading around the Nightingale in a dinner jacket, but it has nothing to do with me.'

'Presumably, he's invited to the reception,' Justin said.

'What reception?'

'Didn't you know? Lord and Lady Hillier are hosting a reception in the Circle Bar for a select number of VIP guests before the rest of the audience arrives.' Justin's eyes searched my face. 'Nell, are you OK?'

I nodded. 'It threw me, seeing Finn so unexpectedly, but I'm all right now. I'm show-ready.' Justin squeezed my hand.

The afternoon wore on. I told Justin and Matt about Marisa and Nicole's falling out. Justin declared that he'd always thought theirs was a toxic friendship that wouldn't last. Matt made a foray for provisions, returning with water and packets of crisps. Conversation grew louder, the cast speculating about Sadie's injuries – it was generally agreed broken bones were preferable to torn ligaments, because ligaments were slower to heal.

We'd been sitting in the auditorium for over an hour when Florence asked, 'Do you think the Gala will go ahead?'

'Absolutely,' Justin said. 'It sounds harsh, but this is why we have understudies and covers.'

'Tonight,' I said, 'Annelise will play Kitty, although I suspect she'd much rather have made her debut in the role in different circumstances.'

'Look – there's Gwen,' Matt interjected. 'Perhaps she'll have news.'

I looked towards the front of the auditorium and saw Gwen and Jonathan walk out of the wings and position themselves centre stage. The cast fell silent.

'Good afternoon, everyone,' Gwen said. 'You're all aware that Sadie Price has had an accident. While she has broken her leg and is badly bruised, I'm very glad to report that she's expected to make a full recovery.' The cast gave a collective sigh of relief. Several people clapped. I saw Leon and Donte exchange a high-five. 'What I want to do now,' Gwen went on, 'is rehearse Kitty's scenes with our First Cover. Annelise, would you join me and Jonathan up on stage? And Cameron too, please.' She peered out into the stalls. 'Cameron – are you out there?'

Conversation sprang up again all around the auditorium, only to stop when Gwen held up her hands.

'Annelise?' she said. 'Cameron?' She walked downstage. 'Does anyone know where our Resident Choreographer is?' No answer came from the stalls. 'Has anyone seen him today?' Silence. 'What about Annelise? Who shares a dressing room with Annelise Kent?'

Eleri called out. 'I do, but I haven't seen her –' She broke off as William entered stage right – accompanied by Finn. The thought came to me, unbidden, that he looked really good in that DJ. To my disquiet, he turned his head and saw me staring at him, before I could look away. Ignore him, I told myself, he is nothing to you. He *rejected* our child.

'I've just received a phone call from Cameron,' William said. 'Seems he and Annelise can't make it in today. Food poisoning. Dodgy shellfish, Cameron thinks.'

Gwen rolled her eyes.

Finn stepped forward. 'Gwen, in Cameron's absence, may I offer my assistance?'

'Hell, yes,' Gwen said. 'I mean, thank you, Finn. Much appreciated.'

'Please give my apologies to Lord Hillier if I don't make it to the reception,' Finn said to William.

Justin leant towards me, and put his mouth close to my ear. 'Cameron and Annelise. That's one backstage romance I didn't see coming.'

'Not now, Justin,' I said. I turned to look at Florence. Most of the cast were doing the same.

'At tonight's Gala Performance,' Gwen said, in a voice loud enough to be heard at the back of the Upper Circle. 'The role of Kitty will be played by Florence Newton.'

Chapter Thirty-Three

'I have to admit that I'm very glad it's not me playing Kitty tonight,' Hettie said to me, as we put on our make-up. 'I'd never accept a job as a cover. Going on in a lead role at short notice isn't something I'd ever want to put myself through.'

I examined my face in my mirror, added a touch more lipstick, and said, 'Me neither.' In the course of my career as a jobbing dancer, I'd often had to perform at a gig after only one sketchy rehearsal, but I wouldn't have wanted to take on the role of Kitty. Not because I didn't know it – after the hours I'd spent watching Samantha from the wings, I knew the part as well as I knew my own track – but because I was aware that my voice didn't have the range to sing Kitty's songs, and that I no longer had the stamina to dance Kitty's solo tap numbers.

With less than a couple of hours to rehearse Florence before the audience arrived, Gwen had opted to have the cast walk through Kitty's scenes and mark her dance numbers – there simply hadn't been time to do anything more. I didn't let it affect me outwardly, but I'd found dancing with Finn watching me from only a few feet away a disquieting experience. I'd avoided looking at him any more than was strictly necessary, but I'd been relieved when Gwen had brought the rehearsal to an end.

While the ensemble had trooped back up to the fifth floor, Florence had been whisked away by Samantha's dresser to the star's dressing room, where she would get into Kitty's opening costume, and where Samantha's make-up artist and hair-dresser would fit her wig and do her make-up. I hadn't had a chance to tell her to 'break a leg' – although, in the circumstances it might have been more tactful to go with 'have a good one.' or 'Toi, Toi, Toi,' which Finn had told me performers said to each other in Germany.

Finn. I gave myself a mental shake. I had to stop thinking about him.

'I know it's a bit early,' Hettie said, 'but are you ready to go downstairs, Nell? It's so hot in here.'

I glanced towards the other side of the room where Marisa and Nicole – who had moved her make-up and hair brush to the far end of the counter, as far away from Marisa as possible – were applying false eyelashes and pinning up their hair, while studiously ignoring each other. I suspected that it wasn't just the stifling heat in the dressing room that Hettie wanted to get away from.

'Sure.' I stuck another pin in my hair, and followed her out onto the landing.

'Oh, my days,' she said, 'you could cut the atmosphere in there with a knife. Are we just going to pretend we haven't noticed?'

'I don't see what else we can do,' I said. 'Anyway, if Marisa doesn't say a word for the rest of the run that's fine by me.' Hettie laughed at that, and we walked down to the wig room, taking rather more care on the stairs than usual.

Wigs and mics fitted, we'd just left the room, when Hettie said, 'Oh damn, I've still got my watch on. I'll have to go back up to Dressing Room Six. See you in the wardrobe village.' With a sigh, she headed back up the stairs. I continued down to the first floor, where it struck me that Florence would still be in Samantha's dressing room, and that it would only take a moment for me to put my head around her door and wish her all the best for her first performance as Kitty. Ordinarily, I wouldn't have dreamt of disturbing one of the leads when they were preparing to go on stage, but Florence was my friend, and theatre etiquette didn't apply.

I trotted along the first-floor corridor to Samantha's dressing room and rapped on the door. There was no answer, so I knocked again, and louder. This time, Florence opened the door. Dressed in Kitty's costume, and with Kitty's make-up and curly red wig, she looked so different that I almost didn't recognise her. Behind her, I could see a rather more luxurious dressing room than the one we shared, with a bed covered in colourful scatter cushions, an armchair, and a carpeted floor instead of lino.

'Oh, Nell,' Florence said. 'I'm so pleased to see you. Come in.'

'No, I don't want to disturb you,' I said. 'I'm just here to wish you all the best for tonight –' Florence pulled me into the dressing room, and shut the door.

'I can't do this,' she said. 'I can't play Kitty.' She paced about the room, her breath coming in short gasps.

Nooo, I thought. *Not again Not now.*

'Of course, you can,' I said. 'You know the part backwards. You could play Kitty in your sleep.'

'I can't –' Florence wailed. She sat down on the bed, her shoulders slumped, her arms wrapped around her stomach. I crouched down in front of her.

'Listen, Florence,' I said, 'you may think that you don't know it, but you're a dancer like me, and once we've learned a role, we never forget it entirely. It's there in our muscle memory. We only have to hear a piece of music for it to come flooding back.'

Florence shook her head. 'You don't understand. I can't play Kitty *opposite Leon as Nathan.*'

'What?' I said, aghast. 'You played opposite him this afternoon.'

'That was different,' Florence said. 'That was a walk through. But tonight – I-I'll have to kiss him.' It finally dawned on me that Florence was stressing about performing Kitty and Nathan's love scene.

'It's just a stage kiss,' I said, 'and then there's the blackout. You'll be fine.'

'I can't go on stage and kiss Leon, and tell him I love him I just can't – not after what happened between us.' Florence was visibly trembling now.

'It's *acting*,' I said. 'Leon knows that. He won't think anything of it. Anyway, it won't be you and him kissing – it'll be Kitty and Nathan.'

'I can't –' Florence said, her voice scarcely audible.

I fought a rising panic. By now, the Gala's audience, in black tie and evening gown, would be entering the auditorium, settling into their seats and opening their souvenir programmes. It couldn't be that much longer before the tannoy summoned all beginners to the stage. I should already be in my first costume – but I couldn't leave my friend alone in this state. For all I knew, she'd bolt out of the theatre.

'Florence,' I said, keeping my voice calm with some difficulty, 'I have to go to the wardrobe village, and you're coming with me –' I broke off at the sound of a knock on the dressing room door. I glanced at Florence. It wouldn't enhance her professional reputation for anyone else to see her like this, but above all else, I had to get her on stage, and I could do with some help. Springing to my feet, I ran to the door and flung it open. Standing in front of me, resplendent in evening dress, was Finn. I'd thought I never wanted to set eyes on him ever again, but at that moment I couldn't think of anyone I'd rather see.

'Oh, I'm so glad you're here,' I said.

'I've a couple more notes for Florence –' He raised his eyebrows. 'Nell, why aren't you in costume?' Seizing his arm, I pulled him inside the dressing room, shut the door and gestured towards Florence, who was still sitting huddled on the bed, staring at the floor.

'It's stage fright, I think,' I said, in an undertone. 'Sort of. She and Leon had . . . a thing, and now she's freaking out about Kitty and Nathan's love scene.' Finn inhaled sharply. In two strides, he was across the room.

'Hey, Florence,' he said, sitting down beside her. 'What's up?'

'I c-can't – I can't go on tonight,' Florence said.

'You have to,' Finn said, in a voice that brooked no argument. 'With Samantha, Sadie, and Annelise out of action, there's no-one else. So, you can either play Kitty tonight or be known for evermore as the dancer who caused the Hillier Charity Gala Performance to be cancelled – throwing away a very promising theatrical career, by the way, because after that, no-one will take a chance on casting you. What's it to be?'

Florence's eyes widened. 'I-I don't want the Gala to be cancelled,' she stuttered. 'I want a career in the theatre.'

'Then you will perform on the Nightingale's stage tonight?' Finn said. Florence nodded.

Over the tannoy, came a disembodied voice that reverberated around the dressing room: 'Florence Newton to the stage, please. Florence Newton to the stage.'

'It's showtime,' Finn said. He stood up, and held out his hand to Florence. For what seemed a hideously long while, although it was probably no more than a few seconds, she just sat there, but then she allowed him to help her up, and lead her out of the dressing room. I followed after them, light-headed with relief. With Finn on one side of her, and me on the other, we walked her downstairs and along the corridors to the door that led into the wings. Finn ushered Florence through ahead of him.

'Do you think she'll be all right now?' he asked me, quietly.

'I honestly don't know,' I said.

'Well, I suggest that you and I leave our troubles at the stage door and work together to do all we can to help her get through the performance. Will you do that, Nell? Will you work with me for the sake of the show?'

'Of course, Finn,' I said, without hesitation.

'So, when you're in the wings stage left, I'll make sure I'm stage right. Are you OK with that?'

'For sure,' I said. 'But shouldn't you be taking your seat?'

'I suspect Lord Hillier would prefer that I made certain that we have a leading lady rather than make polite conversation with his guests in the Royal Box,' Finn said, adding, 'I'll keep an eye on her while you go and get your costume on.'

He went after Florence. I ran to the wardrobe village. Christina got me into my dress, hat and shoes in record time, although, when I reached the wings, the orchestra were already playing the overture. I made my way through the semi-darkness and the press of dancers' bodies to see Florence standing centre stage with Finn. He saw me, drew Florence's attention to my arrival and then went off into the opposite wings. Justin came and stood beside me.

'I thought I was going to be dancing without my favourite partner tonight,' he said. 'What's going on? Why is Finn still backstage?'

'Florence got herself in a bit of a state,' I said. 'I'll tell you about it later.' How fragile Florence looked alone on the stage under the bright lights, her back to the closed curtains.

The overture came to an end. Slowly, the curtains opened, revealing the spectacular Brooklyn Bridge set, which, as always, drew a murmur of appreciation from the audience.

'Have a good one, Florence,' I whispered.

Florence raised her head so that she was looking at the bridge spanning the stage, before pivoting around to face the audience. There was a silence that went on way longer than it should. *Come on Florence*, I thought, *say the line*.

'I-I am in New York City,' Florence said, in a quavering voice. She turned her head, and looked at me. I smiled at her encouragingly. She stood a little taller and, in a much stronger voice, went on, 'It's been my dream for so long, I can hardly believe I'm here.'

The orchestra played the opening notes of *Good Morning New York City*...

Justin and I, and the rest of the ensemble ran on, and then, suddenly, Florence was singing the first verse, her voice soaring with the music, the ensemble tap-dancing around her, singing the chorus. Florence went into the dance, out-dancing everyone else, even if her smile was a little tight... I'd forgotten how good a dancer she is. And then we are all dancing into the wings, running to the wardrobe village, dressers holding out costumes, Marisa yelling at someone to *get out of the way* ... I return to the wings and wait for my cue, looking across the stage to where Finn is standing behind Florence, his hands on her shoulders, bending his head to say something to her, she nods and runs forward ... another song and dance .. . getting my breath back as I watch Kitty and her friends perform *Just For Tonight* . . . Florence sounds terrific, no sign of nerves that I can see . . . I'm back on stage . . . Kitty is meeting Nathan in the speakeasy, relief surging through me when Florence sings their duet without faltering . . . the party scene, the last notes of *She Only Drinks Champagne* fading, the curtain closing, thunderous applause from the audience before they head out to the bar . . .

The interval. I get into my next costume, casting sidelong glances at Florence, who is sitting silently while her dresser and make-up artist fuss around her . . . I agree with Hettie that Florence is doing great, that the show is going great, the audience are great . . . I take Florence a bottle of water, and tell her she's doing a great job, and she thanks me but doesn't smile. I walk with her to the side of the stage, ready for Act II. She's performing brilliantly, she really is, but I wish I knew what was going on in her head . . .

Act II. The raid on the speakeasy, the dancing edgier than before, Justin lifting me, throwing me, catching me . . . another quick change, another dance . . . I am standing with Florence in the wings, feeling the tension radiating from her body as the orchestra plays the first haunting notes of *Dancing In The Moonlight.* Nathan enters stage right. Florence, stage left, doesn't move.

Without conscious thought, I say, 'Five, six, seven, eight,' and I push her out of the wings and onto the stage.

Florence walks towards Nathan. He reaches for her, and she flinches away from him. He holds out his arms, she hesitates, and then she runs to him . . . and then it's no longer Florence out there, but Kitty, dancing in the moonlight, changing from a young girl into a woman before our eyes, melting into Nathan's embrace, the dancing sensual and emotional, speaking without the need for words.

Finn is standing directly opposite me, his attention all on Kitty, his gaze following her around the performance space . . . I love that he is so passionate about his work, and that he cares about his dancers . . .

Kitty's legs lock around Nathan's waist as he spins her round, catching her as she lets go of him . . . holding her wrists, he lowers her to the floor and sinks down beside her . . . Kitty and Nathan kiss.

I look at Finn across the expanse of the stage and the moonlight, and his eyes meet mine. My heart constricts. I can't be with him. I still love him.

Blackout.

Chapter Thirty-Four

The last note of the finale music died away. There was a short silence – as if the audience needed to get their breath back as much as the dancers did – followed by an outburst of clapping and cheering. Justin took hold of my hand, and we ran off stage.

'I'd say our Florence nailed it tonight,' he said.

'She performed superbly.' My heart swelled. 'I'm so proud of her. Ah – here we go again –'

Along with the rest of ensemble, we ran back on to take our bow, followed by the actors playing the named parts, moving to the side of the stage when a drum roll announced that Florence and Leon were making their entrance.

I looked at Florence as she and Leon ran downstage hand in hand, her face lit up by a dazzling smile, and it struck me that tonight, in true theatrical tradition, I'd seen a young dancer become a star. It was a cliché, but that didn't mean it wasn't true. *Years from now*, I thought, *musical theatre cognoscenti will look back and say that they were in the Nightingale on the night that Florence Newton played Kitty in Speakeasy.*

The audience were on their feet now, the applause becoming louder. Florence curtsied, while Leon applauded her, and then she applauded him while he bowed, the entire cast clapping them along with the audience. The music started up again, and we jumped into our supposedly-spontaneous tap dance. The audience went wild, shouting and whistling, and I lost count of the number of curtain calls before the tabs finally closed.

Florence immediately ran over to me.

'Well done, Florence,' I said, and hugged her. 'You were outstanding tonight. You stole the show.'

'Oh, I don't know about that,' Florence said, hugging me back. 'Anyway, I couldn't have done it without you and Finn –' She broke off as the other dancers surged around her, eager to offer their congratulations, Matt lifting her off her feet in a bear-like hug before setting her down again, both of them laughing, Justin, Hettie, and the rest hugging her in their turn. Even Marisa was there, although she avoided the hugging, and her expression was more of a grimace than a smile.

'Nell.' That was Finn's voice. Unnoticed until then, he was standing next to me. 'Florence owned the stage tonight,' he said.

My throat was very tight, but, somehow, I managed to say, 'With your help.'

'And yours.'

The cast were exiting now – Marisa the first to go – still talking non-stop, until only Florence, Justin, Matt and Hettie remained. For an instant, I caught Florence's gaze, and we exchanged smiles before she was swept off by the others, leaving Finn and me alone on the empty stage.

The silence that followed was broken by the sound of the curtains opening to reveal the now deserted auditorium.

'Nell, I know you're angry with me,' Finn said, 'but there are things I need to say to you. Please, can we talk?' A sudden turmoil of emotions inside me threatened to make me cry, but whatever I felt, it wasn't anger.

'I'm not angry with you, Finn. Not anymore.' I sighed. 'I've made such a mess of everything.'

'If anyone messed up,' Finn said, 'it was me.' His grey eyes locked on mine. 'I've missed you so badly these last few weeks. You and Savannah.'

I stared at him. 'Finn – you walked away from us.'

'I won't deny it,' Finn said. 'The night I realised that Savannah was my daughter – discovering that I was the father of a nine-year-old girl – it was overwhelming.'

'I should have told you. I don't regret not telling you ten years ago. I did what I felt was right at the time. But I should have told you now –' My voice cracked.

'I doubt I'd have reacted any differently whenever you'd told me.' Finn raked a hand through his hair. 'I wanted you from the moment I saw you in that first audition – I wanted to be *with* you – but what you were asking of me that night was too much to get my head around.'

I can't do this. It's too much. I need to take some space and time. That's what he'd said to me. I'd demanded commitment from him, but it was too much, too soon.

'I was so stunned to find out that Savannah was mine that I wasn't thinking straight,' Finn continued. 'So, yes, I did walk out. And once I'd calmed down and got myself together, I bitterly regretted it.' Still keeping his eyes on mine, he took hold of my hand. 'I've never been in a serious relationship before. I've never wanted to make that sort of emotional commitment. Not until now.' He placed my hand on his chest so that I could feel his heart beating. My own heart began thumping so hard against my ribcage that I felt he must be able to hear it. He said, 'I've been wretched without you. And when I saw you again today, I understood why. I love you, Nell, and I know for sure that I want a permanent role in your life, if you – and Savannah – will have me.' He let go of my hand, and reached up to run a finger down the side of my face. 'I want to be a father to our daughter. I want us to be a family.'

The man I loved, who had so unexpectedly come back into my life, and who I thought I'd lost, was in love with me. My heart brimmed over.

'I love you,' I said.

'Oh, Nell –' He put his arms around me, drawing me close, and kissed me, a fierce, demanding kiss, that set my blood on fire. I reached up and tangled my fingers in his hair, and he held me tighter, so that I could feel the heat of his body through his clothes, desire lancing through me as his tongue explored my mouth, both of us gasping when he lifted his face from mine.

'I will always love you,' he said, his voice hoarse, and kissed me again.

We were still kissing when the sound of approaching footsteps made us spring apart. I looked wildly around, blushing when I saw the Stage Manager standing just a few feet away, carrying a ghost light – the bulb on a stand that is placed on stage when a theatre is empty.

'Hey, Jerome,' Finn said.

'Just so you know,' Jerome said, evenly, 'everyone else has gone home – except for the ghosts. Don't forget you have to be out of the theatre by midnight.' He placed the stand on the centre stage mark, and vanished into the wings. Seconds later, the lights in the auditorium and the stage lights went out, and we were left with only the ghost light. Its soft blue glow, like the light of a full moon, was just enough to show me that Finn was smiling.

'Will you dance with me, Nell?' he said.

'I would love to,' I said.

Finn took me in his arms. 'I'll count us in,' he said. 'Five, six, seven eight –'

And then I was where I was meant to be, in Finn's arms, dancing in the moonlight.

Chapter Thirty-Five

Three Months Later

It's strange to see Dressing Room Six so bare and empty, with no photos or good luck cards stuck to the mirrors, just as it was on our first day in the Nightingale. Only Florence and me are still here, sitting next to each other, putting the finishing touches to our make-up, as we've done six nights a week since *Speakeasy* opened. Hettie, Nicole, and Jenny, who joined the ensemble after Marisa got herself fired, have already gone to the Circle Bar, where the Company, including Finn, are gathering for the Last Night party.

'I've had such an amazing time in *Speakeasy*,' Florence says, suddenly.

'Same here,' I say. 'Even if sometimes there was more drama off than on stage.' Florence laughs, and returns her attention to her mirror.

My mind drifts back to the *Speakeasy* auditions, the shock of discovering that Finn was the show's choreographer, the undeniable attraction between us, workshopping *Dancing In The Moonlight*, the thrill of finally dancing on a West End stage, Opening Night, the Gala . . .

Me and Finn had spent the night of the Gala at my place, and the next day, after a long discussion about the best way to inform a ten year old girl that she now had two parents in her life – there was no script for this – Finn had stayed there while I'd collected Savannah from my parents' house, giving me a chance to tell her, casually, as we walked home, that he was my boyfriend again. She'd listened without asking any questions, awkward or otherwise. As soon as we were inside the front door, she'd darted straight into the living room – where Finn was waiting for us, sitting on the sofa, running one hand through his hair, and tapping his thigh with the fingers of the other – and asked him if he'd like to watch her dancing school's summer show. He'd said that he would love to, with an enthusiasm that made me want to kiss him, although I restrained myself in front of Savannah.

That was Act I, I thought. *So far so good. Now for Act II.*

'Come and sit with me and Finn, for a minute, Savannah,' I said. She sat on the sofa next to Finn, and I sat on her other side. 'We have a surprise for you.'

'Is it a mobile phone?' Savannah asked.

'No, nothing like that.' I took a deep breath. 'It's about Finn. He – he's your father. Your Dad.' Savannah didn't say a word, but looked from one of us to the other, her eyes wide. I ploughed on, 'Ten years ago, when you were born, he wasn't my boyfriend, so he didn't live with me and you. But now, we – me and Finn – think it would be a good idea if we all lived here together in our house.' We planned to move to a larger family home in the not-too-distant future, but had decided not to make too many changes to Savannah's world all at once.

'I hope you think it's a good idea, too, Savannah,' Finn said, gently, 'because I'd very much like for me, you and your Mum to be a family.'

Savannah put her head on one side, as if weighing up her answer. 'Do I have to call you Dad?'

'Only if you want to,' Finn said. 'If you'd prefer to go on calling me Finn, that's fine.'

'I think I'd like to call you Dad,' Savannah said. To me, she added, 'I'd like to do some painting now.'

I let out a long breath. 'Why don't you paint at the kitchen table while I'm cooking supper?' I said.

'OK.' Savannah jumped up and went off to fetch her paints. I sank back against the sofa cushions, weak with relief. Finn's body visibly relaxed.

'You're through the final,' I said. 'You've got the part . . .'

Now, Florence's voice calls me back to Dressing Room Six.

'I so want to get into Leigh Keaton's new musical,' she says. 'The auditions are next week – but you know that already.'

'Yes, Finn told me,' I say. What Finn has also told me, is that if it were just up to him, the Choreographer of Leigh Keaton's latest West End production, Florence would already have a job. He's sure that the rest of the audition panel will feel the same once they've seen her dance and heard her sing – but it would be unprofessional of me to tell her that.

I will not be auditioning for Leigh Keaton's new musical or any other show. *It comes to us all. Every dancer who has ever turned a triple pirouette or star-jumped higher than their head wakes up one morning and realises they can no longer turn as fast or jump as high.* That's what Miss Rachel said to me – and I've become aware that I'm not dancing as well as I was at the beginning of *Speakeasy's* run. When I messed up a lift – thank goodness Justin caught me before I fell – I knew with startling clarity that while *Speakeasy* was the beginning of Florence's stage career, it was going to be the end of mine. It was my dream to dance in a West End musical, and I've achieved it. I will always think of myself as a dancer – one of many who've danced at the Nightingale Playhouse over the years – but I am giving up dancing professionally. Finn hasn't tried to persuade me otherwise, saying that it's a decision only I can make.

Speakeasy is my last huzzah and I am fine with that.

'I'm so looking forward to auditioning again,' Florence says.

'What I'm looking forward to,' I say, 'is a long lie-in tomorrow, while Finn picks up Savanah from my parents.'

When I'd turned up at my parents' house, the Monday after the Gala, with Finn in tow– Savannah was at school – and introduced him as my daughter's father, their initial reaction was to stare at us, speechless. However much my revelation had stunned them, by the time I'd finished my garbled and apologetic explanation of why I'd lied to them for so many years, my mother was hugging me, while my father was shaking Finn's hand, and welcoming him to the family. As did Marianne, when we told her, insisting that having met Finn at the Gala after-party, she should have guessed Savannah was his, as they're so alike. Finn's parents, once they got over the shock of being informed that their son, who they were only just getting to know again after his return from Germany, has a ten-year-old daughter, have welcomed me and Savannah into their family just as warmly.

Zelda is delighted that we're now together, and that she no longer has to keep my secret – although possibly not as delighted as Justin, who, on learning that Finn and I had a fling ten years ago, declared it the most fabulous backstage gossip *ever*.

'Yes, I'm definitely having a lazy day tomorrow,' I say to Florence. 'What about you?'

'Tomorrow,' Florence says, 'I have a date. With Matt.'

'You and Matt!' I've seen no sign that they've become more than friends. And neither has Justin, or he would have told me.

'He came round to my and Nicole's flat to help me put up some shelves,' Florence says, 'and somehow we ended up kissing. And then he asked me out. Not that I'm rushing into a *relationship* – I've told him I want to take it slowly – but I have to say that he's a great kisser.'

Well, I always did think that Matt should be her leading man.

'You have to let me know how the date goes,' I say, with a smile.

'Naturally,' Florence says, smiling back. 'Now, are you ready to party?'

It comes to me that there's one more thing I need to do before I go to the Circle Bar, where the man I love is waiting for me – hopefully with a glass of fizz.

'You go ahead,' I say to Florence. 'I'll see you there.' She goes as far as the open doorway, but then turns around and comes back into the room, putting her bag down on the counter.

'Thank you for everything you've done for me, Nell,' she says, 'for being my friend and giving me such good advice when I did stupid things, and for sharing your expertise. I've learnt so much about the theatre from you. I haven't forgotten that it was you who persuaded me to go into the *Speakeasy* final, and it was you and Finn encouraging me from the wings who got me through my debut as Kitty. I couldn't have done it without you.'

And then she curtsies to me, the full *reverence*, that dancers perform to show their thanks and respect to those who have handed on their knowledge and love of dance. Suddenly, my chest feels very tight.

'Thank *you*, Florence,' I say. 'That means a lot.' I hope fervently that I can pass on my knowledge of the theatre to the young dancers whose careers I will be guiding in my new job as a theatrical agent, just as I have to my friend.

Florence smiles and makes her exit.

I take one last look around the empty dressing room, check that my little silver dancer is safely in my bag, and then, ready to leave the stage, I go downstairs to say goodbye to Lily Dene.

Acknowledgements

Thank you to Guy, Joanne, David, Sara, Iain, Laura and Marc for the Beta reading, answering my questions about musical theatre and dancing, and for your all round enthusiasm for Dancing In The Moonlight. And thank you to Dino, Rosa and Pippa for making me smile – now you can say your names are in a book.

Thank you to the Romantic Novelists' Association, whose members are always so generous with their advice and support.

Thank you to the Ten Muses for all your encouragement – every author should have a group of awesome writer friends like you.

Thank you to Giulia for sharing your knowledge and expertise.

And last, but not least, thank you to my readers. A book isn't really a book until it's read.

About the Author

Lynne Shelby writes contemporary and dual timeframe women's fiction books with a love story at their heart. Her debut novel, French Kissing, now retitled Meet Me In Paris, won the Woman magazine and Accent Press Writing Competition. Her fifth novel, Love On Location, was shortlisted for a Romantic Novelists' Association Award. She has done a variety of jobs, from stable girl to child actors' chaperone to legal administrator, but now writes full time. When not reading or writing, Lynne can usually be found at the theatre or exploring a foreign city, writers' notebook and sketchbook in hand. She lives in London, with her husband, and has three adult children who live nearby.

Website: www.lynneshelby.com

Also by Lynne Shelby

Meet Me In Paris (originally titled French Kissing)
The One That I Want
There She Goes
The Summer Of Taking Chances
Love On Location
Rome For The Summer

Manufactured by Amazon.ca
Bolton, ON